ALEXA HOPE AND THE AVENUE OF POSSIBILITIES:

A Tale of Teenage Career Choices

GUILLERMINA GONZALEZ

InspireGlobe Publishers

Empowering Readers, Globally

TABLE OF CONTENTS

INTRODUCTION

S tep into the world of Alexa Esperanza—or Alexa Hope, as she's known—a young, bright-eyed seventeen-year-old immigrant standing at the threshold of a world full of endless possibilities and daunting obstacles. Like many her age, Alexa yearns to leave a mark on the world, but struggles to find role models who echo her own story. She battles not only socio-economic disadvantages but also the sharp sting of discrimination, persistently undermining her aspirations.

In Alexa's story, we encounter the essence of adolescence, amplified by her immigrant experience—the desire to stand out yet fit in, to dream big yet stay grounded, and above all, to find and follow her own unique path in life.

However, every cloud has a silver lining, and for Alexa, it arrives in the form of *Latinisimo*, a local radio show hosted by Ella Torres. This unlikely sanctuary becomes her haven, a place where she meets inspiring figures who broaden her horizons and show her that the world is brimming with opportunities, just waiting for her to seize them.

Alexa Hope and the Avenue of Possibilities: A Tale of Teenage Career Choices offers a vivid tapestry interwoven with the tales of eleven remarkable individuals, each a beacon guiding Alexa along her journey. These are not mere characters, but the distilled essence of real people whom the author encountered over a decade of hosting her own radio shows. These remarkable individuals were interviewed again for the purpose of this novel between January and February 2021.

Drawn from a deeply personal well of experience, the novel mirrors the author's own journey—from guiding light Ella, who helps others navigate their lives, to Alexa, the young woman discovering her own potential.

In the shared struggles and triumphs of Alexa and the eleven individuals, young readers, especially those of Latino descent or from immigrant families, will find echoes of their own dilemmas and aspirations. They are invited to explore alongside Alexa, and perhaps, in the process, find their own 'Avenue of Possibilities.' This novel offers a poignant exploration of coming of age, self-discovery, and resilience against the backdrop of the immigrant experience.

Above all, *Alexa Hope and the Avenue of Possibilities* is a celebration of the enduring human spirit, the profound impact of mentorship, and the unwavering belief in oneself. It is a testament to the power of community, education, resilience, and the transformative journey to self-discovery. So, are you ready to walk with Alexa and unearth your own path.

ALEXA'S DILEMMA

The sight of the Rosca de Reyes immediately caught Alexa's attention. "Oh wow, look at that Rosca!" She clutched her cup of hot chocolate. This sweet bread isn't just tasty; it's family history in every bite!

Grinning, she playfully said, "I seriously hope I don't get the Niño Jesús this year!" If I find that tiny figurine again, I swear...

Her eyes wandered, and thoughts of Tía María's infamous kitchen tales for the February second tradition bubbled up. "Honestly, the tamales? That's Tía María's domain," she remarked, rolling her eyes affectionately to all family attending. She couldn't help but think, Man, if Tía María ever gave me her recipe, I'd be unstoppable.

As she took a sip of her chocolate, Alexa felt that familiar, comforting touch of her heritage, like a favorite song playing softly in the background.

As with every family gathering, the air buzzed with the warmth of affectionate hugs, enthusiastic kisses, and animated chatter. The family's patriarch and matriarch, Leonardo and

Cristina, had ventured to the U.S. nearly two decades prior, driven by the universal immigrant dream of a better life.

Their journey to being recognized as the 'Hope' family was filled with more challenges and hardships than most could imagine. Whenever Alexa felt the warmth of her family around her, memories resurfaced of the stories her mother narrated about their home state, Guanajuato—a place besieged by the ominous presence of drug cartels. Her father, Leonardo, had once become embroiled in assisting the combined operations of the Mexican Army and the Drug Enforcement Administration (DEA). This association made him a marked man, with the ruthless drug cartels branding him as a snitch. Her mother had told her that her father, concerned for the future of his young family, made the agonizing decision to relocate north. This meant leaving the comforting familiarity of home and the sorrow of being separated from their elderly parents.

As Alexa pondered these tales, she recalled another thread of her mother's narrative. Cristina had often spoken of her own reasons for migrating. While her brothers had already established themselves in Delaware through a landscaping business, it wasn't merely family bonds that prompted Cristina's move. She had spoken of an electrifying community event, centered around fortifying civilian defenses against the cartels. Amidst this tense backdrop, her father had entered her mother's world. Their serendipitous meeting had evolved into a passionate romance, eventually leading to their marriage.

Her mother's stories always pointed out that in the midst of the chaos and uncertainty surrounding them, Leonardo and Cristina found solace in each other. Their union was further blessed almost a year later with the arrival of their beloved daughter, Alexa. As their only child, she immediately became the radiant center of their universe, the heart that bound their family together. For Leonardo and Cristina, amidst the trials they faced, Alexa was their beacon of immeasurable joy and the precious gem they held dear in their modest, tight-knit family.

Alexa brushed a short curl from her face as she began drinking her second cup of chocolate.

"What about your love life?" Tia Maria nudged her. "You're seventeen and always looking nice Alexa. And those brown eyes... you must be catching some boys' eyes!"

Alexa's cheeks flushed with warmth as a hint of self-consciousness crept in. Glancing at her reflection in the small mirror by the kitchen table, she murmured, "¡Gracias, Tía!"

Casting a glance at her attire, Alexa admired the chic mix of thrift-store gems she'd skillfully curated. Her petite stature occasionally led her to wonder about societal preferences. Would anyone like a short woman? Didn't the tabloids talk about tall women? Yet, her cousins always insisted that her tiny frame was her unique advantage, the key to snagging those incredible fashion bargains.

Didn't Tia Maria know about Rudy? Does she like Rudy? Why is she asking me about my love life? Alexa decided to brush those thoughts aside.

Tía María poured herself another cup of chocolate, her gaze softening as she looked at Alexa. "Mi'ja, you've been quiet. What's on your mind?"

Taking a deep breath, Alexa looked earnestly into her Tía's eyes, her voice tinged with youthful uncertainty. "Tía, so they're pushing us to think about colleges, right? And, I'm just...I dunno, overwhelmed? I can't even figure out what I'd want to major in, and they want answers, like, now. It's all just... a lot. Like being at this massive intersection and not knowing which way to turn."

Tía María smiled gently, stirring her chocolate. "Ay, Alexa, these decisions are never easy. But remember, life isn't about having all the answers right away. It's about discovering them as you go. We'll figure this out together, okay?"

The memory of that meeting with her school counselor, Pete O'Jete, replayed in Alexa's mind, casting a heavy shadow over her heart. His words, dripping with prejudice and laced with thinly-veiled racism, were a sucker punch she hadn't seen coming. "I don't think that you have what it takes to excel in any university, Alexa. You will be better off selecting one that gives you the chance to be near your family, where you can learn a skill that will help you get a steady job as you prepare to raise a family of your own. You might need to help your family, don't you think? I understand Latinos like that."

Every time Alexa replayed Pete O'Jete's words in her mind, it felt like an insidious vine, threatening to choke her aspirations. Could he be right? she wondered momentarily. But then, another voice, deeper and truer, rebelled: Who is he to define my limits?

She recalled the countless times her abuela told stories of their ancestors—of grit, resilience, and triumph. Am I not made of the same stuff? The thought of her family's sacrifices weighed heavily on her, but not in the way Pete O'Jete meant. They hadn't come this far for her to settle. They dreamed big, so she could dream even bigger.

But what if I fail? a small voice whispered. Yet, the very essence of her upbringing was about facing challenges, not evading them. The very idea that she should lower her sights just because someone assumed her background made her less capable was absurd. The spark within her flared.

Who does he think he is, telling me what I can and can't do? Uh-uh, no way. I'm not letting anyone box me in with their little judgy opinions. I'll show him—and everyone else who doubts me. I'm not just some high schooler; I've got goals and dreams. Watch me break the mold and change the game.

"Okay, guys, get your place around the table so each one gets her piece of rosca." Cristina handed the knife to Tía Maria who cut and found the first of several Baby Jesuses inside the rosca.

"Yes! Tía María got the baby Jesus!... Tía María got the baby Jesus." Alexa danced around the table with her cousins, their laughter echoing in harmony. "Now, we'll see you at your place for Día de la Candelaria for your famous tamales Tía. And please don't forget to include atole!"

She could almost taste the rich, steaming atole, its warm, grainy texture filling her mouth, perfectly complementing the savory tamales. She imagined the soft masa of the tamales giving way to the delicious fillings inside—perhaps spicy chicken in green salsa or the sweet tang of a pineapple-filled one.

The evening was coming to an end when Tía María said, "Alexa, I kept thinking about what you said. Ella Torres, a lady we know from community activities, came to mind. You need guidance and she might be able to help you. She's been *Latinisimo*'s host for about eight years now. The program is one of the few local radio shows in Spanish. This one from the University of Delaware's WVUD studios. Go and talk to her."

"Okay, Tía, I will. Is she nice?" Alexa was uneasy talking to somebody she didn't know about something so important for her.

Tía María kissed her goodbye as her family was already out waiting for her in the car. Cristina, Leonardo, and Alexa began collecting dirty dishes and washing them before their favorite telenovela started.

I guess I will have to talk to...what's the name? Ella?

CHAPTER 2

AN ARTS HEALER, LISA BARTOLI

The bright morning light streamed through the windows of the Starbuck's as Alexa rushed to grab her green chai latte. The comfort of the warm cup was just what she needed before the dread of the 7:00 am school bus on a cold Monday in January. Why do I always feel like a massive buzzkill on Mondays? And today, ugh, those literature composition results. Who on earth likes literature…when there's numbers…seriously? Wait…did I even answer that last question correctly? Why can't I shake off that nagging feeling? This is killing me! I shouldn't have binge-watched that series and reviewed one last time. Breathe, Alexa. Just get through today.

Her mind kept flitting back to the recent encounter she'd had at the WVUD studios. "I have no idea why you're here," Ella Torres had said, her face a mask of slight annoyance mixed with curiosity. Alexa had felt a blend of excitement and nerves as she stepped into the studio, having never been in one before.

Total vibe central. First off, that dim lighting made everything feel kinda cozy, but in a pro sorta way. The desks were covered in buttons and screens, giving off major mission-control feels. And the walls? Decked out in those weird, padded soundproofing things. The console…super futuristic. And don't get me started on the headphones. Every time I saw them, I thought, Whoa, that's where the magic happens! Being in there just made everything seem possible. It was the ultimate inspiring spot! I felt like anything could happen in there!

Her thoughts circled back to the *Latinisimo* experience and a recent announcement about the show. Taking a deep breath, she dialed the familiar number while the school bus was parking.

"Hello, Ella? It's Alexa Hope. Remember me?"

The conversation that followed hinted at a potential future Alexa hadn't even fully envisioned yet. Maybe this radio gig could offer a new avenue for her, a break from school and Rudy drama. Only time would tell.

Alexa's memory was gently nudged aside by a familiar touch. Turning her head, she met Rudy's eyes, her on-and-off boyfriend of two years. He was gently tucking a stray strand of hair behind her ear, a fond gesture he often did that always made her heart flutter a bit. Standing in the midst of the school's main hallway, he looked into her eyes, a hint of playful accusation in his own, and said, "Hey Alexa, what was up with Sunday? Thought we had plans?"

"I told you I have a ton of homework," she replied, her tone a mix of exasperation and defensiveness. "Not everything revolves around hanging out, Rudy."

"Yo…" Rudy started, sounding annoyed but trying to get it. "Look, I get the whole video game thing isn't your jam. But for me? It's just how I zone out, you know? Chill a bit. But yeah, we gotta find some 'us' time too."

Looking into Rudy's eyes, a soft blush touching her cheeks, Alexa said, "And honestly? Watching you lose yourself in those video games isn't my idea of a fun time."

He looked hurt, but before he could respond, she quickly added, "I've got choir practice now. Oh, and by the way? Nailed my pre-algebra test in case you wanna know."

She walked away, a heavy sigh escaping her lips. The gap between them seemed wider than ever, a chasm she wasn't sure they could bridge. Tears pricked her eyes as the thought formed. Are we even right for each other anymore?

As twilight approached, the sun's dwindling glow filtered through the large windows of the university cafeteria, bathing the room in a warm, golden embrace. Students were scattered about, some looking relieved to wrap up the week, while others seemed to be gearing up for Friday night activities.

Just a stone's throw away from the WVUD studios, Alexa sat amidst the chatter and clinking of dishes. Having arrived ahead of schedule in her excitement to see Ella, she took a moment to soak in the ambiance of the bustling university space, finding the experience both unfamiliar and intriguing. The smell of fresh pizza wafted from one corner, battling for dominance with the aroma of fresh coffee brewing. In another corner, a taco station had a line of students eagerly waiting for their picks, while the burger and soup counters were also doing brisk business.

Finding an empty spot, Alexa settled onto a chair at a table with a vinyl top that had seen better days. She pulled out her phone, eager to dive into the new game she had recently downloaded: Numbler. It was a math-based game, set up like a crossword, but you'd build equations instead of words. The concept was challenging but intriguing, especially for someone who had a fondness for numbers.

Alexa couldn't help but dive deeper, curious to see where this mathematical rabbit hole would lead her. As she crafted equations, time slipped away. Her focus was interrupted by a familiar voice.

"Hey, Alexa." She looked up, her eyebrows raised in surprise.

"Hey, Ella," she greeted, her voice revealing both surprise and excitement. "Wasn't expecting to see you here but at the studio."

Ella chuckled, "Sometimes I need a break. Plus, the university's tuna melt? Underrated." She unwrapped her sandwich, taking a moment to savor the aroma. "Would you like to have some?"

Alexa smiled, appreciating Ella's down-to-earth attitude. "I remember that show last week. It was pretty intense. How do you manage?"

Ella cradled her coffee cup, taking a thoughtful sip before biting into her sandwich. She chewed slowly, letting the flavors meld as she pondered the answer to the question. "You know," she began, placing her sandwich down and leaning forward her voice filled with quiet enthusiasm, "it's more than just the daily grind. It's the thrill of every interview, the chance to dive deep into someone's story and truly get to know them. I learn something in each interview. That's what keeps me going."

Ella's intense gaze settled on Alexa, and for a brief moment, Alexa felt as if Ella was trying to convey a silent challenge. As Ella continued speaking, Alexa sensed an underlying message. "And equally vital, having the right people alongside you, who support and challenge you in equal measure." A hint of a smile played on Ella's lips. "Sometimes, they might be right under our noses, don't you think?" Alexa caught the subtle wink Ella directed her way, hinting at something unspoken, before Ella stood up. "Shall we go?

Ella opened the radio station door for Alexa as she began, "I have to warn you, a radio show or podcast is hard work." Together, they made their way down the stairs to the basement where the studios were located. "It's a commitment," Ella added.

Alexa felt her eyes widen with a sparkle of excitement. "I totally get that. I mean, sure, 'community activities' would boost my college apps, but honestly? After our chat, I'm, like, super pumped. It feels like it could be such a cool way to learn and put my ideas out there. It's kinda like... a new adventure?" She bit her lip, hesitating for just a moment. "And, well, having someone as experienced as you to guide me? That's just the cherry on top."

Ella studied Alexa for a moment, a slow smile dawning on her face. "You know, if you're genuinely interested and ready to commit, I have a feeling we could make this work. Our 'People Who Make Us Pause' series? It's about showcasing remarkable individuals once every month. The idea is to introduce students on campus to various career paths they might never have considered. We're on the cusp of launching this yearlong series of biographical interviews." There was an unspoken invitation in her tone, and Alexa sensed it.

"And what's a biographical interview?"

"It's about detecting what motivates people to do what they do in a nutshell. Have you ever met somebody that made you pause and then act in response?"

Alexa thought for a minute. "I can't think of anybody right now besides YouTubers."

Ella's voice softened. "Tell me again what brought you to *Latinisimo*?"

"So, I'm in my junior year, and time to think about colleges and stuff, right? My aunt told me, 'You gotta chat with Ella, she knows her stuff.' I'm totally into math and all, but lit, composition, and social studies? Seriously, it's like they're trying to drown us in homework or something. It's just... overwhelming, you know?" Alexa rolled her eyes and sighed.

Ella leaned in slightly, her gaze softening. "You know, at your age, I was a whirlwind of interests, torn in every direction. It was agony not knowing what to pick because I liked... everything." She smiled wistfully, a distant memory crossing her face. "It feels like chaos now, but trust me, things have a way of falling into place."

Alexa's couldn't believe it—Ella, who seemed to have everything figured out, had once been just as mixed up as she was. "Whoa... you're telling me you once felt like me? That's wild! You look like you got everything on lock." Alexa blurted out before she could stop herself.

"Alright." Ella gave a subtle smile, hinting that she might have overheard Alexa's earlier comment but choosing to breeze past it. "Let's give this a go. No promises, but there's always something to learn. Speaking of which, our next guest is Lisa Bartoli, the arts healer. Might be an interesting one for you."

"The arts... what did you say?"

"How about you google her while she arrives. We have some time."

WVUD was at the basement of the university's students' building. The outside was always buzzing with all kinds of students' activities. It made a huge contrast to the quiet inside the radio station. It felt like two worlds divided.

After the staircase, there was another door at the bottom of it. Once inside, a narrow corridor revealed compact offices and four studios to the left after passing the elevator, water fountain, the mini kitchen, and the bathroom to the right. An additional door with heavy security before the studio made it the perfect place to tape simultaneous shows at once if needed. It was obvious that the space was designed to be private and quiet.

In the cozy ambiance of the studio, Ella and Alexa shared the space, each engrossed in their individual tasks. Memories of the narrow trailer where her abuelita lived rose in Alexa's mind. Her abuelita's trailer was always full of life and laughter. Faint echoes of her grandmother's romantic ballads and boleros playing on the radio and the smell of freshly made tortillas on the comal came back to her. There was a sense of warmth and togetherness, even in such a confined space. It was never a quiet place, and she loved that. But she also loved the stark contrast of quiet in this basement studio.

Ella was at the helm of the control board, her fingers gliding effortlessly over buttons, knobs, and sliders. The glow from the board illuminated her face as she queued up tracks and arranged the playlist for the upcoming segment. Every now and then, she'd put on her headphones, listening intently to ensure the audio levels were just right.

Alexa was nestled in a corner, across from Ella, her laptop perched on top of the studio counter. Her screen was filled with tabs dedicated to Lisa Bartoli. Alexa's eyes darted back and forth as she deep-dived into articles, piecing together a comprehensive understanding of their soon to arrive guest. She occasionally jotted down interesting facts on a notepad.

Lisa's organization, Art Therapy Express, had helped more than a thousand children and adults with mild to severe intellectual, physical, emotional, and communication disabilities with special arts education programs. Alexa was particularly intrigued when reading that some programs delivered results through the use of adaptive technology with custom-designed tools.

Oh my gosh, tech in arts therapy? I never imagined it could be used like that!

After finishing her online search about Lisa, tech and arts therapy, Alexa's curiosity was piqued even more about her surroundings. She decided to take a moment to wander around the basement and familiarize herself with the area. A temporary table caught her attention, laden with homemade cookies someone had generously shared. Evidence of crumbles on the blue carpet suggested she wasn't the first to take advantage. As she grabbed a cookie, thoughts of Andy, her best friend and known cookie monster, came to mind.

Man, Andy would've gone ham on these!

The bigger studio for larger group interviews at the center of the corridor was empty, but it had interesting objects, probably a remnant of another program.

I wonder what kind of show would have such odd props. Was it some sort of science program? Or maybe an art installation... She was about to touch the strangest shape she had ever seen when a memory of her mom's voice echoed, warning her about touching things that didn't belong to her. Would it come alive if I touched it? It almost looks like something out of those sci-fi movies Rudy loves. Just then, she heard Ella calling.

"Alexa! Could you please come to the studio?"

Alexa accelerated the pace while eating the last piece of the chocolate chip cookie.

"Shall we talk about the interview with Lisa Bartoli? She's getting here in about fifteen minutes. Since today is your first day at *Latinisimo*...I'd like us to get ready."

Alexa nodded and smiled. She was so nervous. Ella winked in return. "I'm thinking that you should see the flow of an interview, for starters. You have to take care of technical things, such as the sound and making sure the Audacity software is properly recording. You don't want to finish any interview realizing that nothing was captured, right?

"Back to the sound. You need to put the mic about two fingers away from the mouth to properly capture the interviewee's voice," Ella showed Alexa by getting her close to the mic. "Once ready, you check the sound and then begin asking the questions you have in mind."

Alexa's mouth dropped along with her stomach. Would she have to ask questions? Her throat went dry at the prospect of asking someone she didn't know questions. "Am I asking…"

"Relax, Alexa. I'm just explaining part of the process when taping a radio show and you have to run the show yourself."

Alexa exhaled, feeling the pressure evaporate. "Ella, I'll be right back."

Alexa staggered outside, gasping for a breath of fresh air to calm her racing heart. That had been a moment of sheer terror. Emerging from her panic, Alexa took deep breaths to steady herself. As the anxiety began to ebb away, she spotted Lisa approaching. Lisa's infectious smile instantly lightened the weight in Alexa's chest. That same familiar face she had seen while googling shone back at her, radiating warmth and understanding.

"Hi! I'm Lisa, and you are?" Lisa extended her arm, offering a handshake.

"I'm Alexa, Ella's intern for the next year." Alexa smiled back. "She's ready to interview you. I'll take you to the studio. I hope you don't mind that I'll be listening."

"Not at all," Lisa said. "I love working with students."

They walked together back to the studio. "Hey, Lisa! So good to see you again!" Ella's smile made it evident they knew each other. "Congratulations on winning the Governor's Award for the Arts, by the way! I think that was probably the last time I saw you. So well deserved! Shall we get started?"

Lisa nodded.

Alexa saw Ella placing the mic as she had described minutes ago. The interview began. Alexa was thrilled.

"Lisa, you have dedicated your professional life providing an outlet of creative expression to a population normally not associated to the arts, people living with all sorts of disabilities. I believe you are an arts healer. Could you tell us why you do what you do?"

Lisa's easy smile quickly appeared. "That's a beautiful way of defining who I am. I have been blessed my whole life sharing my passion in a way that is so well received and getting as much in return—or more—than I give. Our participants and artists have taught me more in life than I have ever taught them. They are the teachers, not me."

Lisa's enthusiasm was contagious. Alexa was eager to know the origin of such passion. Ella's next question went exactly there.

"I can tell you enjoy what you do, Lisa. How and when did it start?"

Lisa stopped for a minute, obviously racking her memory to find the exact time when everything started for her. "I was in my teenage years. I had a distant relative with cerebral palsy. It triggered my interest. I saw how much she was capable of and how her parents interacted with her. That kind of opened my eyes up to people with severe disabilities, their capabilities. I ended up doing my internship at her school.

"I found the arts because I was not exactly an athletic person." She looked down at her body and then back to Alexa and

Ella. They all shared a good laugh realizing that they were not necessarily runway material.

"I found something called art therapy and thought I could make a living at this instead of being an artist. The niche just felt right to me. I got the job that put me through graduate school by dialing the wrong telephone number."

Alexa sat up straighter. Ella leaned forward. "What do you mean by that?"

Lisa nodded, giggled, and continued, "I called about a job that I had seen for an art therapist. It was the wrong number, but the person who answered got interested. It was a residential facility for people with emotional disabilities. I was able to work weekends and go to graduate school at the same time."

"So, Lisa, please help us understand more about the nature of your work. What would you say your work is?"

"As you know, I founded Art Therapy Express in two thousand three. We serve children and adults with mild to severe intellectual, physical, emotional, and communication disabilities within special education in school, hospitals, and nonprofit organizations. We try to create a safe and empowering space for people to express themselves, connect with peers, and feel joy through the power and creativity of the arts. We frequently use custom-designed tools and equipment. When we started, we only had basic adaptive equipment, made from store-bought stuff, like jerry-rigged Velcro arm cuffs.

"Let me give you the example of one of our participants. Her name is Haley Shiber, who has cerebral palsy. She cannot speak or use her hands. But she paints bright canvases using a brush attached to her head or a robotic device to her arm. She communicates with her computer and always says that art makes her happy and that she looks forward to our classes."

Alexa recalled the art classes she was taking in school. It seemed boring compared to this. Wow, I've never thought about art that way. It's more than just... expression. It's a lifeline for some.

"Another example of my work is when I invited Dwayne Szot. He was a guest artist in an event where we created a mural that stretched across the floor of a gymnasium. He provided paint rollers that could be attached to wheelchairs and walkers."

That's insane! Alexa thought. Art's like... it's their voice, their escape. This is deep.

"I remember Dwayne saying that he always enjoys the happiness he sees in every participant's eye. Can you imagine that? We all need to be creative. It is so important to be able to reach out and leave our mark, or write our name in poetry, some chalk on the sidewalk."

Alexa was amazed. I always get hyped about a catchy song or an amazing picture, but this? It's next level!

Lisa paused for a moment then continued, "I, like Dwayne, love to see how happy they are at least for a moment."

The interview continued. The connection between the arts, therapy, and arts healing was making sense to Alexa. Lisa was doing what she loved. Her passion and gratitude for her work captured Alexa's mind. I've only painted one thing and I didn't enjoy it. Maybe I just need someone like Lisa to help me.

Alexa looked for Lisa's feed and quickly typed into her Instagram: Tech+art therapy today=mind blown! #ArtsMeetTech #NextLevelInspo Check out #ArtTherapyExpresswithLisa to see the magic.

"Lisa, I have seen your family very much involved in your work. Would you like to explain how?"

Man, how does Ella whip out these questions on the fly like that?

Lisa mentioned her husband but particularly her daughter Shayla. "From the time she could walk, she's pretty much been by my side. She's known participants in the program that have been with us for twenty years. She doesn't see disability. Do you know what I mean? They are friends. They are family."

Whoa, Shayla's really in deep with all this. Guess when you see your mom totally rocking her passion, it's hard not to get inspired. Lisa's like her own personal superhero.

"Many thanks for your time today! We have to let you go since you have a commitment to attend." Ella made a quick pause. "*Latinisimo* audience, that was Lisa Bartoli, Executive Director of Art Therapy Express. Lisa's interview is part of our monthly series 'People Who Make Us Pause.' I'll see you next week to discuss why Latin America is embracing populism with Dr. Julio Carrión. But, if interested in another remarkable individual from 'People Who Make Us Pause' please tune in the last Friday of each month. Until the next one!"

Alexa felt the interview had gone in a blink, but she remained pensive.

"So, Alexa, what is being an arts healer to you?" Ella's question brought back Alexa to the present time.

"Lisa's words just hit different. There's like all these artists out there, right? Some in wheelchairs, some dealing with their own stuff, but they're all creating these masterpieces. It's like Lisa's giving them a mic or something. I like it!"

Alexa was going to say something else when Rudy's text arrived: *Here! Front door.* "I have to go. Rudy, my boyfriend, just texted me. He's here to pick me up." Even Alexa could hear the annoyance in her voice at his unexpected arrival.

Before letting Alexa go, Ella said, "I'll leave some suspense for you. Next time we are going to interview a president. I'll text you soon as to who it is, but see if you can guess! I have to edit the interview before I go. I'll show how you to do it next time. Happy weekend, Alexa!"

As Alexa stepped out of the studio, her heart still raced from the adrenaline of the experience. Being so close to the action, witnessing an interview firsthand... It's way different than just listening to it. She reflected on Lisa's words, her stories, the passion in her voice. How effortlessly Ella led the conversation... Alexa thought, a mix of admiration and wonder swirling inside her. And to think, maybe someday, I'll be the one asking the questions. She smiled at the prospect, a budding excitement for the future possibilities in the world of radio.

Alexa walked outside to meet Rudy. "I figured I better come to pick you up to go home before you texted." A proud Rudy opened the door while Alexa climbed the last stairs before the outside door.

Alexa squeezed his hand and kissed him, happy to see Rudy after all. What would Rudy think if she wanted to be an art therapist? Would he find it stupid? Would he be intrigued? She shook the thought from her mind. "Yes, let's go. I'm starving, and those carnitas tacos are calling my name! Is your mom doing salsa verde or the habanero one."

CHAPTER 3

A PRESIDENT OF A UNIVERSITY, HAVIDÁN RODRÍGUEZ

Ella's mention of interviewing a president indeed piqued Alexa's interest. A president of what? she kept thinking when entering her school. The frigid February air in Delaware was unforgiving. As Alexa rushed through the school entrance, she regretted her choice of jacket the moment she stepped outside, but she had been running late. It had seemed so chic when she'd picked it out this morning, but in the biting cold, its thin fabric offered little protection.

Opening her locker, an envelope caught her eye—her name written across it in familiar, meticulous handwriting. It was from Pete O'Jete, the school counselor. A man with an impenetrable demeanor and a thinly-veiled prejudice that had soured their previous interactions. While his role was to guide students, particularly during the stressful college application process, their meetings were often charged with tension, his biases apparent.

Dread knotted in her stomach. What did he want now? She'd done her best to stay off his radar. Carefully opening the envelope, she found a formal note requesting a meeting later that week. She groaned internally. Another lecture laced with his subtle jabs was the last thing she needed.

Appointment to review college applications with Pete O'Jete, Friday 9:00 am.

"Great, just the kind of pep talk I needed to start a weekend," Alexa muttered, rolling her eyes as she slammed her locker shut. "Thanks, O'Jete."

After homeroom and several classes, it was finally time for lunch. She was starving. Andy met her in the cafeteria line. A text from Ella arrived as soon as they sat down at a table.

Hi! President=Havidán Rodríguez. University at Albany. First Latino. Please begin researching him.

"What's that?" Andy took a big bite of his chicken salad sandwich.

"We're interviewing the first Latino president of the University at Albany for *Latinisimo*."

Alexa caught the flicker of surprise in Andy's eyes. "Latin… what? What are you talking about?"

"You seriously didn't know? My bad, I thought I told you! I've teamed up for this radio gig at the University of Delaware. It's called *Latinisimo*."

Andy glanced at Alexa with a mixture of surprise and amusement. "Wait, you're going on the radio? And what's *Latinisimo* all about?"

Alexa smirked, shaking her head. "Ugh, I can't believe I didn't tell you. It's hosted by Ella Torres. And guess what? We're gonna interview Havidán Rodríguez. I've got to do some digging on him now."

Andy grinned, "Hold up! You're co-hosting a radio show? That's wild! How did I miss this?"

"Life's been a whirlwind lately with Rudy and the whole Pete O'Jete situation," she replied with a shrug. "It's been... a lot."

Andy nudged her. "Look at you, making moves! But, why the radio gig?"

Alexa smiled wistfully. "Started as a way to get advice about college. But after seeing the interview with Lisa Bartoli, that arts healer, I was hooked. She was part of Ella's 'People Who Make Us Pause' series. It's about showcasing genuine, impactful folks, not just the 'look at me' crowd."

Noting Andy's impressed expression, she continued, "When *Latinisimo* announced they were looking for a student host, I jumped at the chance. Ella was on board, so here I am. It's a fun project and it'll look great on my college apps for community service."

Andy's eyes lit up. "That's awesome! Mind if I help you with the research on him? I got curious to tell you the truth. We can compare notes later."

Alexa's smile wavered for a split second as she considered the stark contrast between Andy's genuine enthusiasm and Rudy's obliviousness. "Thanks, Andy," she whispered, the weight of that difference heavy in her chest. "It means more than you know."

Alexa wanted the week to slow down, but before she realized it she was knocking on Pete O'Jete's open office door.

Sporting his signature oversized plaid jacket paired with faded brown khakis, Pete O'Jete was unmistakably known among the students—and rarely for anything positive. His tenure in the education system was a tapestry of short stints at different institutions, a trail of less-than-glowing reviews shadowing him.

To most, especially those who looked like Alexa, his ever-present scowl and not-so-subtle biases were like a looming dark cloud. The undercurrents of his prejudices, veiled as professionalism, were clear. Most students made it a point to sidestep him, avoiding the downpour. But with him being her assigned school counselor, Alexa had no choice but to walk into the storm.

"Hello, Mr. O'Jete. Can I come in?"

"What? Oh, sure, Alexa. How are you making out on college applications? What about the SAT?"

"I'm exploring engineering options, as math is my thing. My grades are great—"

"Wait, engineering? For you? Are you sure? It's one thing to have good grades in math, but thinking about engineering is an entirely different story." Pete glanced down at a piece of paper in a folder with her name on it, sighed and looked back up. "Have you explored something less demanding? Like I suggested last time?"

Alexa's memory of that conversation was very present. The pain was still there. "Yes, I remember the conversation. Thanks for your help." Alexa was being sarcastic, but O'Jete didn't perceive it.

"I'll continue exploring engineering options. My grades will help. Perhaps a recognized university? And, regarding the SAT, I'm thinking about taking it in July. Is there something else you think we should talk about?" She clutched her backpack tighter, giving her fingers something to do so she wouldn't do something she'd regret.

Mr. O'Jete looked annoyed. "Seriously, Alexa. I mean, Ivy League universities, or any well-known universities, tend to prefer people with history. A legacy. Have your parents attended any universities?"

Images of her mom and dad working at odd hours to make ends meet came to Alexa's mind. She was getting angrier by the minute. She looked down; her knuckles were white from clenching her bag. "No, they have not. I'll be the first one attending college."

Mr. O'Jete was looking at his computer and typing. "I thought so. I have some information about alternative, less highly-selective universities for you. I just emailed them to you. Check them out. I'm always here for you. You know that, right?"

Alexa smiled, recognizing his half-commitment for people *like her*. "Yes, Mr. O'Jete. Thanks for your help."

She left his office, trembling and mad as hell. Who does he think he is? Clearly, he couldn't care less about me!

As Alexa exited O'Jete's office, her eyes met Rudy's, who was waiting just outside. The weight of the meeting was evident on her face, a silent storm that Rudy read all too well. Without uttering a word, he gently took her hand, his silent gesture offering a momentary refuge.

The rest of the day was uneventful. Rudy pulled his car up to Alexa's house at the end of the school day, the engine idling softly. He turned to her, concern evident in his eyes. "You okay?"

Alexa sighed, her shoulders slumping. "It's just... O'Jete."

He gave her hand a reassuring squeeze. "Don't listen to him. You're way out of his league."

She smiled weakly, taking comfort in his words. This was the Rudy she loved. "Thanks, Rudy."

As Alexa looked out the window, she noticed Andy pacing back and forth on her front door, clearly waiting for her. "Looks like Andy wants to chat," she chuckled.

Rudy followed her gaze, nodding. "He's a good friend. Talk soon." He leaned over, giving her a quick peck on the cheek letting her go.

Alexa immediately forgot about the O'Jete incident and concentrated on Andy's news.

Andy bounded over with excitement in his eyes. "Alexa, this dude's legit! President since two thousand seventeen, runs the Hispanic Leadership Institute, and he worked for the University of Delaware as director of the Disaster Research Center. Sent you the deets."

Alexa grinned. "Dang, Andy! Thanks for the quick assist. Seems like he's done a lot, right?"

"Totally! Making waves for sure. By the way," Andy said, his voice dropping a bit, excitement replaced by concern, "Saw you with Pete earlier. You good?"

"Not really. You know him."

"Don't let the guy get to you. He's not worth it. You just do your thing."

"You always see the bright side of things. That means a lot to me. Thank you."

"Any time, Alexa. See you soon." Andy left after implying he needed to see somebody without much elaboration.

The unmistakable aroma of albondigas in tomato sauce floated through the air as Alexa stepped inside. As much as the comforting scent was a balm to her senses, she couldn't entirely mask the strain of the day on her face.

"Hey, Mom," Alexa greeted, attempting a smile, but her eyes betrayed her.

Her mom paused, setting down the sock she was mending. She studied her daughter with a keen, knowing gaze. "¿Tienes hambre? I can heat up some tortillas to go with the albondigas I have ready for dinner. They're delicious. Tough day, mi'ja?"

Alexa needed to unload the difficult day she'd had with O'Jete. "Mamá, the counselor asked me about where you guys went for college. I know you didn't go. He thinks that I don't have much of a professional future. He insists that I shouldn't dream and keep my sights low...." Alexa's voice cracked, halting her words mid-sentence. She felt a tear slide down her cheek, followed by another. Her mother immediately wrapped her in a comforting embrace, holding her close as she allowed the flood of emotions to flow.

When Alexa had cried as much as she needed to and calmed down, her mother sat her down. "Alexa, what dad and I have done to survive isn't what we want for you. We've told you that your education will take you to places. It'll be the key for your success. Please keep at it and let us worry about the rest, okay?"

"¡Pero Mamá! I want to go to college. My math grades are great and I want to keep learning. He practically thinks I should drop out of high school since I can't get there because you guys didn't go to college at all."

Cristina stood to check on dinner and returned with a noticeable grimace.

"What is it, Mom? O'Jete's always like that, but this time he offended *you*. I know you both work a lot all the time. I want to be the best student I can to give you something back."

"Oh, Alexa, always aim high. We're here for you. But, can I ask you a question? What kind of documents do you need for college application?"

"Let me get the list I just got from O'Jete." Alexa went back to her room and retrieved it. "They ask for valid government-issued photo ID, such as driver's license, social security card, or birth certificate."

As Alexa delved deeper into her story, she could see her mom's fingers tightening around the edge of her seat. The room grew thick with tension, each word making it more palpable. Alexa hesitated for a moment, trying to gauge her mother's reaction before pressing on.

"They also ask for high school transcripts, three letters of recommendation, SAT scores, statement of purpose, essays, and certificates for extra-curricular activities. This is where my work with *Latinisimo* will come in handy!"

"Alexa, I don't know how to tell you this, but you need to know. You don't have those papers."

Alexa dropped her hands, the paper rustling against her clothes. "What do you mean by those papers, Mom?"

"You… we're here without papers. We overstayed our visa when we first came years ago. We don't have a passport… because we never became American citizens. We made the decision to come to the U.S. and stayed for a better life. You were just a baby when we arrived. I'm so sorry, Alexa!"

After saying that, her mother's eyes welled up with tears, and her hands trembled slightly. She took a deep, shuddering breath, trying to steady herself before looking into Alexa's eyes, searching for understanding or forgiveness. There was a weight to her gaze, a mix of fear, regret, and hope.

Alexa stood still for what seemed like an hour but was only minutes, absorbing her mom's words. She couldn't believe what she was hearing. Oh, gosh! I'm illegally living in this country! Her dreams, aspirations, friends, and everything she was fighting for seemed to crumble right in front of her eyes. It was too much. She began sobbing uncontrollably. "Why did you lie to me? Why are you telling me this now?"

"We didn't want to cut your dreams short, Alexa!" Her mom's instincts kicked in and, next thing she knew, her mom was embracing her, consoling her, protecting her like she had always done, until now.

"We have everything, a decent life here, work to provide what's needed. You're doing so great in school. We're so proud of you! We don't understand how the school system works here. We didn't study here, Alexa!" Her mom stopped, as she was now crying her eyes out seeing Alexa's dreams shattered.

After a few minutes, her mom was able to continue. "We didn't know if you wanted to go to a university, but we'll do whatever it takes for you to continue. In fact, your dad and I follow all news on the DACA Program. You qualify as a dreamer, Alexa! You do have a future!"

"I'm not sure about that. People hate illegals in this country! I don't even know if I can continue. Maybe O'Jete's right and I should go for a less demanding option after all."

Each step toward the front door felt heavier than the last. The sting of O'Jete's words combined with her mom's revelation made the room feel smaller, her world closing in. It was as if the dreams and aspirations she had meticulously built were now standing on the edge of a precipice, teetering perilously. A bleak future loomed, with her hopes now seemingly out of reach. Just as she reached for the doorknob, desperate for a breath of fresh air, her phone buzzed with a message from Ella: *Doing okay? Have not heard from you. Need help?*

Taking a deep breath, Alexa pressed the call button next to Ella's name. It only took a couple of rings before Ella picked up.

"Alexa? Hey, what's up?"

"I just... Ella, everything's such a mess right now." Alexa's voice trembled. "I'm running behind."

Ella, even without knowing the specifics, sensed the gravity of the situation. "Hey, deep breaths. Whatever this is, you're not alone. Remember, every problem has a solution. Do you want to talk about it?"

Pausing for a moment, comforted by Ella's words, Alexa replied softly, "Not now, but soon. I'd appreciate that, Ella."

"Of course. Whenever you're ready. Just know I'm here for you." Ella replied warmly, offering an unexpected lifeline to a distressed Alexa.

Speaking with Ella provided Alexa a much-needed sense of purpose amidst the chaos of her day. This brief escape shifted her focus, even if just momentarily. Turning her attention back to the research on Havidán Rodríguez, she was pleasantly surprised. Alexa uncovered a wealth of information, especially interviews. In New York and among the Latino community, he was quite the prominent figure. Starting with the university's official records, his impressive credentials left her astounded. After compiling her findings, she promptly sent an email to Ella detailing her discoveries.

Ella returned the email with a text. *Great info! Tks! It'll be Zoom. Link here. CYsoon!*

On the day of the interview, Alexa's gaze lingered on Ella as she set up the Zoom call. Her own recent revelation cast a shadow over her thoughts, making her wonder, what would Ella think about it. As she pondered on her own college future, she couldn't help but let her worries seep into the moment.

"How are you doing? Everything okay on your end? You seem pensive."

Alexa nodded. "Kinda. I'm better now. I'll share with you later. So, how does it work with a Zoom interview instead of at the studio?"

"It's similar except for the need to conduct the interview remotely. The preparation and research on the interviewee are the same, actually. I'm thinking about beginning with what motivated his career."

She was finishing the sentence when Havidán opened his camera and microphone. "Hello, Ella! So good seeing you! It has been… how many years?"

The familiarity took Alexa by surprise.

"Hola, Havidán! I believe last time we saw each other was at a Board meeting probably five years ago, or perhaps at an arts event. Let me introduce Alexa Hope, *Latinisimo*'s intern for the next year. She conducted great research on you. Are you okay if she takes notes and keeps an eye on the time?"

"By all means! By the way, Ella, I am afraid that an unexpected meeting with the Hispanic Leadership Institute just emerged. I should have a solid hour before I have to leave. Is that okay?"

Ella understood that time was of the essence and began the interview with an open-ended question. "What made it possible for you to become a university president, Havidán?"

Havidán smiled. "The funny part is that I never expected to go to college. I never expected to get a PhD, let alone be a president of a major research university. I was actually advised to become an automobile mechanic rather than attend college. As it turns out, I joined the U.S. Air Force, completed college, later earned a doctorate in sociology, and was appointed the twentieth president of the University at Albany in June two thousand seventeen."

Alexa's ear perked up. Did he get the same advice I had? And… he became president of a university! She quickly typed a message in the chat box. *Ella, please ask about 'becoming a mechanic advice.' Why was that?* Ella responded with the thumbs up emoji.

Havidán explained further. "I grew up primarily raised by a single mother in the Bronx. She drove a taxi in New York City to support our family. My mother instilled in us the love to work hard, to get educated despite the fact that she never went to college. She was just sixteen, a baby herself, when she had me. For us, education was the way to move up socially and economically and make contributions. So, thanks to her, here I am."

Gosh, it's like hearing mom: 'The only thing we ask of you is to study, good grades. Education will open doors for you.'

The interview continued, exploring Havidán's many professional facets, including being Disaster Research Center Director at the University of Delaware along with related activities, some recognitions, awards, and publications.

"From our work together," Ella said, "I know how proud of your heritage you are and how it's been a motivator in every step you've made. Could you please make the connection for us, being president and being Latino?"

"One of my colleagues used to introduce me and said, 'Havidán Rodríguez is an excellent President of the University at Albany… who happens to be Latino.' Not that I was Latino and, therefore, am president. We have to make sure that diversity and excellence come out in the same sentence, because when we promote diversity, we do not minimize our standards. Diversity increases excellence, right?"

As Havidán spoke, Alexa's eyes widened momentarily on the Zoom call, taken aback by his words. Diversity, excellence, and… being Latino is like a bonus? The newfound concept began to seep in, challenging and reshaping her internal narrative. This empowering perspective was a refreshing twist, one she had never entertained before.

"I'm incredibly proud to be Boricua, from Puerto Rico." Havidán paused then added, "Latinos have to lead by example and make sure that we are seen as role models. I'm not concerned about the work I do. I *am* concerned about the work that should represent very well the Latinx community.

"As Latinos we need to establish greater participation in nearly every profession. Did you know that Latinos are particularly underrepresented in the sciences, technology, engineering, and mathematics, for example? People sometimes refer to them as STEM. We also need more senior administrators in institutions of higher education, where they can serve as role models for students."

Watching him command the screen with undeniable authority, Alexa was struck by how polished and professional he appeared. His voice, with its deep timbre, coupled with the intentional pauses and eloquent intonations, was captivating. Wow, he's totally on point. Why aren't there more Latinos out there like him, making big moves? Isn't he, like, the ultimate boss goal? Being a university president is so legit!

As she mulled over this, Alexa felt a rush of pride. It wasn't just about looking up to Havidán; it was about wanting to see herself and others like her in such major roles. Despite the chaos of the day's discoveries, right now, that anxiety was eclipsed by a vision of potential futures. Havidán wasn't just some guy on a screen; he was an inspiration for young Latinos like her. Gripping her mouse, a little tighter, she felt a spark of hope and determination.

To Alexa's dismay, the time allocated for the interview was quickly coming to an end. She was getting nervous and sent another message in the Zoom chat, refreshing Ella's memory on the question about overcoming negativity. Ella texted back, *Thanks—asking.*

"So, Havidán, how do you respond to an advice like 'become an automobile mechanic'? I'm sure it impacted you, didn't it?"

Havidán reflected for a few seconds. "Yes, it did. I still remember. I was about fifteen years old when my advisor recommended that I better have a backup plan because apparently, at that time, I was not college material." He paused again. "Perseverance. My mother taught me by example. Not too long ago, she actually completed her high school degree herself. That is what I did. I persevered, and here I am."

Alexa found herself hanging on to every word, absorbing the layers of Havidán's journey. The struggles, the discrimination, the climb to success—it resonated deeply with her. A spark of recognition lit up within her as she thought, We have a lot in common! He was also discriminated against, and yet he's a president of a university. He's the whole enchilada!

Ella asked Alexa if there was something missing or anything she wanted to ask. Alexa blinked in surprise, momentarily caught off guard. She hadn't expected to be directly included. Regaining her composure, she unmuted herself and said, "I was looking forward to that last question. Everything was covered, Ella. Thanks!"

"Many thanks for your time today, Havidán! We know you have to go. Have a great rest of your day!"

Havidán said goodbye and disconnected, but Alexa and Ella stayed on Zoom.

"What do you think, Alexa?" Ella asked.

"Listening to Havidán was just... eye-opening. You know I've been having a rough time, but hearing his journey and struggles, it's like I saw a bit of myself in him. If he could push through all that and reach where he is now, maybe I can too. This was exactly the boost I needed today. Seriously, thank you so much for this!"

"Glad to hear! Next time will be a chemist and nonprofit leader. Her name is Lourdes Puig."

As Ella's voice brightened, sharing details about the next guest, Alexa felt a spark of excitement. "That's cool, Ella! I've actually been thinking a lot about maybe going into the STEM field, particularly engineering, like Havidán mentioned."

A hint of surprise flashed across Ella's face on the screen. "Really? You're into engineering? Wow, having Lourdes on 'People Who Make Us Pause' is going to be super timely then. Catch you in a few weeks. Don't forget to do a bit of homework on Lourdes. Thanks for being awesome today!" Ella gave Alexa a warm smile before disconnecting.

Alexa felt a surge of warmth. Being acknowledged like that meant the world after a rough day. Ella's genuine appreciation made Alexa feel seen, not just as a student, but as someone with potential. It was a comforting conclusion to a tumultuous day.

CHAPTER 4

A CHEMIST AND NONPROFIT LEADER, LOURDES PUIG

Just two months into her gig as co-host of *Latinisimo*, Alexa was amazed at how much she'd already absorbed. With only two interviews under her belt, the impact on her was huge. Working alongside Ella, she not only picked up the ropes of hosting a show but was also blown away by the real-life tales their guests shared. The arts healer and the university president, from different worlds, had stories of grit, determination, and heart that went beyond any cultural label.

For Alexa, these weren't just interviews; they felt like peeks into real-life adventures of chasing dreams and overcoming odds. She saw bits of herself in their tales, feeling like she was part of this bigger narrative of chasing big dreams. More than just learning the art of interviewing, Alexa was getting life lessons and a good dose of inspiration.

The next interview was getting closer, but she had not heard from Ella yet. She decided to text her. *Hi there! Any news on the next guest?*

Ella responded quickly. *It'll be Lourdes Puig, chemist, former DuPonter, Board President of Aspira Academy. Not much online. Please research.*

Alexa had all intentions of looking up Lourdes, but being a dreamer was weighing heavily on her.

Alexa's thumb hovered momentarily over her phone screen as a headline caught her eye: "DACA Developments: What's Next for Dreamers?" She tapped on the link, skimming through the article. Being a dreamer in the U.S. ... it's more than just a status, she thought, pausing on a quote from an activist. It's about yearning for a life without shadows, without fear of being uprooted from the only place that feels like home. She screenshotted a section detailing upcoming policy changes, feeling the urge to share with someone who'd understand.

Quickly, she texted it to her mom, adding, *Check this out. You are right!* A few moments later, her phone buzzed with a notification. Opening the message, she saw a simple heart emoji from her mom. She felt hopeful.

The lunch bell rang out, punctuating the midday bustle. As students rushed towards the cafeteria or their favorite lunch spots, conversations about upcoming tests, weekend plans, and school gossip mingled in the air. Amidst this familiar noontime chaos, Alexa walked with a sense of introspection. She had recently discovered more about the dreamer status, and it provided a glimmer of hope in her complicated world. Every so often, she'd pull out her phone, rereading her mom's text and smiling faintly at the heart emoji. Alexa's heart was heavy, but this new knowledge and her mom's unwavering support gave her a touch of resoluteness amidst her emotions.

It was during this introspective moment that Andy found her. "How are you doing?"

Alexa met Andy's eyes, her cheeks warming with a hint of embarrassment. The weight of everything threatened to bring her to tears again, but she held on. "It's... it's complicated," she admitted, her voice wavering.

"What's wrong?" Andy's concern was evident.

"There's so much I need to tell you." Alexa shared her dreamer status and how her parents had kept that secret. It was a painful conversation.

"I feel for you, Alexa," Andy muttered while embracing his friend. He let Alexa talk.

"But you know... you have options. I know of at least one more student in a similar situation here at school. Let's check."

Swiftly, Andy keyed in 'dreamer' on his phone, and a flood of results populated the screen. Skimming the top hits, he started relaying the essential bits. But just as he was diving deeper, the intercom's staticky voice interrupted, "Students, please make your way to your next class."

Caught off guard, Andy hurriedly summarized the main points for Alexa. The urgency meant neither had a moment to even think about grabbing lunch.

"Undocumented students... Deferred Action for Childhood Arrivals, or DACA... Close to one million students affected in the U.S.... No federal law barring college attendance... Colleges decide admission and in-state versus out-of-state charges... Mostly treated as international students... Limited financial aid dollars." Andy's gaze lifted from the information he was skimming, and seeing his expression, Alexa felt a pang of anticipation.

"Mom always said I had options," Alexa began, her voice trembling with emotion. "I had a hard time believing her, but what you've just shared, Andy... it's starting to resonate. I cherish my Mexican heritage, but in my heart, I'm also American.

This country is all I've ever known." The warning bell sounded, signaling the imminent start of the next class.

Once the class ended, and as the hallway next to the computer lab thrummed with students eagerly discussing their day, Andy gently led Alexa to a quiet corner near a cluster of lockers. Her eyes shimmered with unshed tears, and she bit her lip, willing herself not to unravel amidst the crowd.

Andy, sensing her distress, softly said, "Hey, it's going to be okay." He discreetly pulled out his phone, ensuring that only Alexa could glimpse the screen. "After we spoke earlier today, I did some additional research. There are options for you."

Swallowing hard, Alexa leaned in closer, her voice trembling with a mix of embarrassment and hope. "What did you find?"

Andy quickly scrolled through his screen. "There are private scholarships. They're designed for situations like yours. They don't just cover tuition, but other expenses as well—housing, meals, even books. And Alexa," he paused, glancing into her eyes, "your journey, your story… It's powerful. It could move mountains in an essay."

Alexa's eyes misted over, touched by the depth of Andy's compassion and support. "You did this for me?" She managed a weak smile, her voice quivering. "I… I'm overwhelmed."

Gently patting her back, Andy responded, "Of course. You're not in this alone. And this DACA thing? We'll dive deep into it. Together."

She closed her eyes for a moment, letting the weight of her gratitude sink in. "Thank you, Andy. You have no idea what this means."

As they began to walk back towards the classroom, Alexa felt the knot in her chest loosen slightly. She was grateful, so incredibly grateful, to have such a supportive friend by her side.

The school day drew to a close, the atmosphere grew heavy with the scent of impending rain. Clouds, gray and melancholic, mirrored Alexa's mood, gathering in the sky and casting a somber shade on the campus. Near the bus exit, Alexa and Andy were waiting.

Soon, the sound of Rudy's voice cut through the murmur of students. "I swear, I don't get these school folks," he vented, joining the duo. "O'Jete keeps harping on about universities, the SATs, life after high school. It's like, what if I haven't figured it all out yet?" He was about to launch into another rant when a flurry of notifications from his game, Skyrim, diverted his attention. Almost instantly, his complaints about school were forgotten, replaced by the allure of the virtual world.

Alexa bit her lip, suppressing a sigh of exasperation. She'd hoped to bring Rudy up to speed sharing her feelings, but as she watched Rudy engrossed in his game, it was clear where his priorities lay. With a resigned shrug, she exchanged a knowing glance with Andy, a silent acknowledgment of the vast differences in their focuses. The contrast between Rudy's and Andy's attitudes made Alexa's heart sink.

Andy quietly said, "I know. Let's go."

It was a busy time at school and the days were going fast. Towards the end of the week, *Latinisimo*'s pending episode came to Alexa's mind. She remembered that she needed to work on Lourdes Puig's information to be ready for the interview. She googled the name but couldn't find much. She texted Ella: *Need Lourde's email & cell. No info = have to email/call her.*

Ella texted back with Lourdes' email and a number to call. Alexa wasn't sure where to begin and felt the need to connect with Ella for guidance. She texted immediately: *Have time for a quick WhatsApp?*

Ella texted back: *Yep!*

Alexa's eyes darted across the screen, reflecting her confusion. She hesitated, biting her lip. "Hey Ella... I'm not sure where to even begin with this. Can you help?"

Ella leaned in, her face softening with understanding. "It's alright. So, for Lourdes, start with an introductory email. Mention that you'll be calling her soon and that it's to prep for the interview."

Alexa frowned slightly, scribbling notes. "But what exactly do I ask about? Just her life?"

Ella chuckled. "That's a start. Dive into her professional background too. LinkedIn is your best friend for this. You can gather something about her career from there."

Alexa's eyebrows raised in playful mischief. "So, it's kinda like online detective work? A little pre-interview stalking session? Cool!" She laughed, but her face became serious again. "What about the program? Should I ask her about any specific elements she wants to include?"

"Absolutely." Ella nodded. "Perhaps see if she has any preferred music for breaks? And remember, it's just some research to be prepared and able to ask relevant questions, right?" she added with a wink.

Alexa replied with a smile. "Thanks. And yeah... about her being a chemist... I find that intriguing. As you know, I'm into sciences, especially engineering."

Ella's smile was encouraging. "See? You've already got a connection there. Just take it one step at a time. I've got your back, and I'm here if you need any more guidance."

Alexa promptly drafted an email to Lourdes, suggesting a phone call and outlining its purpose. She looped in Ella by cc'ing her. Within a short time, Ella chimed in with her support in the email thread. A few days later, the call with Lourdes was scheduled.

"Hi, Lourdes! This is Alexa, Ella's intern for *Latinisimo*."

"Hi, Alexa! Glad you're calling." Lourdes' voice held a warmth and excitement. "How can I be of help? I have to admit, if not for Ella, I probably would have declined any interview request."

"Really? Why's that?" Alexa asked, genuine curiosity lacing her voice. "I mean, I'm glad you didn't say no, but what made you hesitant in the first place? Alexa paused for a moment. Is this a good time to chat?"

Lourdes paused briefly, her laughter tinged with a hint of nervousness. "Well, you see, I've always been the type to work quietly in the background, making things happen without seeking attention or applause. Stepping into the spotlight and sharing my personal journey? It's quite out of my comfort zone, to put it mildly."

Alexa tilted her head, her youthful curiosity evident. "Honestly, with all these YouTubers and influencers these days, it's like everyone's just chasing clout without really doing anything cool. It's wild to talk to someone who's actually awesome and isn't all about the likes and follows."

Lourdes raised an eyebrow, then let out a genuine laugh, her eyes sparkling with amusement. "Oh, Alexa," she said, shaking her head, "I can see why Ella speaks so highly of you. Refreshingly candid! It's true though, isn't it? So much noise out there, it's hard to distinguish the real stories from the fake ones."

"It is a challenge to get the real ones!" Smiling Alexa pressed on. "So, I saw on your LinkedIn that you're a chemist, which is super cool. But what caught my eye was 'community leader' and how you're into helping young folks succeed. What's the story behind that? I'm super curious!"

"I have a bachelor's in science with a concentration in chemistry, and a doctoral degree with a specialization in analytical chemistry from the University of Michigan in Ann Arbor. All of that with a full scholarship, which helped a lot! A few years later, corporate America hired me, and I was able to apply my background in different assignments. I enjoyed each one of them, including management."

Alexa's eyes gleamed with genuine curiosity. "That's seriously cool!" she began, "But I gotta ask, what made you shift from the world of chemistry to diving deep into helping young people and supporting nonprofit organizations?"

"I have a passion for education. Switching to helping others started as a consequence of volunteer work related to my daughter. Since she was born, it was about her catechism, girls sports and the like. When she got to high school, she needed less of me. I had more time for other people. I thought she could share me." Clearing her throat with a light-hearted giggle, Lourdes shifted the conversation. "We'll definitely dive deeper during the interview. But for now, I'm curious about you, Alexa. What lights your fire? Have you chalked out plans for after high school?"

Alexa hesitated for a moment, her voice faltering slightly. "Well, Lourdes…I mean, I really enjoy math, and I've been doing well in my science classes. But when it comes to deciding what to study in college and everything... it just feels overwhelming, you know?"

Lourdes replied, "Oh, Alexa, I've seen this so often. While I was volunteering with Aspira, an organization helping high school students, many of them grappled with choosing their future paths. A select few had it figured out, but for most, it was quite a challenging decision. How about we delve deeper into this after our interview? I'd love to help."

"Thank you so much! I'd really appreciate that." As Alexa ended the call, a rush of excitement surged within her. Alexa briefly closed her eyes, imagining a cozy café meeting with Lourdes, filled with engaging stories and warm cocoa. She felt hopeful as she confirmed their next meeting, looking forward to their conversation.

Alexa immediately dialed Ella after finishing her chat with Lourdes. "Ella, you won't believe this. She's not just a chemist," she exclaimed, her voice bubbling with enthusiasm.

Ella, a bit taken aback, responded, "What do you mean?"

"She's a CE!" Alexa announced triumphantly.

"A... CE?" Ella echoed, puzzled.

Alexa couldn't help but laugh. "Yeah, Lourdes is a Chemist who Educates! It's like the universe is dropping hints right in front of me!

Alexa hesitated for a brief moment, her enthusiasm dimming slightly. "It's just, there's this thing... it's personal and has been on my mind a lot lately. It makes me question if I'll even be able to pursue everything I dream of."

Ella, sensing Alexa's change in tone, probed gently. "What's up? You can always talk to me, you know that, right?"

Alexa took a deep breath. "I know, Ella. I promise I'll share soon. But talking to Lourdes... it gave me a burst of hope. Despite the uncertainties, I feel like there's a path forward."

Ella replied with warmth, "Alexa, whatever it is, I'm here for you. Always. But for now, let's get pumped for the interview! Thanks for connecting with Lourdes. See you at the studio."

The day of the interview was a sunny Friday in March. As Alexa stepped into the studio, the weight of the secret she'd been harboring pressed on her. Her boots echoed softly against the floor, and her outfit—jeans paired with a light jacket—suited the brisk yet sunny March day in northern Delaware. She paused, absorbing the familiar studio surroundings, appreciating the serenity before the onset of the interview's hustle.

Ella soon walked in, holding a drink. "You know, this is just divine, Alexa," she started, flashing her signature grin. "Pumpkin spice and two espresso shots, all immersed in the silkiest almond milk ever. Doesn't that sound like sheer perfection?"

Alexa chuckled, the tension momentarily forgotten. "Honestly? That sounds dreadful. I'd much prefer a frozen chai green tea topped with whipped cream."

Ella laughed heartily. "Clearly not your cup of tea. Or, in this case, coffee." She set her drink aside and looked at Alexa more intently, noticing some underlying tension. "Hey, you alright?"

Alexa took a deep breath. "Ella, there's something I've never shared with you. With everything that's been happening... I found out from my mom that I'm undocumented. You know, one of those 'illegals' living in the U.S. We've looked into it, and I might qualify for DACA. Basically... I'm a dreamer."

Ella's playful demeanor shifted instantly. Her eyes widened slightly, absorbing the gravity of the revelation. Without a word, Ella stepped closer and wrapped Alexa in a warm, comforting embrace. Alexa felt a rush of emotions as she leaned into Ella's hold, feeling the balminess and understanding radiate from her. For a moment, they stood like that—two friends, connected by a newfound depth of trust and empathy.

Finally pulling back, Ella looked Alexa in the eyes. "It's not a piece of paper or a status that defines you. It's your spirit, your tenacity. Thanks for trusting me with this."

Their moment was interrupted when the studio door softly clicked open. Lourdes walked in, her eyes catching the empty cup of coffee in Ella's hand. "Is Ella trying to convince you about the quality of her pumpkin concoction?" Lourdes teased with a smile. "Please, don't fall for it. I tried it once and couldn't sleep for hours."

Ella rolled her eyes playfully. "I don't like flimsy stuff! But enough about coffee. Are we ready for the interview? Alexa, any musical preferences for our breaks today?

In the gently illuminated WVUD studio, the subtle lighting accentuated the disarray of items from Alexa's well-worn backpack. Amidst crumpled notes, a few stray pens, and the faint scent of an old fruit snack, Alexa's fingers frantically searched for her memory stick. Just when she was about to voice her fear of having lost it, her fingers brushed against the familiar plastic shape. Pulling it out with a mix of relief and triumph, she offered it to Ella, exclaiming, "I thought I'd never find this! Lourdes is from Puerto Rico, so I thought of Daddy Yankee's 'Gasolina' and Ricky Martin's 'Livin' La Vida Loca.' They might be older songs, but they're total bangers!

"Sold!" Lourdes said.

This time, Alexa checked the mics and volume while indicating to Lourdes where she should sit.

"Great job, Alexa." Ella placed the memory stick in its slot. She closed the door and adjusted the console, making sure that

Audacity was recording properly. A dry run confirmed that everything was in place. She opened the session with the pre-recorded program intro and welcomed the audience.

"Lourdes, help us understand the person behind your successful professional life. You recently retired from a multinational corporation but are giving back to the community, particularly in education. What motivates you to do what you do?"

Lourdes leaned forward, her eyes shining with passion as she gestured emphatically with her hands. "I've always felt this deep connection with education. It's transformative. I yearn to pave pathways for students, to uplift them. Remember this— everything can be taken from you: your home, your possessions, even the shirt off your back. But education? It remains undeniably yours, forever unclaimed by anyone else."

The intensity in Lourdes' eyes, coupled with the animated gestures of her hands, captivated Alexa. The fiery spirit, the undeniable Latina energy in Lourdes, felt so familiar, so reminiscent of mom and, more recently, of Havidán. As Alexa's thoughts drifted to her impressive grades, a surge of pride welled up. All those heart-to-heart lectures, maybe there was truth in them, she pondered. I'm actually nailing this!

Ella explored Lourdes' community involvement. "What organizations have you belonged to?"

Lourdes remembered a few. "At the University of Michigan, we had a Puerto Rican Association. I led that association for several years. The objective was to enhance the voice and the presence of the Puerto Rican community there. We always finished all events with a dance. Obviously, anything Latino, typically Puerto Rican, you need to have the salsa night," she said.

"Perfect segue for our first music break, Lourdes. Let's dive in!" Ella announced.

As the sultry rhythms of a salsa track began to envelop the room, Lourdes' fingers gracefully traced the air, mimicking the beat in a dance all their own. Alexa caught the gesture, a silent yet passionate connection to the music. It wasn't long before all three found themselves swaying, their hands waving in tandem to the rhythm, laughter echoing and eyes gleaming. A shared, joyous moment that quickly came to an end.

Bringing the conversation back to a more recent time Lourdes added, "I am part of the American Chemical Society. I still want to keep a little bit of the technical connection. A year ago, I was nominated to the board of the Delaware Foundation for Science, Math, and Education, or DFSME. I've been participating in one of the grants committees advancing science, given my technical background."

"On that front," Ella began, "our research indicates that despite making up nearly half of the U.S. workforce, women are still vastly underrepresented in the sciences, technology, engineering, and math fields. In nineteen seventy, women constituted thirty-eight percent of all U.S. workers but only eight percent of STEM workers. By twenty nineteen, women made up forty-eight percent of all workers, but their representation in the STEM fields was only twenty-seven percent."

Lourdes nodded. "And these are the workers who play a key role in the country's innovative capacity and global competitiveness. Still a long way to go for women on this front."

Alexa's brows shot up in surprise. Wait, that's kind wild when you think about it. Like, half the brainpower in the country is being overlooked? She quickly pulled out her phone and started typing. "Sorry, just need a sec," she muttered, then added to her Instagram story: Almost half the workforce is women, but where are they in STEM? Let's change this! #GirlsInSTEM

#TimeForChange. She looked up, a smirk on her face. Done. Maybe somebody else will start thinking about it too.

"Now, going back to the connection with your background and the salsa nights," Ella said, "let's bring Aspira back to the conversation."

Alexa shifted in her chair, her attention riveted on Lourdes. The ambiance of the room was snug, and the muted lighting cast a soft glow, highlighting the gentle lines of experience on Lourdes' face. As Lourdes began her tale, Alexa could see the depth of her commitment reflected in her eyes and the subtle gestures that accompanied her words.

"When my daughter entered her teenage years and began driving on her own, it felt like she didn't need her mom quite as much," Lourdes began, her voice tinged with a hint of nostalgia. "That void led me to Aspira. It's an organization that sprouted in New York more than sixty years ago. From its roots, it has since branched out across the nation. I've heard tales of its bustling hub in Washington, D.C., but my journey intersected with Aspira around the idea of birthing the Aspira of Delaware chapter in the mid-two thousands. Our mission was clear: shepherd Latino high school students through the intricate dance of college applications."

Lourdes paused, taking a momentary breath, her eyes distant yet shining with memories. "There were days, especially Saturdays, when I found myself up and about at seven in the morning for Aspira. Admittedly, there were fleeting moments of doubt, moments where I questioned—'Why am I doing this?' But each year, without fail, there would be at least one or sometimes two students who would provide the answer. To them, our role transcended beyond guidance. We were their confidants, their mentors, and often, the steady hand they needed amidst their chaos."

As Lourdes spoke, Alexa felt a pull, a connection. Here was a woman who had taken paths Alexa could only dream of. In Lourdes, she saw a hint of the strength and resolve she yearned to harness within herself. Out of the corner of her eye, she felt Ella's gaze, perhaps recognizing the deep resonance of Lourdes' words were having on her.

"But you are still related to Aspira somehow, is this correct, Lourdes?"

"Yes, I am the President of the Board of Las Americas Aspira Academy. It's a dual-language, full-immersion Spanish charter school in North Delaware. I've been the board chair for the last seven years."

"How did Las Americas Aspira Academy begin, and where is it now?"

"It started with three hundred students. I was involved with Aspira, the organization, but not part of the school board at that time. I became the Chair two years later, when there were five hundred students. We currently have over one thousand students. We're kindergarten to ninth grade right now, and will continue to add a grade every year for the next three years until we complete the entire K to twelve program. The alignment of leadership and staff has been crucial in the whole process to facilitate growth. I truly feel honored to have had the chance to lead the organization all these years and to have found the means and resources to support the school's expansion."

Lourdes began recounting the deliberate and persistent efforts that had brought the school to the cusp of introducing the twelfth grade. All the while, Alexa leaned in, absorbing every word with rapt attention.

Ella leaned back, clearly impressed. "What an achievement, Lourdes! Building a school from scratch is truly remarkable."

After a brief pause, she asked, "Anything else you'd like to touch upon before we wrap up?"

Lourdes replied warmly, "I'm simply thankful for the opportunity to share on *Latinisimo*. Having both you and Alexa here makes it all the more special."

Ella quickly shut off the mics and secured the recording. Looking up, she beamed. "Lourdes, that was a fantastic conversation. Thank you so much!"

Lourdes flashed a grateful smile. Her gaze then landed on Alexa. "Speaking of fantastic, Alexa and I have a pending conversation. Would you care to join?"

Ella gave a regretful shake of her head. "I'd love to, but I need to edit this down and then dash to a dinner commitment. Rain check?"

Lourdes nodded understandingly. "Of course."

As Ella focused on her editing, Lourdes gestured to Alexa, hinting towards the upstairs cafeteria. The aroma puffing from it was especially inviting on Fridays, thanks to the specials that always drew a crowd. This time the scent of fresh nachos was practically irresistible.

While making their way up, Alexa, with youthful curiosity, asked, "Lourdes, you mentioned something about 'alignment of leadership and staff' during the interview. What does that mean? How does that help things?"

Lourdes paused for a moment, searching for the right words to make it relatable for Alexa. "You know how in a group project, when everyone is on the same page, understands their role, and works towards a common goal, it just... flows better? And how it's so much harder when everyone is doing their own thing without coordinating?"

Alexa nodded, recalling the many school projects she'd been a part of.

"It's like that on a larger scale," Lourdes continued. "When the leadership and staff are aligned, they understand the school's vision and work seamlessly together to achieve it. Everyone knows their part, and they trust each other to play it. That's what makes growth possible and smooth. Think of it as the ultimate group project, where everyone is in sync."

Alexa's eyes lit up in comprehension. "Oh, I get it! It's like making sure everyone's energy is directed in the same way. That makes sense."

As they reached the cafeteria, Lourdes pointed to a corner stall. "How about some nachos? They smell fantastic, don't you think?"

Alexa's eyes sparkled with excitement. "Yep! But with tons of jalapeños. I love a good kick."

Lourdes chuckled. "Maybe not tons of jalapeños if that's okay with you. Let's get a medium plate and share it. Sounds good?"

They placed their order and, once it was ready, picked it up. The heaping plate of crispy nachos drenched in cheese with jalapeños was too much to resist. The two of them dug in, savoring every bite. To Alexa, it didn't feel like she was with a seasoned professional; it felt like she was sharing a snack with a friend who just happened to prefer fewer jalapeños.

"Lourdes, did you know that you're a CE?"

"What's a CE?"

Alexa's eyes brightened as she responded, "You're not just a chemist, are you? You're a Chemist who Educates. You really love education, don't you?"

With a warm smile, Lourdes nodded. "I see what you did there... yes, I am truly passionate about education. I suppose I am a CE, then. Now, Alexa, let's delve into where you stand and where you aspire to be, shall we?

Taking a deep breath to steady her nerves, Alexa began, "Lourdes, you remember our chat earlier about college, right? My advisor keeps suggesting university might not be for me. He says I might not be cut out for... well, much. But I have this knack for math, and I just can't ignore it. Why did you choose chemistry?"

Lourdes leaned in, her attention solely on Alexa. "First off, never let anyone define your capabilities. And as for chemistry and engineering, while they remain predominantly male fields here in the U.S., many female students excel remarkably. Sometimes even outperforming their male peers."

Pausing to enjoy a nacho, sans the jalapeño, Lourdes continued, "So tell me, what draws you to STEM, especially when you talk about your affinity for math?"

Swirling a nacho in the cheese, Alexa pondered. "I think it's the intrigue. I've always wanted to know how things tick. Math is like this... puzzle, waiting to be solved. I just don't know where I fit in this STEM world."

Nodding, Lourdes said, "STEM's beauty lies in its vastness. From delving into the cosmos in astrophysics to decoding the human genome. Every branch has its mysteries."

Feeling more animated, Alexa admitted, "Exactly! I adore puzzles. It's just choosing one avenue feels daunting. And then there's the whole dilemma of ensuring a good career and all."

Lourdes chuckled softly, "Ah, the perpetual balance of following your heart and being pragmatic. STEM is versatile, innovative. Most of its branches guarantee a stable career. The trick is finding which branch sings to your soul. Like anything else really."

Alexa, sipping her drink, wondered aloud, "And what made chemistry sing to you?"

With a reminiscent smile, Lourdes explained, "Chemistry, to me, was the heartbeat of science. It's everywhere—our food, the makeup we wear, the air we breathe. I was smitten with the idea of deciphering the world, molecule by molecule."

A spark in her eyes, Alexa mused, "That's genuinely captivating. I should probably dive deeper, maybe shadow some professionals, get a feel of different fields. Like continuing what I started here at *Latinisimo*, right?"

Lourdes' eyes shimmered with encouragement. "That's it, Alexa. Dive in, immerse yourself, and you'll undoubtedly find your space in STEM. As mentioned before, I had a fulfilling job in corporate America. Being a chemist opened up possibilities for me. It will for you!"

Alexa felt a lump in her throat. Mustering the courage, she locked eyes with Lourdes, her voice wavering slightly. "Lourdes, have you worked with dreamers?"

Lourdes paused, her gaze keen on Alexa, picking up on the unspoken undercurrents of the question. "Alexa," she began gently, as if sensing the vulnerability in Alexa's eyes, "have you thought about the opportunities available for dreamers at top universities?"

Alexa hesitated, "I've thought about it, but I don't know if they'd even consider someone like me."

Lourdes' eyes held a hint of surprise. "Why would you say that?"

Taking a deep breath, Alexa replied, "Financially, it's a strain. I'm not sure if we can afford it. And... the dreamer thing."

Lourdes leaned in, her tone earnest. "Did you know, Alexa, that the Massachusetts Institute of Technology has a scholarship specifically for families in dire need? It's actually considered a grant, meaning it doesn't need to be repaid. What's more, there's no obligation for you to work while you study."

Alexa's eyes widened. "Really? But such prestigious institutions..."

"Yes," Lourdes interrupted gently, adding, "Institutions like MIT, and even Ivy Leagues such as Harvard, Princeton, and Yale. They recognize potential and are willing to invest in students like you. They'll cover everything—tuition, housing, dining, books, even personal expenses. All you need to do is apply."

Alexa was visibly moved. "That's... that's incredible, Lourdes. I had no idea." Alexa's eyes brightened with anticipation.

Lourdes paused. "Alexa, if Ella believes in you enough to want you as an intern for a year, it's evident that you have what it takes to succeed. No one should be allowed to snatch your dreams away. If it's math or engineering that excites you, then chase it with everything you've got!"

"You sound so much like Ella... and my best friend Andy!" Alexa exclaimed with a smile.

Lourdes laughed. "Well, Ella and I are friends for good reason! No surprises there, right? As for Andy...I already like him! I'm here to support you too!"

They said their goodbyes outside the cafeteria, parting with the assurance of staying connected. As Alexa walked towards the university's public transportation stop, her steps were buoyed by the newfound hope and warmth infused by their heartening conversation.

As the bus rumbled beneath her, Alexa's thoughts drifted back to the discussion with Lourdes. Their exchange had lasted for more than an hour, each moment rich with insight and understanding. Lourdes' warmth and receptivity still lingered with her, especially when she had offered her number for any future queries. The weight in Alexa's chest had lessened, replaced by a comforting thought that in Lourdes, she had found both a mentor and a friend.

Staring out of the window, the city lights blurring, Alexa mused, this is great! More than great! Taking that chance with Ella led me to something... someone... invaluable. Lourdes could be my personal CE! A text was in order.

Hi! On the bus home. Met Lourdes today. She's amazing! She gets me. She'll guide me in all this. Will tell you more at home.

Her mother texted back: *Can't wait to hear all about it. So proud of you, Alexa. ¡TQM. Con cuidado m'ija!*

CHAPTER 5

AN ACTIVIST AND ARTS EDUCATION ADVOCATE, RAYE JONES AVERY

As the school bus rumbled along the streets of Wilmington, Alexa's eyes were drawn to a colorful local mural splashed in vivid hues, illuminated by the soft glow of the April morning sun. The intricate blend of shades and shapes seemed to dance, infusing a sudden burst of excitement and joy into her soul. She hadn't noticed it before. The unexpected trill of her phone ringing from inside her backpack momentarily broke the artistic trance.

She quickly fished out the phone, her eyes still glued to the vibrant panorama outside the window. "Hello?" she answered.

"Alexa, get ready for a treat!" Ella's voice buzzed with excitement on the other end.

Distracted by the sprawling art, Alexa blinked, pulling her gaze away to focus on the call.

"I'm sorry, Ella. What did you say?

"Our next interview. ¡Pilas Alexa! She's an activist creating positive change. Her name is Raye Jones Avery. Please get some info. She is also a singer. I will send the two songs that won her the Individual Artist Fellowship for a Jazz performance from the Division of the Arts. One is 'Higher Love' and the other is 'Visiting Room.' I cannot tell you enough how many times I have heard 'Higher Love.' Tell me what you think. Talk soon!"

As Alexa scrolled through Ella's email, she plugged in her earbuds, immersing herself in the rhythmic beats of the suggested songs. Suddenly, the music was interrupted by a familiar voice. "Alexa… hello! Got a sec?" It was Andy, sliding into the seat next to her, his expression a mix of frustration and hope. "I really need to run some class stuff by you before we get to the lab today. Is that okay?" Andy pulled the textbook out and pointed to the section related to class. Can we talk about the method to obtain… what's the name of the thing?"

"Do you mean ethane?" Alexa said with a warm, empathetic smile. She could see the confusion clouding Andy's face, making him look almost helpless, a stark contrast to his usual confident demeanor.

"Yeah, ethane! Ugh, so what's the extra step to get it from… uh… what's the name of that other thing?" Andy's words tumbled out in a mix of frustration and desperation. "Why is this stuff so freaking hard? Even the names are like, impossible."

Alexa let out a light, understanding chuckle, seeing her normally unflappable friend so clueless. "Hey, it's cool, Andy. I get it, organic chem is like learning Martian sometimes."

After giving Andy's arm a reassuring squeeze, Alexa leaned closer to his open book. "What exactly do you not understand about the process?" She listened carefully as Andy shared his doubts. "Okay, look here, Andy," Alexa said, her finger tracing the intricate diagrams on the page. She was trying to be a calming guide for Andy through the complex world of molecules and reactions. "This is the process to obtain ethane."

Her explanations were clear, concise, making the material more accessible to her friend. Andy's face lit up with growing understanding, "Oh, got it! You make it sound so easy." The stress from before visibly melting away.

Alexa reached for her earbuds, eager to pick up from the song she'd paused just moments earlier. "Ummm, nope. Too jazzy. Not my thing."

Andy's curiosity piqued. "What's kinda jazzy?"

Alexa pulled one earbud out and handed it to him, her eyes watching his face as he listened. The transformation was instant; the tapping of his fingers on his knees, the slight bob of his head, and the smile spreading across his face. She knew then, this song had found a fan in Andy.

"I love her voice. Good arrangement, too. Who's this?"

"Her name is Raye Jones Avery, an activist who sings."

"What do you mean… is she an activist or a singer? The music is good!

"Apparently both… don't know. Just got the info."

The bus's steady rumble accompanied Alexa's gaze as she watched the morning sky gradually brighten, trees whisking by in swift succession. The low hum of her classmates' chit-chat played like background music. Andy sat snugly beside her, their shared chemistry textbook sprawled open. Its pages softly reflected the muted bus light.

Pulling into the school, Andy snapped the textbook between them shut. As the bus hissed to a stop and the doors groaned open, Alexa and Andy stepped out, welcomed by the crisp morning breeze. But before they could make their way to the building, a familiar figure blocked their path.

"Hey, Alexa!" Rudy called out, his face beaming with a cheerful grin as he approached them with a lively bounce in his step. Without hesitation, he gently cupped Alexa's face and planted a sweet kiss on her lips, his eyes sparkling with affection.

Caught off guard but pleasantly surprised, Alexa returned the kiss, feeling a warm flutter in her chest. Andy, standing beside them, awkwardly shuffled his feet, instantly interested in examining the cracks in the pavement, giving her and Rudy their moment.

Breaking away from the kiss with a playful wink, Rudy called, "Just a little good luck for the day, babe!" He dashed toward the school, laughter trailing in his wake. Alexa felt the blush grow on her cheeks.

Babe. The term hung in the air even after Rudy's departure, an unwanted guest in Alexa's mind. It clashed, oddly, with the affection it had always signified before. She mechanically mustered a smile, pushing against the unease bubbling beneath her surface.

Andy, oblivious to her internal conflict, teased her with a goofy grin. "Well, well, looks like someone's day just got a whole lot better, huh?"

Alexa shot Andy a "Can you believe this?" look, her eyes filled with exasperation. "Remember when 'babe' used to give me butterflies?" she whispered, hoping Rudy wouldn't overhear.

Andy glanced between Rudy and Alexa, nodding slightly. "Things change, don't they?" he replied in a low voice, sensing Alexa's annoyance.

"Yeah." Alexa sighed, watching Rudy's carefree stride. "And sometimes not for the better." Alexa watched Rudy turn back towards them. Then, out of nowhere, Rudy popped a question that felt completely disconnected from their previous conversation.

"So, when are you guys taking the SAT?" he asked, like nothing had happened. Alexa exchanged a quick, 'Is he for real?' look with Andy. They were both thrown off by Rudy's random question, especially since he acted as if their previous encounter never happened.

"Thinking late June early July," Alexa replied, not missing a beat. "What about you, Andy?"

"June too," Andy chimed in. "Got my essay drafted and I've scheduled a review with O'Jete next week. So, fingers crossed."

Rudy barely seemed to process their responses. Absorbed in his phone for a beat, he pocketed it with a shrug and an air of indifference. Without another word or a backward glance, he walked away once again.

Alexa watched him go, biting her lip in frustration. "He asks, then doesn't even care about our answers." Rudy's flippant attitude was becoming harder to ignore. And every dismissive gesture like this deepened the rift she felt growing between them, making his casual use of "babe" feel more like a slap than a term of endearment. As Alexa pondered her next steps, new possibilities for her essay and future began weaving through her thoughts, inspired by her recent chat with Lourdes. Yet the image of Rudy, walking away with his hands shoved deep into his pockets and his future carelessly dismissed, lingered like a shadow over her newfound clarity and excitement.

It was a peaceful day at school for Alexa, filled with notes, lectures, and laughter with friends. However, as she sat at her desk later that evening, the pages of her math and chemistry homework spread before her, her mind kept drifting away from the equations and formulas. The looming interview with Raye for *Latinisimo* tugged at her thoughts, splitting her focus. The glowing numbers on her digital clock seemed to tick away faster, reminding her of the approaching date.

She couldn't help but steal moments in between her academic tasks to scour the internet for more information about Raye. It felt like borrowing time from one part of her life to feed another, but Alexa didn't mind. The thrill of working for *Latinisimo* and the opportunities to learn and grow it presented were irresistible draws.

It was relatively easy to find information on Raye. A singer, a curator, an educator, an activist, and a mentor. Her involvement with the local community was far and wide. Apparently, she had recently retired from Christina Cultural Arts Center (CCAC) as their Executive Director after almost thirty years of service to pursue artistic interests.

Alexa was intrigued about Raye's change of pace. Who retires just like that to be an artist? It doesn't make sense!

Alexa sent Ella what she had found before going to sleep. She couldn't help but asking Ella the same question she had thought about.

Ella answered: *Got it! Let's discuss before the program. Cafeteria next to studio, 4 pm. Cythen!*

On the day of the meeting, Alexa's heart fluttered with a mixture of excitement and anticipation as she walked towards the familiar cafeteria adjacent to the radio station. The place held a warm spot in her heart, filled with the memories of her enlightening conversation with Lourdes weeks ago.

Meeting Ella there an hour before the program, Alexa was met with an unexpected sweetness. "I bought a green chai latte for you today, Alexa. That's what you like, isn't it?" Ella's voice was warm, her hands carefully holding a medium-sized green drink topped with a generous swirl of whipped cream.

Taking in the inviting latte Ella handed her, Alexa felt a rush of gratitude. The delightful aroma floating from the cup mingled with the ambient scents of the cafeteria. Sipping the creamy drink, the last worries she once held about Ella disappeared.

With every laugh they shared and idea they exchanged about the upcoming program, Alexa's fondness for Ella deepened. She marveled at the unexpected ease she felt in Ella's presence. I actually like you, Ella… a lot! she admitted to herself, her surprise turning into contentment. The newfound connection made Alexa all the more eager about their collaboration on the *Latinisimo* project.

"I kept thinking about your question. How about if we start with Raye's upbringing and segue into her community service in both the arts and education? She is also a Governor's Award recipient. Coincidentally, she received recognition at the same time Lisa Bartoli did."

"You know, I'm really curious about how Raye sees herself." Alexa's voice softened into a contemplative tone as she cradled the warmth of her green chai latte, taking sweet sips that intermingled with her reflections. Memories of Lisa's serene and calming aura wrapped around her thoughts, much like the delicate blend of spices from her drink enveloped her senses.

"Like, what would she say about that?" Alexa mused, her words tinged with the same glow of excitement she felt when discussing Raye. The gentle smile playing on her lips seemed to echo the comfort she felt in Lisa's presence. To Alexa, Lisa's art was a delicate whisper, a nudge towards genuine self-expression.

"Hey, do you think Raye's art is like, the total opposite of Lisa's? Like, is it loud where Lisa's is all soft and whispery? Does her art yell and challenge everyone while Lisa's just calms and heals?" Her head tilted slightly as she awaited Ella's response, her eager eyes bright with anticipation for their upcoming interview with Raye. The chai latte's sweet remnants lingered on her palate, echoing the pleasant thoughts dancing in her mind.

Ella considered Alexa's questions. "You're onto something, Alexa. It would be fascinating to explore these contrasts in the interview."

Alexa's eyes brightened at the thought, anticipation bubbling within her. "Yeah, let's delve into that. I'm super curious to know how Raye sees her own art, her own impact."

Her eagerness lingered in the air, blending with the rich aroma of their surroundings. The transition from their cozy, informal discussion to the forthcoming interview was marked by Ella's composed tone. Her voice gently yet firmly broke through the noise of the bustling cafeteria, pulling Alexa back to the present.

"Good point, Alexa. Let's make sure to ask her. Are you ready to head to the studio now? It's about time for the interview."

The sun dipped below the horizon, painting the sky with hues of pink and orange as Alexa and Ella approached the glass doors of the radio station building. Their reflections danced on the glass as they pushed through, stepping into the softly lit interior, the quiet hum of the building embracing them. Their footsteps echoed in the hallways, adorned with framed posters of upcoming university events and internship opportunities, as they made their way to the studio.

As they neared their destination, Alexa and Ella spotted Raye seated on a flimsy chair outside their studio door, finishing up a phone call. Adjacent to their studio, another was buzzing with activity, a live broadcast in session. Through the slightly ajar door of the neighboring studio, the hushed tones of a broadcasted conversation and the subtle hum of electronic equipment echoed in the corridor, spilling from the speakers placed above.

Ella's voice broke the hushed ambiance as they approached Raye. "Hi, Raye! How are you?"

Raye's head snapped up, a bright smile illuminating her face. "Hi, Ella! I am doing great. It's so good to see you!" Her words imbued warmth and familiarity.

The introduction flowed effortlessly. "Same here. Raye, meet Alexa Hope. She's *Latinisimo*'s intern for the year. Alexa, Raye and I have worked together in a not-so-distant past." As Ella and Raye fell into easy conversation, their laughter mingled with the quiet of the building.

Feeling the need to steer the conversation towards the program, Alexa chimed in, "So, Ella, about the music for the program. I downloaded the two songs you mentioned but found an intriguing one to consider 'Make me over'." She handed over a USB flash drive to Ella.

"Good job, Alexa!" Ella complimented, taking the flash drive from her.

"No problem." Alexa smiled. "My friend Andy liked 'Higher Love,' actually. I connected with 'Make me over' for some reason."

Hearing the mention of her songs, Raye's eyes lit up. "Oh wow, that's awesome to hear!" she beamed. "'Higher Love' is about a first love that lasts forever as a marriage. I'm really glad Andy liked it!"

Her genuine warmth made Alexa feel even more connected to the upcoming interview, eager to learn more about Raye and her creative journey.

Raye then shifted her gaze to Alexa, eyes filled with friendly curiosity. "And you, Alexa? Why did you connect with 'Make me over'?"

Alexa's heart stumbled over the question, catching her off guard. Her mind was instantly flooded with images of Rudy. His easy laugh and playful wink filled her thoughts, his laid-back 'whatever' attitude clashing with the passion and purpose she heard in Raye's songs. A swirl of emotions tugged at her heart. Was Rudy's chill vibe really okay, or was the determined passion she heard in 'Higher Love' more appealing than 'Make me over'?

Alexa took a deep breath, a move to gain time and collect her scattered thoughts. "Um, Raye, 'Make me over'… it's deep," she managed to say. Her mind sneakily slid back to Rudy as she spoke. The melody didn't really hit the right notes for her, but the words, oh the words. "This woman… walking away from an unhealthy relationship, seeking to be made over, renewed…" she added, her voice a soft echo of her inner turmoil and wonder.

As they stepped into the studio, it was like crossing into another realm. The outside world, with all its noise and bustle, seemed to fade away, replaced by an almost sacred calm. The studio felt like a sanctuary, a haven where the chaos of everyday life simply couldn't reach.

"Raye, do you mind taking a seat here?" Alexa gestured to the plush chair in front of the microphones. Her hand was steady as she adjusted the mics, ensuring they were at the right height and angle for Raye. The familiar, rhythmic pattern of setting up for each interview filled her with a sense of confidence and empowerment. She was feeling in her element here, a place where she could contribute and make a real difference.

As Raye settled in, Alexa's fingertips grazed the dials of the soundboard, making minor adjustments with a familiarity that made her heart swell with pride. She took a moment to soak in the scene, her pulse dancing to the hum of the equipment around her.

Ella, seated across from Raye, meticulously scanned the system, ensuring every detail was in place for the recording. Her eyes danced over the screen, checking that Audacity was primed to capture their conversation. The glow from the computer screen filled the room, casting a shimmering light that made everyone's faces seem like they were caught in a moment of quiet anticipation.

"We're starting the recording, guys. Get ready." Ella's voice broke the silence, composed but brimming with underlying exhilaration. As the recording light blinked on, the room pulsed with an electric energy of stories ready to unfurl.

"Welcome to *Latinisimo*! Today, we resume our cherished series, 'People Who Make Us Pause.' With us today is the phenomenal Raye Jones Avery, known to many as an unwavering education activist and recently, a celebrated singer. Welcome, Raye!"

"Thanks, Ella! It's always a joy to be in your company. I appreciate the opportunity for today's interview!" Raye said warmly, mirroring Ella's sentiment.

"So, where did the activist in you begin?"

In the corner, Alexa's lips curved into a soft smile, a subtle pride blossoming within her. She felt a flicker of accomplishment as she recognized her subtle impact on the opening query of the interview, bringing the spotlight onto the depths of Raye's journey and conviction. The conversation flowed, a river of words and emotions.

"I am a child of the Sixties," Raye said. "We were very neighborhood-oriented and instilled with the value of serving, although not in traditional ways. You didn't throw paper on the ground. You just swept your porch. You swept the street. You kept the streets clean. Everybody helped everybody on our block."

Then she addressed the question. "I remember being involved in passing out literature about activities in the community about upcoming elections. I've been involved in all those kinds of activities, particularly with my father, since I was nine or ten years old."

"Interesting, Raye. So, is your activism influenced by your upbringing, since you mentioned your dad?"

"My father was a mathematician and an older student at Morgan State University. He taught at Bancroft in Wilmington for twenty-five years. He was a revered and brilliant guy who taught me through poetry. He would recite an African author who said, 'March to the beat of your own drum,' and from Invictus, 'I am the captain of my ship, I am the master of my soul.' He was teaching me to be an individual and not to follow the crowd.

"My father was an avid reader. Whatever book he couldn't put down, I couldn't wait for him to finish so I could read it. I ended up majoring in English literature."

"What about your mom, Raye?" Ella asked.

"She was a full-time teacher, raised in the South, and always eager to help others. After a lengthy career, she retired but later returned to train the inaugural teachers at Kuumba Academy, a school that integrates arts into education. Now at eighty-eight, they still seek her advice on her training methods."

Raye paused. "She had so many kids! Some of my siblings had a rare disease called Metachromatic Leukodystrophy, which causes babies to regress in development. I was the second-born child. I wasn't supposed to be in charge yet life made me do it somehow. I know how to take charge. I've been misunderstood as a result of it.

"I decided then that having fewer kids was probably a good idea. After the second one, I'm like, this is it! I'm not going to be like my mother with a bunch of kids." Raye words were heavy in the air, carrying a mix of regret and resolve.

Alexa was completely absorbed in Raye's story. She felt drawn in by the honesty in Raye's voice, which vividly brought to life the journey she had taken, with all its highs and lows. It was as if Raye was sharing a secret with her, allowing Alexa a glimpse into her private world of reflection. Moments like these were precious to Alexa, where real, unscripted, and profound conversations unfolded.

Raye then shared what caught Alexa's attention even more. "I didn't make good choices in my personal life. I'm not talking about my kids, but I didn't make good choices in my relationships with men." Her voice held a tone of self-awareness and acceptance, a recognition of past mistakes and learned lessons. "That's a part of my story when I'm talking with people, privately, families, and women in particular. I don't sit in there like I'm some saint."

Raye's words reverberated in the room, a testament to humility and raw openness. Alexa's heart beat with newfound respect for Raye. The audacity it took for one to lay bare their faults, transforming them into signals of hope for others, was an inspiration Alexa found herself drawn to. In the candid glow of Raye's confession, Alexa felt a deep human connection, a gentle reminder of the intertwined tapestry of emotions and experiences that bound all lives together.

However, as the quiet truth of Raye's statements permeated the air, a charged silence hummed in Alexa's ears, sending her heart into a tumultuous dance. The echoes of Raye's pain resonated within her, forcing her to confront the swirling tempest of her own emotions. Images of Rudy, awash with laughter and a carefree radiance, cascaded through her mind. Her happiness from those moments, now hidden behind growing shadows, started to fade under the tough light of painful truths.

Alexa couldn't breathe right. A giant lump of feelings stuck there, stubborn and heavy. Her chest hurt, a sharp kind of pain, and her stomach felt like it was twisting up into knots. That pain, as real and hard as the floor beneath her feet, suddenly made things super clear, even with all the chaos swirling around inside her head. Rudy's not for me, I know it!

Inside, Alexa was shaking, the sobs sitting heavily in her chest, threatening to spill over. This big sadness wrapped around her, making the future she'd imagined with Rudy fade away like a daydream in the harsh light of reality. And it was all too clear, wasn't it? Her path was veering off in another direction, away from Rudy and the tangled mess their relationship had become. Her slightly trembling hands betrayed the emotional storm she was sailing through, yet she managed to keep it from showing too much.

Even with her inner chaos, Alexa clung to the ongoing conversation, like it was a lifebuoy in the wild sea of her emotions. Raye's calm, steady presence was a subtle comfort, a gentle anchor amidst the tidal wave of pain and confusion. As Ella's voice, clear and focused, wove through another question, Alexa took a slow breath, quietly willing her heart to hold it together. Engaging in the interview was her momentary shield, keeping the emotional storm at bay, if only for a little while. Her internal struggle was still there, bubbling beneath the surface, yet she managed to paint on a serene exterior for the outside world to see.

"Where has your activism taken you, Raye?"

"I was a chartering member of the board of directors for the Metropolitan Wilmington Urban League. I'm one of the founders of Kuumba Academy. I'm still on their board, and I'm a charter member of the Coalition of One Hundred Black Women and former president."

"Community service and activism are interconnected in your case, aren't they, Raye?"

"There's no separation between my work life and my community service. I've always worked in a community-based service role and in causes that I care about. Those causes frequently didn't have budgets." She paused for a minute.

"Let me say it this way: a white woman with a high school diploma will earn in excess of nearly a million dollars more than I will earn, despite my level of education, because there's a racial wealth divide. I didn't intentionally choose to go into a field where I would take a vow of poverty, but that's basically what I did. I'm pretty highly educated, but my asset portfolio doesn't say that."

Listening to Raye talk about unfairness and struggle, Alexa felt a jolt in her chest. Her own troubles with Rudy suddenly mixed with a new anger about the bigger picture stuff Raye was sharing. Quietly, her hands balled into fists under the table. Something about Raye's tough but hopeful story nudged Alexa. Maybe, just maybe, she could find a way to navigate through her own messy feelings too.

Glancing over, she noticed Ella, too, was visibly affected. Her fingers clenched around her mic, a subtle sign of the surge of emotions coursing through her in the studio. Alexa's eyes lingered on Ella, finding an unexpected kinship in their silent, shared frustration. In that glance, Alexa sensed Ella's decision before the words even left her lips.

"I see... Let's take a quick music break," Ella announced, her voice carrying a slight tremble. "It's time to listen to another of Raye's original songs, 'Visiting Room'."

The abrupt intermission was a small reprieve, a chance for them to gather their thoughts, rein in their emotions. The music filled the air, a comforting melody that contrasted sharply with the turmoil within Alexa, yet offering a momentary escape from the painful discussion.

The music hummed in the background. Alexa's eyes were moist, mirroring Ella's, who had a taut expression as she took a sip of water. The anger was palpable in the dim light of the studio, a shared flame that burned within each of them.

Raye's voice cut through the charged silence, her tone soft but steely. "It's a cruel world out there, but remember, every time we speak up, it makes a difference, however small." Her words didn't gloss over the harsh realities but carried a weight of quiet strength and resilience.

Alexa felt the echo of her words within her, a resonating chord that cut through the fog of her turmoil. She wasn't alone in this fight. They were all threads in a larger narrative, each making a small but crucial difference. Seeing that knowing look in both Raye's and Ella's eyes gave Alexa a quiet kind of courage. It was like they were silently saying, 'We get it, and we're in this together,' even when facing super tough stuff.

Ella set her water bottle down, her eyes meeting Alexa's with a silent agreement and newfound resolve. The anger was still there, but now it was a fuel, a driving force propelling them forward in their shared mission as they prepared to return to the live conversation, their voices united, stronger and more determined.

"And we're back to *Latinisimo* where we are having a conversation with the education activist and musician Raye Jones Avery. I can't conclude this rich interview without asking, what influenced you to take the path you have selected?"

"I'm going to give you two major events. The first one was the day that Dr. King was killed. He was trying to do good for all people, and for black people in particular, so that really influenced my life's advocacy to better the conditions for African Americans in this country. I was no more than ten or eleven years old.

"The next pivotal event that I can remember was helping Jim Sills get elected as the first African American mayor for Wilmington. I actually felt like I felt when Barack Obama was elected. I felt like there was some hope for black people and with that euphoria, we could actually see improved conditions in significant ways. Those kinds of experiences have kept me hopeful and kept me engaged, despite some real lows."

As Raye spoke, Alexa could feel the weight and importance of the moments being shared. She took a deep breath, trying to imagine the rollercoaster of emotions Raye must have gone through.

"About seven or eight years ago, I had made a personal decision that I would not speak publicly anymore about race, racism, or any aspect of advocacy in the public education space until we started to see some transformation." Raye paused, allowing the weight of her words to sink in. Alexa could feel a lump forming in her throat, sensing the pain behind the decision.

"I broke my silence because of Congressman John Lewis. He said, 'Don't give up.' This is a lifelong battle, and we must never give up. We must not be silent about the things that matter."

Alexa felt a tightness in her chest, Raye's words hitting her hard. She blinked rapidly, trying to control her emotions. Wow, she thought, Raye's strength and passion were truly something else. It made her think about the power of never giving up, no matter how tough things got.

"I was about to ask about the reason you had stopped advocating for education, Raye, so thanks for providing that answer naturally. Now, what's the thing that makes you feel the proudest?"

"I count Kuumba Academy as a singular accomplishment. We're into the twentieth year since its foundation. My introspection tells me that I've made a difference there. I just got a letter last week from a former student, a young white man now in the military, married and a parent himself. He found me on Facebook. He sent me a private message telling me about the impact that I had on his life. You never really know until they come back and tell you. I'm now thinking of a song where it says, 'Let the work I've done speak for me.'"

"And I'm sure that's how people are going to remember Raye Jones Avery," Ella said. "Many thanks for your time today! I love to keep learning from you!" Ella turned back to the mic. "And many thanks, *Latinisimo* friends! That was Raye Jones Avery, artist, educator, activist. We'll see you a month from now to continue the 'People Who Make Us Pause' series. Until then, have a great rest of your week."

Alexa took a mental note of how smoothly Ella had closed the session.

Ella closed the mics and thanked Raye, who was about to leave the studio, when she looked in Alexa's direction.

"What about you, Alexa? What are you passionate about?"

Raye's interest in her caught Alexa by surprise again. She didn't know how to answer. "Well, I don't know. You're passionate about education, about helping people. I like math, sciences and things that aren't complicated."

"I found math and sciences kind of complicated." Raye smiled at Alexa. "Education and helping people were the things I grew up with. I don't think much of it. I just feel the need to do something about it. To level the playing field, if you will. The point, Alexa, is to be in love with the things we do. To be passionate about causes or activities that truly move us. Hope you find what motivates you! It's important. Let me know if you want to talk."

"I will. Thanks, Raye!"

Raye finally left the studio, saying goodbye to both of them.

Alexa felt something special about Raye, a welcoming and nurturing spirit that grew stronger as the interview progressed. She was captivated by Raye's personality. She kept reflecting on the interview as well as about the role models *Latinisimo* had presented so far. She was also unexpectedly confronted about the future of her relationship with Rudy. She didn't notice Ella looking at her, puzzled.

"You kept thinking, Alexa. I can see it in your eyes. Are you okay?"

"What, Ella?"

"I wonder what you're thinking. You were miles away."

"Well, Raye's life and career path. She's inspiring. She made me think a lot. Can we talk about it later? Rudy's picking me up in a few minutes and I have to hurry."

Alexa said goodbye to Ella while thinking that a heart-to-heart conversation with her boyfriend needed to happen soon. One thing was for certain, a career path was on the horizon for her. A relationship with Rudy might not be.

CHAPTER 6

AN EDUCATION LEADER, YAMIL SÁNCHEZ

Rudy's car was wrapped in the soft glow of the fading afternoon light, quiet and shadowed as Alexa climbed in. There was a peculiar tension in the air, unspoken but palpable.

"Hi, babe! How was your radio thing?" Rudy asked, his eyes remaining focused on the road ahead as he pulled away from the Perkins building back entrance.

Alexa's jaw tightened almost imperceptibly at the pet name, her voice firm yet controlled as she responded, "Please don't call me 'babe,' Rudy. You know I don't like it."

Rudy merely shrugged, nonchalant. "Okay, okay. Anyway, who did you guys talk to today?"

Alexa let out a shaky breath, feeling a genuine smile breaking through the tension she had felt earlier. "Today's interview was amazing. We had Raye Jones Avery." She found herself sharing with a rush of enthusiasm, the air around her seeming to lighten. Her voice was tinged with admiration and respect. "She's not just an activist, but a singer too! The way she blends art and education to really make a difference... it's inspiring. Just being in the same room and listening to her taught me so much." Alexa's words tumbled out eagerly, reflecting the profound impact that *Latinisimo*, and guests like Raye, were having on her.

But Rudy's response, while accommodating, lacked genuine interest. "That sounds cool, Alexa. Should we go home, like, right away? There's a Warcraft tournament tonight. I *have* to be there."

Alexa and Rudy sat side by side in the car, yet they might as well have been miles apart. Alexa gazed out the window, seeing her own reflection mixed with the passing scenery, her mind swirled with admiration for Raye's powerful words and a growing heaviness at what was unfolding in the car. Even though Rudy was just an arm's length away, it felt like a wide, silent canyon had opened up between them, swallowing all the words they weren't saying. The car rolled on, moving them forward, but emotionally, it was like they were stuck, neither of them speaking a single word for the entire drive.

As they stepped out of the car, the crunch of gravel underfoot on Rudy's driveway was sharp in the quiet evening. Alexa paused, a wave of emotion halting her as she turned to face Rudy. The cool night air, filled with the chorus of distant crickets, seemed to accentuate the turmoil brewing within her. Alexa felt a sudden tightness in her chest, her fingers instinctively curling into a small fist.

"So, ready for the Warcraft tournament tonight? I really *have* to be there!"

"What? You *have* to be there?" The realization of his priorities made Alexa's heart hurt. But hadn't she seen this coming? "More video games Rudy… really?

Rudy shuffled awkwardly, eyes darting. "Yeah, babe—uh, Alexa. Why are you mad at me all the time?"

Her heart pounded in her ears, her emotions teetering on the brink of spilling over. Underneath the driveway's solitary lamplight, Rudy's face looked almost foreign, shadowed and distant. It was in that moment that Alexa felt a wellspring of words rise from within her, a need to crack open the silence and air out the struggles that had been suffocating her. The question brought back the discussion Alexa was trying to avoid. The time to talk was now.

"To tell you the truth, I'm not happy about this." Alexa's hand went back and forth between them.

"About what?"

"You… me… us. It's not working, Rudy. It hasn't been working for a while. I like you but it's like we live on different planets. I don't like videogames the same way you do. I want to go to college despite being a dreamer. It'll be complicated, but I want to try. What do you want?"

Rudy's voice broke through the stillness. "Why… wait, Alexa?" They stood beside his car, the ambient light from his porch painting a soft glow across the driveway, making his eyes look so much deeper, so much more vulnerable.

"I can… I can make money now, Alexa. I don't wanna sink under books and debts, and what? For an uncertain future?" His voice wavered, a subtle crack exposing the fear beneath his casual demeanor.

Alexa, her heart swaying with each of his words, couldn't summon a response. Her mouth opened slightly, but no words tumbled out. His face, softly illuminated by the ambient light, shifted through emotions she hadn't seen before, feelings she hadn't known he'd hidden. Rudy sighed, deep, deflated, his shoulders drooping under an invisible weight. His eyes found hers, exposing a rawness that caught her breath.

"It's like we're on different planets, Alexa. I get it, okay? You deserve to be happy, and maybe I'm not the one for that right now."

Silence enveloped them, its presence almost tangible as it stretched out, filling the space with unspoken regrets and swallowed words. They looked at each other, and for a fleeting second, she saw a flicker of their shared past, their laughter, their camaraderie.

And then, he spoke, barely above a whisper, "So… is this where we say goodbye?"

Alexa's heart hammered against her chest, her breath hitching as she tried to maintain her composure. Blinking rapidly, she gave Rudy a nod, her voice a hushed breath. "Yes. I'm so sorry… goodbye, Rudy."

But he stepped closer, desperation lining his features. "Alexa, please!" His voice, rough and thick with emotion, held her in place. "I see things differently. Doesn't mean I don't care; doesn't mean I don't want you to be happy."

His hands gestured, almost reaching out to her before retracting, as if he was battling the urge to pull her close one last time. "I just need you to understand where I'm coming from, too."

Tears rolled down Alexa's cheeks, but she stepped back, whispering a fragile, "I'm truly so sorry. Goodbye, Rudy."

Alexa turned onto the familiar path leading home. Her steps were slow and heavy as she made her way down the driveway, feeling the weight of the evening in her heart. The night around her was still, with only the sound of her quiet footsteps and the occasional choked sob breaking the silence. Each step felt like peeling away layers of a shared past.

Reaching her front door, she found her mom waiting. Their eyes locked, conveying volumes in a silent exchange. In her mom's gaze, Alexa found understanding and quiet support. Words were unnecessary; the comfort of her mother's presence was a balm, offering solace and space in equal measure.

Alexa moved silently through her home, the happy murmurs from her family in the living room a poignant contrast to the emotional turmoil within her. Her bedroom, a haven that had witnessed countless secrets and joyous moments shared with Rudy, now became a sanctuary for her sorrow. With hands trembling slightly, she typed out a message to Andy: *We broke up. Sad. Talk on Monday?* Her pillow absorbed the quiet sobs that followed, providing a soft place to land amidst the crashing waves of heartache.

An early text from Ella woke Alexa on a sunny Saturday morning. *Check this old interview with educator Yamil Sánchez. lmk your thoughts.*

Alexa took a quick look on LinkedIn as a distraction to ease some of her pain. Yamil appeared to be an executive in a school district in New Jersey. He had been head of the school and worked for United Way, among other positions. *Interesting guy! Young for a PhD, right?* She texted Ella back.

The chill of the Monday morning hung in the air as Alexa stood by the bus stop, her eyes feeling dull, lacking their usual spark. She could hear footsteps approaching, and then Andy's voice broke through her distant thoughts with a simple "Hey, there."

Alexa barely managed a half-smile, her gaze never quite meeting his. "Hey, Andy."

He leaned beside her, giving her space yet offering silent solidarity. "Tough weekend?" he ventured, softness threading his voice.

"Yeah," she whispered, tears threatening. "Told you we broke up."

Andy shook his head. "I kind of felt it coming. Paths diverge, you know?"

"It's *Latinisimo*, Andy. It's... changed my perspective. I want more."

"You still care for him?"

She paused. "I do. But while he's immersed in games, I'm aiming higher. We're just in different places."

As students passed by, laughing, Alexa felt her heart constrict. Andy's comforting arm found its way around her.

"It hurts," he acknowledged gently.

Alexa leaned into him. "Wish it didn't sting this bad."

On the bus ride home, Alexa lost herself in research on *Latinisimo's* next interview, trying to drown out the hurt. But when her phone buzzed with a text from her mom—a heart emoji followed by 'Thinking of you'—warmth spread through her. Mom... always knows when I need her most, she thought, her heart swelling with gratitude. A simple emoji, yet it feels like the biggest hug.

As Alexa read up on Yamil's background, she discovered he had been at the helm of Kuumba Academy, a school co-founded by Raye Jones Avery. Despite the student population being predominantly black or Latino, the charter school boasted a graduation rate hovering around ninety percent, a remarkable feat surpassing Delaware's average. As she read further, Alexa felt a spark of excitement when Yamil began discussing the intricate relationship between math and reading, emphasizing the patterns inherent in both. This subject resonated deeply with her, causing her heart to race with anticipation.

She quickly shot Ella a text thoroughly engrossed by the newfound connection: *Whoa, math & reading connected? A Latino deciding in education? Pumped for this one!*

In the hustle of a typical mid-week school day, Alexa was hunched over her phone, flipping through pages about Yamil's story whenever she got the chance. She was so engrossed that she didn't even notice Andy until she spotted the worried look he always had when something was up. He was right next to her, dodging the usual hallway traffic of kids getting to class.

"Hey," he began, his voice gentle, eyes filled with worry. "How're you holding up?"

Alexa met his gaze, feeling the warmth of his concern. "Hi, Andy. Here googling Yamil Sánchez, our next guest at *Latinisimo*."

"Who's this Yamil? That's a name I never heard before. Do you need help with him? I have five minutes to spare before class."

"He's a big shot in education. I just found out he was appointed Chief Administrative Officer at Reading School District after a leadership position at United Way of New Jersey."

"Look, I found an article," Andy said. "He got unanimous approval from the Reading School Board on his hiring as assistant superintendent in October two thousand and nineteen. Looks like eighty five percent of students there are from minorities, Latinos being the majority."

Andy kept scrolling his phone and found another fact about Yamil. "This one talks about his Puerto Rican roots and the responsibility he feels to help the community. Interesting guy. Have to go. I just sent you some links. Talk later?"

Alexa quickly assembled the info on Yamil and shot an email to Ella right before taking the bus back home. The thought of interviewing someone as accomplished as Yamil gave her a buzz of excitement.

Ella texted back: *Let's meet before the interview. Perkins cafeteria? Want a drink?*

Alexa responded: *Bringing mine, cythere thks!*

On the Friday of the interview, the buzz outside the Perkins cafeteria was palpable. Students flowed in and out in a whirl of activity. Some were engrossed in animated discussions, while others were busily setting up booths for various clubs and initiatives. The atmosphere was electric, filled with the typical energy of a bustling university campus.

Within this setting, Ella and Alexa approached the cafeteria, each holding their drink. They found a spot where they could easily keep an eye on the studio entrance.

"Ella, there's something so captivating about Yamil's story," Alexa began. "Being Latino and rising so high, yet staying so connected. Can we explore the core of that bond during the interview?"

Ella's eyes shone with agreement. "Definitely. Yamil has this rare blend of achievement and humility. He's based in the New Jersey projects, where his family's journey in the States began. And the fact that he chose to work there? It's like his heart beats in sync with his community."

Amidst their conversation, Ella's gaze shifted beyond Alexa for a brief moment. "Isn't that Yamil by the studio entrance?" she inquired, pointing slightly. "He looks a bit disoriented with all this activity."

Alexa followed Ella's gaze and noticed Yamil, who indeed seemed out of place amidst the busy campus backdrop. Recognizing the urgency, Ella handed her empty cup to Alexa. "I'll go get him. Could you please help with this?"

With swift strides, Ella approached him. "Yamil!" she called out, her voice cutting through the din, waving to get his attention. "Over here, the studio's this way!"

Upon hearing his name, Yamil paused, locating Ella's voice amidst the hubbub. He then changed direction, heading towards them with a grateful nod.

"Hello there! How are you?" Ella caught up to him.

"Hi, Ella. So good to see you!" he said. "I was worried I might not make it in time. It took longer than I thought to come to Delaware from my office. I forgot the mess that I-95 can be."

Alexa had caught up with them both and extended her hand to Yamil. "Wow!" she said. "You're tall!"

Yamil gave her a solid handshake while smiling. "Yes, I've been told. And you are?"

Alexa realized that her candid comment might not have come off as very professional. "Sorry, Dr. Sánchez, I'm Alexa, *Latinisimo*'s intern."

"Good to see you, Alexa. But, please, call me Yamil. I'm Dr. Sánchez for official purposes only, not among friends."

Ella directed the group to the studio. "Yamil, did you decide on the music for the interview?"

Yamil extended a flash drive with his music selection. "I'm a Boricua at heart, but I expanded my music selection for you guys. How about Selena Gomez's 'Baila Conmigo' and Maluma's 'Amor en Coma'?"

Wow! What amazing musical selections. Alexa set up the mics and adjusted them for each person. Who knew he had great taste in music.

Armed with the music and after the usual preparations, Ella started the interview.

"Welcome to *Latinisimo*, Yamil! We were just discussing the significance of your Latino identity in all that you've accomplished. We'll delve into that in a bit." Ella paused purposefully. "But first, for our listeners, let's get acquainted with your background. And for that, I'll pass the mic to my co-host, Alexa Hope, who's looked into your journey. Over to you, Alexa."

A nervous lump formed in Alexa's throat, causing her to briefly lock eyes with Ella, silently communicating her surprise and slight panic. She hadn't expected to be thrust into the spotlight so suddenly. But Ella's firm, encouraging gaze said it all: You got this.

Drawing strength from Ella's faith in her, Alexa scrolled through her phone, quickly finding her notes. Taking a shaky breath, she began. As she spoke, her initial hesitation faded and by the end of her segment, her voice resonated with confidence and authority.

From the corner of her eye, Alexa stole a glance at Yamil. He had an earnest expression, his sharp eyes fixed on her as she spoke, absorbing every word. There was an air of wisdom about him, a result of years of experience and hard-earned success.

Yamil looked genuinely impressed, a warm smile lighting up his face. "That was an impressive rundown, Alexa. You really captured the essence of my journey. Thank you!"

As the musical interlude started, Ella leaned in closer, her eyes sparkling with amusement and pride. "Nicely done, Alexa!"

Beaming, Alexa replied with a mock-exasperated tone, "Thanks, Ella! But seriously… you almost gave me a heart attack. A little heads-up next time… pleeease!"

Ella laughed softly, giving Alexa's arm a reassuring squeeze. "You were brilliant, Alexa. Welcome to the live radio and podcasting world!"

Once the music faded, Ella refocused the interview. "So, Yamil, in your own words, how has your Latino identity influenced and inspired your work?"

"You see, Ella," Yamil began with fervor, "recent political events have pushed me. They've made me realize I need to be louder, to stand up, to rally for our rights."

Yamil's chuckle carried a hint of self-deprecation as he relayed his mother's words. "My mom says I should've been a lawyer, you know?" he said with a smile. "Says I have a knack for defending others, making sure they're treated right. Guess I've just always found my stride in leading, being the voice for those who need it."

Alexa felt a sudden surge of interest at Yamil's words. Instinctively, she leaned forward, zeroing in on every syllable he spoke.

Yamil paused, choosing his words carefully. "Especially for people like me." As he said this, his gaze fixed intently on Alexa. The intensity of his eyes felt like a jolt, making her heart skip a beat. It was as if he was silently challenging her to rise up, to amplify her voice for their community. "Many don't feel they can speak up, especially in areas where people of color aren't usually in leadership roles.

"I've been who I am all my life. I've been an advocate, I've been outspoken, I've been a voice for our community, always. As a person of color, I can say this loudly and clearly now. We're often made to jump through extra hoops."

Caught in the magnetic pull of Yamil's conviction, Alexa whispered under her breath, with a smirk. "That's what I'm talking about, someone speaking truth to power."

As Yamil delved deeper into his advocacy, Alexa's admiration grew. His words painted a clear picture of the need for stronger

Latino representation in leadership roles. Without hesitation, she began typing a brief Instagram caption:

@ Latinisimo with Yamil Sánchez. Latino voices needed. Championing what's right & bringing others along. #CommunityLeadership #LatinosInPolitics

She quickly snapped a candid photo of Yamil, his face alight with passion, and attached it to her post. His eyes, burning with intensity, locked onto hers as he spoke, almost urging her to truly grasp his message.

"Why is that, Yamil? What do you mean by extra hoops?" Ella asked.

Yamil's fingers drummed rhythmically on the table, the weight of memories evident in every tap. "I've always felt like I was going against the wind. You see, I went to Villanova University intending to be a pediatrician, a dream I'd nurtured since the age of five. There were only seven of us who graduated with a chemistry major."

Alexa's eyebrows rose in surprise; her gaze, however, never left Yamil. She could see a flicker of nostalgia in his eyes.

"In my senior year, I interned in the ER at the local Reading hospital. The internship almost broke me because I wasn't able to disconnect emotionally from the suffering. I learned that emergency room doctors needed to be able to emotionally disengage. I couldn't, which made me realize that I couldn't be a doctor after all. I had a career decision to make. By then, I'd already spent four years studying chemistry. I also loved working with children."

Alexa could imagine Yamil in a lab coat, the weight of each patient's outcome pressing on him. She could feel his disappointment and disillusionment.

"Fate has a sense of irony," he continued, "because in nineteen ninety-five, the Reading school district was actively seeking bilingual chemistry teachers. They were so desperate, they even went to Puerto Rico for recruitment. And that's how I first connected with the school district."

Ella chimed in, her voice filled with curiosity, "The same one you work for at the moment?"

Yamil nodded. "Yes. To be hired, I needed to get my certification as a teacher. I thought, if I need to go back to school to get eighteen credits, why not get a master's? So, that's what I did. I graduated in two thousand and eight with a Master's in secondary education, curriculum, and instruction. In twenty ten, I started my doctorate at Lehigh University in curriculum and instruction."

There was a spark in his eye, which caught Alexa's attention. He was passionate about his journey. And just as he seemed to be peaking academically, life threw him another curveball.

"I was recruited for a job in New York, where I worked for the Committee for Hispanic children and families, overseeing youth development programs throughout the Bronx. It pulled me away from my doctorate. The job was so demanding that I had to take a break. The break was short enough that I could come back, but long enough that the faculty was upset with me that I was gone."

Alexa could almost visualize Yamil's struggle, standing defiantly against a rigid academic system, every nuance of his face displaying the fight he'd waged.

Ella's voice broke into her thoughts. "This is where the extra hoops come in, right Yamil?" She paused, glancing down at the program schedule. "But before we dive deeper into that, let's give our listeners a musical treat. Stay with us, everyone!"

A short chime signaled the start of a music break. Soft, melodic tunes began to play in the background, offering a gentle interlude for listeners.

As the first notes of the song filled the studio, Ella took off her headphones, letting out a relaxed sigh. "Whew, that was intense." She turned to Yamil. "You have an interesting story!"

He nodded, his eyes reflective. "Thank you, Ella. Life hasn't been a straightforward path, but every challenge has made me stronger."

Alexa, silently absorbing the conversation, gave a supportive smile. Yamil's ability to overcome difficulties really struck a chord with her.

Yamil chuckled, "It's been a journey, that's for sure. By the way, I love that song. It's been stuck in my head for days after choosing it for todays' interview guys."

Alexa chimed in, "Oh, same here! It's one of my favorites. Maluma is so Latino music these days!"

Ella smiled. "Music has a way of doing that. But alright, let's gear up for the second half. Everyone good?"

Both Yamil and Alexa nodded.

As the last notes of the song faded, Ella signaled to pick up from where they left off. "Alright, we're back on air. So, Yamil, you were saying about your discussions with the faculty..."

He took a deep breath, re-immersing himself in the narrative. "I had an uphill battle to be readmitted. I petitioned all the way to the president to be allowed to come back and finish, even though I had left in good standing academically and financially. They made it very challenging. There were some tears that were shed, and some honest, uncomfortable conversations with the faculty and my advisor. I pushed through all of it. I was too invested to even think that I couldn't do it."

As Yamil recounted his challenges with the university admiration ignited within Alexa. Hearing about his struggles, the unfair hurdles thrown his way, made her fists clench tightly beneath the table. Every word intensified the heat rising to her cheeks. What the heck… why always fighting! Does it end? How can he be so cool?

"In the end, I think everyone saw my work ethic. Eventually, one of the committee members apologized for the experience that they made me go through and welcomed me as a colleague."

Alexa looked at Yamil, she could feel a spark light up inside her—like they were both in on a secret challenge against every unfair rule and every big shot like Pete O'Jete who thought they could push people around. Her heart raced a little faster, not just from the drama but from the thrill of standing up for what's right. So, this is what it feels like, she thought, her inner teenage rebel waking up. Yamil's got a point. There's a whole world of Petes out there. Bring it on—I'm so ready for this!

"When I thought I was done with school, I was recruited to join the school district. Part of the opportunity was to be prepared for any kind of future opportunities. Believe it or not, the President of the Department of Education didn't recognize my doctorate as enough qualification to be a school district superintendent. I had to go back and take an alternative path to get the certification. I explored and opted for a flex MBA.

"So, the lesson learned in education these days is to be smart about how to pay for school. I took a loan and now I'm paying the consequences. I should've taken tuition reimbursement or some kind of scholarship."

"Yamil, what other lessons learned could you share besides being smart in how to pay for education? 'People Who Make Us

Pause' is a series about presenting career choices for youngsters like Alexa."

Yamil's voice softened, "You know, my resilience, it's a gift from my mom. I share it with my students as much as I can." As he spoke, his eyes misted over with a deep sense of reverence and gratitude. In that vulnerable moment, Alexa could clearly see the profound appreciation and love Yamil held for his mother.

"She was born in Padilla, Puerto Rico, and went to school until eighth grade. Despite her limited English when she came here, she didn't let her language barrier keep from working. She figured out not only how to raise kids but also help her family on a limited income."

Yamil's face sweetened while thinking about his mom. "I picked up my work ethic from her, by going with her to a lot of the house cleaning she did. I let my students know what my mom did to be able to earn money, which was an honest work's pay. There's something that she's given us, pushing us to go beyond what she was able to accomplish academically. We're a close-knit family. I grew up in a very poor home financially, but we were not poor emotionally."

A pang of nostalgia hit Alexa, and her eyes welled up, thinking of her own mom's sacrifices and enduring love. The similarity in their stories made her heart swell with a mix of pride and sentiment.

Yamil then tried to answer the question more directly. "I grew up in a modest wooden house, its walls worn and weathered, topped with a rusting tin roof. Many folks would think people who grew up like that wouldn't be able to accomplish the things that I've accomplished. I'm the first and only one in my family to have a doctorate. This is a motivation. Now, I think my nieces and nephews see that as a possibility. My advice, if I can provide some, is that I'm not the exception. There are others like me, and there could be plenty more like me."

When Yamil looked at Alexa, she could tell he really believed what he said. She felt a lump in her throat and his words touched her deeply. She swallowed, feeling emotional, her eyes shining. She nodded in understanding, a silent promise forming.

If he can rise above his circumstances, then so can I. And so, can many others.

Ella, sensing the nearing end of their airtime, smoothly chimed in, "Such powerful words to end today's episode. Thank you for joining us on *Latinisimo*, friends. That was Dr. Yamil Sánchez, Chief Administrative Officer at Reading School District, wrapping up our monthly series, 'People Who Make Us Pause.' Stay tuned every week and especially for our monthly specials. Have a wonderful week!" With a final nod to Yamil, Ella switched off the mic, concluding their segment.

Beyond the glass partition, the neighboring studio buzzed with life. Another show was in full swing, the host speaking animatedly while their guest responded with fervor. Yamil, Alexa, and Ella watched for a moment, the clear window offering them a ringside view. It was a reminder of the vibrant, interconnected world of live radio, where one conversation ended only for another to take its place.

Yamil began to gather his belongings—a mix of documents and personal effects. Feeling a tinge of hesitation but wanting to ask him something, Alexa glanced towards Ella and said, "Yamil?"

Catching Alexa's glance and understanding the unspoken intention, Ella smiled warmly. "Take your time, guys. I've got to head over and coordinate our next interview with the station manager. It's going to be a remote one. Happy weekend to both of you!"

The weight of their recent conversation still hung palpably in the air, felt more intensely now in the quiet aftermath. Yamil paused, looking up, eyebrows raised inquisitively.

Alexa hesitated for a split second, finding the right words. But as they walked side by side, nearing the exit that led to the elevator, he broke the brief silence. "So, Alexa, what's on your mind?"

Alexa was grateful for the opening, easing what felt like an awkward buildup. "I'm in the process of deciding what to study. I mean, I see friends grappling with the same decisions, unsure where to go, what path to take. I'm leaning towards engineering since I've always had an affinity for math and sciences. But hearing your journey today, I wonder... How did you decide to become an educator?"

"Well, everything started with my sister-in-law. She inspired me to do what I do because she was doing it. I enjoy helping kids and inspiring them to achieve their potential. Find a role model who inspires you. Give yourself time to find what you like. Tell you what, here's my number in case you want to talk later on. Please reach out whenever you need."

As the warm hues of the Friday evening sky in May painted the horizon, Alexa was grateful for Yamil's genuine concern and promised to call him if she ever needed advice. She started her walk towards the bus station and felt the absence of Rudy, her now ex-boyfriend and once-constant chauffeur. She felt her heart aching again, yet found a way to regain some strength. Alexa thought that she could persevere just like Yamil had done. The interview with him had been her day's highlight, despite finding herself alone on a Friday evening.

CHAPTER 7

A FILMMAKER, SHARON BAKER

June had turned Alexa's cozy bedroom into a warm summer hideaway. Without an air conditioner, the room felt toasty, like the inside of a freshly baked pie. A fan twirled in the corner, blowing around the summer-scented air. Alexa sat on her bed, staring out the window, daydreaming. Bright sunbeams danced into the room, making fun shapes on the floor. Outside, birds chirped happily, singing their summer songs.

The buzz from an incoming text drew Alexa out of her contemplative state. Picking it up, she saw Ella's text, the words shining brightly on the screen, *Hi! Doing OK? Next guest, filmmaker = Sharon Baker.*

While she was thrilled at the prospect of meeting a filmmaker, the looming SAT was like a gray cloud over her excitement. She quickly replied to Ella: *Hi! Excited about it… w/SAT stressedtomax! I'll get back to you soon!*

Alexa felt like she was lost in a maze, and suddenly, the idea of Lourdes Puig popped up like a signpost pointing the way. She quickly dialed Lourdes' number, her fingers fidgeting with her hair while waiting. The moment Lourdes' familiar voice answered, it felt like finding a secret shortcut out of the maze.

"Hi, Alexa! Great hearing from you. Has it really been that long since our interview?"

Between the rhythm of Lourdes' words, Alexa could faintly hear the muffled sounds of city traffic painting a bustling backdrop to their conversation. Imagining Lourdes amidst her busy day made Alexa appreciate the call even more.

"Everything alright? How can I assist you?" Lourdes inquired.

Taking a deep breath, Alexa put Lourdes on speaker, freeing her hands to fidget with a pen on her desk. "Lourdes, I need to decide on colleges. Ever since we interviewed you at *Latinisimo*, engineering has been on my mind. Could we meet to discuss? You might be the clarity I need right now."

"Of course!" Lourdes responded, her voice briefly overshadowed by what sounded like a car horn. "Sorry about that. When are you available?"

While clicking on her smartphone to pull up a calendar, Alexa asked, "Do you have any free slots this week, Lourdes?"

"I'm juggling a few things with Aspira Academy at the moment… and I'm actually driving now as you probably heard," Lourdes admitted. "But, I have an idea. Why not meet there tomorrow? I have a gap between two meetings. Saves me the back-and-forth. How about two p.m.? Are you familiar with Aspira's location?"

Typing swiftly, Alexa quickly located the address. "Is it the one on Ruthar Drive?"

"That's the one! See you there!"

As Alexa ended the call, her room fell silent again, but her heart was aflutter with anticipation. Meeting Lourdes in person, discussing her future, it all felt like a step in the right direction.

While trying to research Sharon Baker, Alexa's thoughts drifted to the enriching conversations she had on *Latinisimo*. She reminisced about Yamil, Lourdes, Lisa, and Raye—each representing a unique journey shaped by the challenges they overcame and the institutions that played pivotal roles in their growth. Yamil, from his modest beginnings to earning a doctorate; Lourdes, whose drive led her to DuPont and eventually to helm Aspira Academy; and both Lisa and Raye, who found transformative experiences at the University of Delaware.

These reflections shifted her focus to where they studied. While the allure of Ivy League universities was tempting, she realized that she should prioritize institutions renowned for engineering. MIT, Caltech, Stanford, and UC Berkeley popped up in her search. Each institution had its own unique offerings, but all shared a reputation for excellence in engineering.

As Alexa tapped swiftly on her smartphone, compiling her notes, a wave of determination surged within her. Eager to present her findings to Lourdes, she paused momentarily, her fingers freezing over the screen. What if Lourdes thinks I'm aiming too high? she thought, her thumb unconsciously tracing circles on the phone's surface. Taking a deep breath, she pushed past the uncertainty, reminding herself that seeking Lourdes' insight was the very reason she needed to talk to her.

The day after, Alexa stepped into Aspira Academy after a long bus journey, and for a split second, she felt like she was entering a different world. The reception area was huge, not like any school she'd seen before. Everywhere she looked, there were pops of bright blue and sunny yellow, which instantly lifted her mood.

To one side, massive windows stretched from floor to ceiling, revealing the industrial park beyond at the intersection where the school was located. The cars driving by gave a sense of hustle and bustle, even from within the calm of the building. Their movement was a sharp contrast to the stationary room she stood in, but somehow, it didn't feel out of place.

There were sitting areas around, kind of making it feel like a cozy waiting room or a café corner. And she couldn't help but notice the potted plants scattered around. They added a fresh, earthy touch to the place, breaking the monotony of urban life just outside the window.

As Alexa soaked in the surroundings, a constant ebb and flow of students added life to the scene. They moved with purpose, their backpacks swaying to the rhythm of their steps. Some chatted animatedly, their laughter ringing out, while others seemed engrossed in their thoughts, perhaps contemplating an upcoming test or project.

Every so often, a student would glance her way, giving her a quick nod or a smile. Their easy confidence made her wonder about the kind of environment Aspira nurtured. The place was alive, vibrant, even amidst the serenity of the reception area.

A friendly staff member approached her. "Alexa? Lourdes is expecting you. Follow me," she said with a warm smile in an accented English. As they navigated through the corridors, the energy of the academy was palpable. Alexa followed her guide, anticipation building with each step, eager to reconnect with Lourdes in what appeared to be such a dynamic setting.

Soon, they approached a classroom where chaos seemed to rule: chairs precariously stacked atop desks, evidence of a recent cleanup or perhaps a hurried gathering. Walking into the room, Alexa felt a swirl of apprehension. She hesitated for a brief moment, taking in Lourdes' composed demeanor amidst the surrounding disorder. How can she be so cool in all this chaos? Alexa wondered.

Lourdes had stopped typing on her laptop when heard the door opening. "Hi, Alexa, glad to see you! Please have a seat and give me a minute." Alexa searched for an available chair and brought it closer to Lourdes.

Lourdes looked up, and upon catching Alexa's slightly overwhelmed expression, chuckled. "Oh, this mess? It's a bit chaotic, I know. Sometimes things don't go as planned, and we have to adapt. We have to make the best of where we are, don't you think?" Her warm eyes and understanding smile immediately put Alexa at ease.

With an encouraging nod, Lourdes motioned for Alexa to begin. Gathering her courage, Alexa rushed into her inquiry. "I was hoping to get your advice on colleges. I've been looking into universities renowned for engineering like Stanford University, MIT, Georgia Institute of Technology, and California Institute of Technology."

Lourdes' eyes lit up, a mixture of admiration and understanding upon hearing Alexa's ambitious plans. She closed her laptop gently and, with a graceful motion, slid a nearby chair closer, indicating she was ready to give Alexa her undivided attention. "I see," she began softly, "Those are exceptional choices. But before we dive into that, where are you with the SAT?"

"I registered for the SAT at the College Board website less than two months ago." Alexa pictured the time when Rudy was asking everybody where they were on that front. "I created an account and scheduled in July at a location nearby. The website made it easy, so I'm good there."

Lourdes' eyes studied her for a moment before she leaned forward, fingertips tapping lightly on the desk nearby. "Good in what sense, Alexa? The SAT requires tons of preparation. I'm sure you already know. Are you prepared? This is early June already and I wonder…"

Alexa's grip on her bag tightened, and she consciously had to remind herself to breathe. "I'm good to go, Lourdes. I've dedicated weekly hours for SAT preparation and I've been practicing with several tests already. With that and my three-point-five GPA, I believe I should be okay."

Seeing Alexa's determination, Lourdes' face softened. She shifted in her chair, bringing it closer to Alexa, a gesture of intimacy and reassurance. "Yes, you're on the right track, Alexa. And a solid GPA does make a difference."

She paused, a thoughtful expression playing on her face. "Remember, the essay is now considered optional by many institutions. Nowadays, you'll receive a passage from an author taking a stance on an issue, and your task is to analyze their argument. It's scored separately from the rest of the SAT."

Quickly, Alexa pulled out her smartphone, tapping in a quick note to remind herself to further look into the essay changes. She glanced back up, noticing the earnestness in Lourdes' eyes, which put her at ease.

"I did come across that on the College Board website," she replied, her voice carrying a hint of gratitude. "I initially hoped to leverage the 'old' essay format. But I believe my experiences with *Latinisimo* have prepped me well for this new challenge. I'm actually thankful for it."

Lourdes leaned forward, her eyes filled with genuine encouragement. With a nod of approval, she voiced her support for Alexa's choices, pushing her to apply. Throughout the conversation, Lourdes exuded a warmth and understanding that touched Alexa deeply. As their talk drew to a close, Lourdes reached down beside her and handed Alexa a small yellow book.

"I brought this book for you. I want you to have it. It's about a successful Filipino immigrant, Jose Antonio Vargas, who happens to be undocumented. He wrote *Dear America: Notes of an Undocumented Citizen*. He's a Pulitzer Prize journalist who overcame countless adversities like you. He's now a frequent keynote speaker, sharing his story whenever he can. I want you to read it and make it yours. Adversity is only a bump in the road. Don't let anybody write your story. You can do it, Alexa!"

Holding the small yellow book close to her chest, a surge of emotions welled up in Alexa, catching her off guard. Growing up, charting her path, and all the anxieties that came with it seemed to momentarily lift, replaced by a growing confidence, thanks to Lourdes' support.

"Thanks, Lourdes," Alexa's voice quivered, the weight of her gratitude making her words tremble. "I'll dive into this book as soon as I get home. You know, talking with you, it feels like I've found a missing piece to a puzzle I wasn't even aware I was trying to solve. Suddenly, a future in engineering seems so tangible, and I'm... I'm just overflowing with hope."

As Alexa made her way towards the door, a rush of vulnerability swept over her. She paused, turned around, and without thinking, wrapped her arms around Lourdes, drawing her into a tight embrace. The intensity of the moment hung between them, a shared understanding of dreams and the challenges of youth. After what felt like minutes, Lourdes gently pulled back, locking eyes with Alexa and whispered with a sincerity that sent chills down Alexa's spine, "You've got this, Alexa."

On Friday, two days after her helpful meeting with Lourdes and right after school, Alexa sat at her family's small kitchen table. The rustic surface bore the marks of countless family meals and discussions. The rich aroma of a freshly baked corn cake, a cherished recipe from her mom, wafted in the air, mingling with the sweet scent of cinnamon. Every inhalation brought a swell of nostalgia and warmth. It smelled like home. Alexa felt a deep sense of belonging, anchoring her as she navigated the challenges and dreams of her budding future.

Feeling a surge of positive energy, Alexa eagerly started her research on Sharon Baker for *Latinisimo* at the kitchen table. Deep in her findings, the unexpected ring of her smartphone broke her concentration. It was unusual for her to be alone at home on a Friday evening. Where's everybody? Seeing Ella's name flash on the screen, she quickly answered.

"Hi, Alexa! Hope it's okay to call you. I was a bit worried about you. Is the SAT prep coming along well? If you can't help with the interview with Sharon, I understand."

"Thanks for checking in." Alexa replied, her voice warm with gratitude. "I'm all good. Chatted with CE today, and she was seriously awesome."

Ella's confusion was palpable over the line. "You talked to who, Alexa?"

Alexa shared the conversation she had had with Lourdes Puig.

"I'm so happy you talked to Lourdes. She's a mom at heart, plus a chemist with a successful career. She can indeed help you. Listen, how about if we do some research together to save you some time? I can send you a Zoom link right away and spend a few minutes together on this."

They spent time exploring Sharon's website Teleduction, where they found she had produced a documentary depicting the lives of Latinos in Delaware, *Estamos Aquí*, alongside other interesting pieces. Then they found more articles mentioning industry awards in categories such as documentary, cultural programming, public affairs, and directing, but also from film festivals. Her programs had appeared on PBS, APT, the History Channel, BRAVO, National Geographic worldwide, and many regional cable outlets.

"She embodies everything an independent career woman should be. Get ready for a real trip with this interview! See you soon."

Drawn to the allure of Sharon's world of filmmaking, Alexa's curiosity spiked. She had never known a filmmaker personally. Diving deep into her online research, Alexa stumbled upon an interview. In it, Sharon spoke passionately about her love for social justice and storytelling, revealing how she seamlessly intertwined these passions throughout the companies she had established.

Exhausted after a long day, Alexa reflected on her findings. Looks like Sharon uses a camera like a tool to tell stories. I might not become a filmmaker, but I still like what she does. She barely finished her last thought before falling asleep.

The Friday of the interview, Alexa was engrossed in the studio cabin, adjusting the console, mics, and software when she felt a presence. Looking up, she found Sharon, earlier than she had expected. A quick buzz from her phone showed a text from Ella, saying she was caught in traffic and would be a few minutes late. *Pls take care of Sharon.* Alexa's heart rate picked up a notch. She was face-to-face with the filmmaker she'd recently researched, and now she had to step up, at least for a little while, in Ella's absence.

Alexa introduced herself and told Sharon about Ella's delay, asking if she was okay with waiting a little bit. Sharon luckily had saved the evening for *Latinisimo* and only had plans for dinner with her husband in a nearby restaurant.

"We're okay, Alexa, don't worry. If we're a bit late, I can call Frank to change the reservation for later. Tell me about yourself, besides being *Latinisimo*'s intern. What do you do?"

Alexa explained her journey to decide on a career path and her difficulties finding the right choice. An interesting conversation ensued.

"Sharon, how did you find your calling to become a filmmaker? It looks like you have a connection with social justice."

"Actually, I started in radio and then evolved, realizing I was interested in films. I started my career in my early twenties. I had a job as a radio talk show host in Wilmington at Delaware's WILM. I did a nightly live talk program called *News Talk*, and I really delved into all the issues of the day.

"When I was doing talk radio, there were no other women. I had kind of a deeper voice, so people didn't realize how young I was. I started on the talk show because I needed a little job I could do at night when the kids were still young. It wasn't such a little job, as it turned out. I started before Ken Burns, but he got the budgets."

Alexa felt a pang of embarrassment for not knowing, and hesitated briefly before admitting, "And who's Ken Burns?"

Sharon leaned in, offering Alexa a reassuring smile. "He's a renowned director. Some people would say, 'Oh, but you never had a lot of commercial success.' Yet, I have traveled to Africa, China, Guatemala, some of the most remote villages, Europe, and extensively throughout the U.S. I've met people from all corners of the globe. That experience, for me, is priceless. I was torn between arts and public service. So, I brought them together."

Alexa's senses became immediately alert when the studio door creaked open, revealing a slightly flustered Ella. Alexa could feel a gust of cooler air from the corridor waft in, carrying with it a faint scent of some kind of food from the break room. Ella's hurried footsteps on the studio's floor were a testament to her rush.

"I'm so sorry for being late, traffic was a mess," Ella announced, her eyes darting to where Alexa and Sharon sat. There was a light sheen of perspiration on her forehead, making her skin glisten under the studio lights. "But I see you two started without me."

Sharon let out a soft giggle, the sound light and airy in the studio's otherwise silent ambiance. "We were just getting acquainted," she remarked, her gaze lingering on Alexa with evident admiration. "Glad you arrived! She's impressive, Ella. You sure you want to keep her all to yourself?"

Alexa felt a blush warming her cheeks at the unexpected praise. She tried to gauge Ella's reaction, noticing the corners of her lips tugging into a playful smile.

Laughing, Ella responded, "Absolutely! Hearing about merging public service with art is intriguing. Shall we begin there? Now, about the music for our program..."

Sharon's nod was accompanied by a genuine, warm smile, making Alexa feel more at ease. "That sounds perfect," Sharon agreed with Ella's song choices.. Drawing Alexa back into their conversation, she elaborated. "As I was saying, I was coming up in an era where if you weren't part of the problem, you were supposed to be part of the solution. As a Boomer, we grew up with the murder of John Kennedy, Bobby Kennedy, Martin Luther King, the battles over the war in Vietnam, Buddhist monks lighting themselves on fire to protest. That stuff stays with you when you're a kid."

Once they settled on the appropriate music choices, the interview began with the public service angle Sharon had brought up before once Ella shared briefly who the guest was.

"Sharon, your career as a filmmaker began after being a radio host. But somehow it was an attempt for public service, wasn't it? Could you please share with us the connection between filmmaking and public service?"

"I was a theater major but also took law courses thinking about going to law school. That was, until one day after we'd done a moot court, or trial exercise. I told our very famous professor that I couldn't possibly represent the defendant because he clearly had committed the crime and was a loser. He said, 'I think you better go back to theater because that's not the way it works here.'"

Alexa, Ella, and Sharon laughed in unison before Ella continued. "I guess that was the end of law school for you, but what about politics?"

"My dad and mom were involved in politics. He even thought of running for public office. He described the Washington of the fifties as a place where there were bad and good guys, but also a degree of respect that people had for one another. I believe that some of this awful anger and divisiveness is the last bit of the Civil War being fought. It's about racism, hatred, and white supremacy that the nation never dealt with."

"As we take a short music break, I'd like to thank Sharon for sharing her insights. Stay with us, *Latinisimo* listeners, we'll be right back," Ella announced smoothly.

With the mics temporarily silenced, the energy of the room shifted to a more relaxed ambiance. Alexa, feeling the urge to capture the essence of the moment, swiftly began crafting her Instagram post.

Noticing Alexa's fingers dancing over her phone's screen, Sharon leaned in with genuine curiosity. "Whatcha doing there?"

With a soft chuckle, Alexa tilted her phone slightly so Sharon could see. "Just wanted to share a piece of today with my Insta followers. I find your journey really inspiring."

Sharon's eyes crinkled in a sincere smile. "It's an honor to be part of someone's digital memory. Stories are meant to be shared, after all."

Buoyed by Sharon's encouraging words, Alexa confidently tapped 'post'. The room was momentarily filled with the soft hum of equipment and the distant, muted beats from the music playing during the break.

Ella checked the timer, signaling that the break was nearing its end. She caught Alexa's eye, communicating silently about the transition back to the interview.

Alexa, inspired by Sharon's previous answer, scribbled down a quick question and passed it discreetly to Ella. She got a nod of approval.

Ella adjusted her headset, cleared her throat, and as the last notes of the song faded, she took the lead. "Welcome back to *Latinisimo*. We've been having a thoughtful conversation with filmmaker Sharon Baker. Sharon, your insights about the political environment from the past until now are truly enlightening. Alexa here has a question she'd like to suggest. Go on, Alexa."

With a mixture of excitement and nervousness, Alexa took a moment before asking, "Sharon, with your family's background in politics and the pressing issues of our times, have you ever considered running for office yourself?"

As Alexa posed the question, Sharon's initial composure shifted subtly. Her eyes, which had been steadily meeting Alexa's, widened just a fraction. She took a slightly deeper breath than before, and her fingertips drummed momentarily on the table, betraying a moment of introspection. For that brief second, Alexa could sense the weight of memories and decisions Sharon had made in the past.

"I was encouraged to run for office at some point, but my children were very little, and I didn't want to leave them to go through all that. Radio allowed me to take care of them better. About ten years ago, I was thinking about getting in the game, but I had a business to run and employees to take care of. I started to say, I am too old for that."

"Are you serious," Ella said. "It's perhaps what many career women like you had to face, right?"

"Isn't that the truth?" Sharon answered.

Hearing Sharon, Alexa felt the real side of adulting—tough choices and all. She nodded, her face serious. So, running a business while managing family life can be complicated. You're forced to make choices. Alexa pondered, Will I be ready when the time comes?

"Please tell us about services to the community since politics was not in the cards for you after all."

"We have always gravitated towards nonprofit organizations and causes focused on social justice, rather than corporate interests. In reviewing our portfolio of work over the last thirty years, it's clear that we've represented all the nonprofit organizations in Delaware. The reality is, these organizations often didn't have enough funds to fully realize their ambitions. While our production business was able to meet payroll and complete projects, profiting and saving extensively wasn't always possible. I've been involved with many organizations, offering in-kind services and serving on various boards. Most of my contributions, I believe, have come from adding value to communication projects for nonprofits across the state. I've always had a particular fondness for 'value-adding' in this way."

As Sharon talked about her work, Alexa heard the term 'value-adding' and wondered what it meant. She quickly pulled out her phone under the table and googled it. With a fast read, she got it—it was about making things better for others, not just making more money. Satisfied, she slipped her phone away and focused back on Sharon.

"I don't need tons of money. I just need to fund the next project. If we had enough money to meet the payroll, and get the project done... but never enough to profit and save too much. We gravitate to nonprofit organizations and causes that focus on social justice issues more than corporate. We did some interesting corporate work that took us all over the place."

As Sharon spoke of not chasing profit, Alexa nodded, getting the gist—doing good mattered more than making big bucks. I like that.

Mid-nod, her attention snagged on some commotion in the studio next door. Through the glass, she saw silhouettes bustling about, a whirl of activity against the flashing lights. It was like peering into an ant colony, each shadow moving with purpose she couldn't understand.

She tried to glue her focus back to Sharon, to be the attentive listener she aimed to be. But her eyes betrayed her, darting to the studio drama. It was a losing battle, the ebb and flow of the next room's energy too chaotic to ignore.

Projects, not profits... Alexa mentally repeated Sharon's words, trying to anchor her thoughts. But the visual buzz next door was like a TV left on, diverting her attention without permission. She squinted, curious yet frustrated, her concentration fractured.

Sharon said, "We did a project in China, with President Carter on village elections. I remember standing with a translator, outside of a humble little home, with the farm field right there talking to this woman. She was complaining about her husband and that she could not get her daughters to concentrate on their schoolwork, and I said, 'I know just how you feel.'"

Ella could not resist. "We've all been there and done that. Families are the same regardless of nationality, right, Sharon?"

Sharon laughed in agreement.

"Talking about family," Ella said, "Frank, your husband, and you have worked together on various projects. Your family has always been present in your career. Could you please share more about them?"

"I've been married to the same person for many years. That's a feat unto itself! My husband Frank and I have many things in common like theatre, arts, folk music, and a total love for our children. Our three hearts are Peter, Ned, and Kate. I came from a very large Irish American clan. My grandparents came over here in the late nineteenth century. I grew up with a group of people that had all kinds of stories. I had so many cousins that I didn't need any other playmates. There was storytelling and lots of music and singing and raising voices at the dinner table."

As Sharon recounted the stories of her family, Alexa's mind danced with images of raucous reunions and the rich tapestry of her own storytelling. She could almost hear the echoes of her family's tales in Sharon's words, the shared immigrant heartbeat resonating within her.

"Frank and I both have theater and music backgrounds, and we like to write. We started creating radio commercials and jingles. Shortly after getting married, we started the very early roots of our production company Teleduction. It was never easy, but enabled me to be around the kids when they were growing up."

"It seems that the arts are a constant connector in your life. Could you explain how?"

"I chose the arts and evolved into the work that I do now. It was the right choice for me, because I've had the opportunity to shed light on so many interesting people. We have told wonderful histories about John Dickinson, about Fort Delaware, about the Vitrola Museum, about Hagley, about all different aspects of Delaware's history."

Oh… yes! I remember it! Alexa's memory of the Hagley Museum flashed in her mind with clarity. She could still picture the machinery, the massive water wheel, and the intricate models that demonstrated the DuPont family's business acumen. It had been a school trip a year ago, but the way the museum connected the dots between history, industry, and innovation had truly impressed her. The realization that a business could have such a longstanding impact on a community had lingered with her long after the visit.

"At one point, I looked around and saw people like Charles Parks, Jack Lewis, and Helen Sloane and thought, 'Oh my God, they could suddenly die and then nobody would really know their story.' So, I put together a series called 'Through the Eyes of the Artist.' We raised enough money to cover the cost of having them tell their stories. They're now preserved forever for anybody who wants to know how significant these Delaware artists were. I'm very proud of that."

"That is another constant in your work, Sharon, the state of Delaware," Ella said.

"As part of my local production company, I have been to every small town in this state at one time or another, working with local communities, and I have met some wonderful people. I think Delaware is a state of possibilities. The production we've done that's maybe better known outside of Delaware is 'Whispers of Angels,' about the Underground Railroad. We used all historic locations here in the state. Twenty-two years later, it's still airing all over the world and on American Public Television."

Wow! TV… that is something… Underground Railroad… I've heard that in class. Alexa's eyes flicked across her screen, absorbing facts about Delaware's part in the Underground Railroad. Listening to Sharon, she felt a swell of pride. It hit her—Sharon had brought her home's hidden stories to life. She's really shown us the soul of Delaware.

"How do you connect both social justice and the state of Delaware?" Ella asked.

"Through my work, I had the opportunity to really get to know the African American community. I also ended up teaching at Delaware State University for five years, and I learned a lot more when I got there. We did three or four major documentaries that focused on Delaware's connection to black history.

Alexa's interest deepened with every word about the African American community. She could almost picture the documentaries Sharon mentioned, visualizing scenes that would make history come alive on screen. The dark parts of the state's history — the intolerance and discrimination. And sadly… still exist.

"We also started to get involved with the now called Latinx community, and I learned more there. It's really broadened my understanding and appreciation of people from all cultures, American and non-American. I have to pause though, Ella, and tell you that I'm still trying to learn Spanish. Our new project, already funded, is about the dreamers. It is called 'United We Dream,' and it's about DACA recipients." Sharon reflected for a minute and continued. "We really are the same and we want the same things in lives. So why does anybody hate anybody?"

As Sharon spoke about dreamers and DACA, Alexa's fingers paused mid-scroll on her phone. Her heart gave a quick jolt, a mix of shock and connection hitting her. She blinked hard, trying to focus, her mind racing. Whoa… she's talking… that's real for me! Alexa felt a sudden, intense connection to the conversation, her own reality reflected in Sharon's words. She gets it!

Watching Ella, Alexa caught the slight shift in her expression, a quick flicker in her eyes as they moved between Alexa and Sharon. It was like a quiet nod, an unspoken 'I get it' about how close the topic hit Alexa. After a second, Ella, with a small nod to herself, turned back to Sharon, keeping the interview on track.

Ella smoothly transitioned the conversation, her voice steady yet infused with curiosity. "You've had so many milestones in your career. Is there one that you'd say is your crowning achievement?" She paused for a brief moment, a thoughtful look crossing her face. "But before we dive into that, let's take a quick music break. Hold onto that thought, Sharon. We'll pick it up right after this." With a swift motion, she put the musical segment, allowing the conversation a moment to breathe.

As Ella announced the music break, Sharon expressed her relief. "Oh, thank goodness for music breaks. I could use a quick pit stop."

Ella, with a quick smile, directed her. "Just next to the elevator, Sharon. Can't miss it."

Alexa jumped in, "I'll walk you over."

They made their way through the studio's narrow hallways. The carpet felt damp under Alexa's feet, a reminder of the recent flooding. She made a face. "Watch your step. These carpets got a few surprises after the last heavy rain. They smell funny for starters."

Sharon chuckled, stepping gingerly. "I'll take your word for it."

Reaching the restroom, Sharon thanked Alexa. "Appreciate the guide through the maze here."

Alexa laughed. "Anytime. Adds a bit of adventure to the day, right?"

Sharon returned promptly from her brief break. Ella welcomed back their listeners. "And we're back with Sharon

Baker," she announced, her voice bright and engaging. "Before our musical interlude, we were about to dive into one of Sharon's proudest moments in her career. Sharon, care to pick up where we left off?"

"Sure. We had an opportunity to participate in the Mid-Atlantic Emmy competition. I must say, it was intimidating competing against big broadcast stations. We won nine Regional Emmys, a number of them in Public Affairs for productions we've done for nonprofits like the YWCA.

"I remember the day. We got all dressed up and went to these award events in Philadelphia. When they called out the winner Teleduction, everybody looked around puzzled. Who the hell are they? Where did they come from? Our little guerrilla team from Delaware won! We always try to put an extra level of creativity into the storytelling."

As Sharon shared the vivid memory of her triumphant moment, Alexa's eyes sparkled with excitement. She caught Ella's eye, giving her a subtle but eager nod, signaling her desire to jump in. Ella, understanding the unspoken message, smoothly wrapped up Sharon's anecdote and turned towards Alexa.

"Alexa, did you have something you wanted to ask Sharon?" Ella said, offering her the floor.

Alexa leaned forward, her enthusiasm evident. "Yes, thanks, Ella! Sharon, hearing about your experiences, I'm just so curious..." She took a brief pause, gathering her thoughts for the question that had been forming in her mind. "As a filmmaker, what makes a good story?"

"Good question Alexa! These days thanks to the Internet, a lot more people are able to tell their stories. We're bombarded with so much content, but you have to dig your way through the bad stuff to get to the good stuff."

Sharon sat back with a thinking face. "High-powered animation or sensational imagery can certainly help to enhance a program. For me, the secret sauce is found in the underlying story. I'm interested in people, how they think and feel, and what they have to say. That's the foundation on which to build a unique story."

The interview ended as Ella thanked Sharon for her time while wishing the *Latinisimo* audience a great rest of the week. Sharon left the studio and Alexa soon followed after her, telling Ella she wanted to ask Sharon another question.

Sharon held the elevator doors when saw Alexa rushing to catch up. "You're still thinking, Alexa. I see it in your eyes. What's on your mind?"

As Alexa stepped into the elevator, she wrinkled her nose at the musty scent that hung in the air, a leftover from the recent flood. The gray, cushioned walls looked tired and worn, making the space feel even more enclosed. She glanced at the colorful posters advertising student events, their brightness a stark contrast against the dull surroundings. In her mind, she couldn't help but think how the elevator's dreary interior could use a bit of a makeover, but her attention quickly shifted back to Sharon, eager to hear more of her insights.

"I keep thinking about the 'secret sauce' of a good story and connecting that to my decision about studying engineering. And also, about the SAT requiring criticizing a passage by an author. You shared how your career has evolved while accommodating your family needs. Were you clear about what you wanted?"

"Not everything is always clear." Sharon's words resonated with Alexa as they ascended. "I've been driven by my interest in people and their stories. I made choices based on what felt right, sometimes saying no, other times diving in. It's about finding what excites you and feels right. Be open to opportunities and find your true motivation. You'll find your path, Alexa. And if you need guidance, I'm here."

There was more Sharon wanted to say. "Let me tell you something kind of spiritual, can I?"

Alexa nodded, curious to hear as the elevator doors slid open.

"Have you ever heard that little quiet voice kind of telling you what to do? Then unexpectedly, the path is right there, so clear! Sometimes you hear somebody saying something, perhaps not even related, and all of a sudden something clicks and you find yourself saying. That's it! I know what to do!"

As Sharon's words echoed Alexa found herself nodding in agreement. Each interview on *Latinisimo*, every conversation with inspiring individuals like Sharon, had left her with a similar revelation. It was as if those interviews had quietly been a piece of a puzzle clicking into place in her mind. Yeah, she thought, a sense of clarity washing over her. "That's exactly how I've been feeling."

As Alexa stepped out of the radio station, the chiller than usual summer evening air brushing against her face, she glanced back to see Sharon in the distance, waving goodbye. A sense of awe enveloped her. She had just conversed with a filmmaker who, beyond her impressive career, had revealed a depth of heart and understanding that Alexa hadn't anticipated.

I just met a filmmaker with a heart she thought to herself. The realization that it wasn't just the storytelling, but the heart behind it that truly made Sharon's work resonate, struck Alexa deeply. It was a perspective she would carry with her, a newfound understanding of what made stories—and people—genuinely impactful.

With each step away from the station, the words Sharon had shared lingered in her mind. This day, like so many others woven into her journey with *Latinisimo*, had etched something special into her heart. Alexa smiled softly to herself, feeling grateful and inspired as she watched Sharon's figure fade into the distance. This was more than just an interview; it was a gift of insight and inspiration at the end of a long week and a complicated school year.

CHAPTER 8

A RESEARCHER AND DEAN, MARIA ARISTIGUETA

The humid July air hung heavily around the local pool, where Alexa and her friends gathered to celebrate their latest accomplishment: the SAT results. It was a typical scorching summer day in Delaware, the kind where the air felt like a warm, wet blanket. The vegetation around the pool area was lush and green, offering a refreshing contrast to the heat.

"Guys, we're finally done with the SATs!" Alexa beamed, her voice tinged with excitement and relief as she kicked her feet in the pool, sending ripples across the water.

Andy, lounging on a deck chair with sunglasses perched atop his nose, grinned at her. "Totally nailed it, didn't you, Alexa? Always knew you were the brainy one among us."

Alexa laughed, splashing water playfully in his direction. "Oh, stop it, Andy. But yeah, feels good to be done. And hey, no more classes!"

The others in the group nodded in agreement, sharing in the sense of accomplishment and freedom. "It's like we can finally breathe again, right?" Andy added, stretching his arms behind his head.

"Yeah, seriously. Feels like we've been under pressure forever," one of their friends chimed in, floating by on an inflatable raft.

Alexa smiled, soaking in the moment. The sun was shining, school was out, and the whole summer stretched out before them, full of possibilities. The stress of exams seemed like a distant memory now, replaced by the simple joys of a summer day spent with friends at the pool.

"And some of us are visiting colleges next week!" added Jessica, splashing water with her hands. "I'm checking out Vo-Tech. They have some cool programs plus I'm not sure I want the college thing and all."

Alexa nodded enthusiastically. "I've got a few university tours lined up too. It's all getting real, you know?"

The group shared after high school plans, their voices mingling with the sounds of laughter and water splashes. The atmosphere was light, filled with the buzz of teenage dreams and aspirations.

"Can we just talk about Mr. O'Jete for a second?" Andy blurted out, rolling his eyes dramatically. "Was it just me, or was he on a whole other level of annoying this year?"

"Ugh, tell me about it," Jessica chimed in. "His pop quizzes were like, the worst. And his jokes? Cringe city!"

"Let's not ruin the vibe talking about him," Alexa quickly interjected, wanting to keep the mood upbeat. "Today's about us and our future!"

Cheers erupted as they clinked their soda cans together, toasting to their achievements and the exciting journey ahead. They talked about the universities they wanted to visit, the programs they were interested in, and the new experiences awaiting them.

As the sun began to set, casting a golden hue over the pool, the friends decided to take a group selfie. They squeezed together, making funny faces and peace signs as the camera captured the moment.

"Best summer ever!" shouted one of them as they all jumped into the pool, creating a big splash. Laughter filled the air as they swam and played, savoring the carefree joy of their youth.

The next day, on a sunny Sunday afternoon, Alexa was surprised by an unexpected visitor. Rudy had stopped by her house. She hadn't seen him since their breakup, and her heart fluttered with a mix of emotions as her mom opened the door.

Cristina poked her head out briefly, her tone friendly but hurried. "Alexa, Rudy's here. Sorry, I can't stay, the chicken for our mole is almost ready. You're welcome to join us if you'd like."

"Thanks, Mrs. Hope. I'll just talk to Alexa for a bit," Rudy replied, his voice betraying a hint of unease.

Alexa stepped outside, squinting against the bright sunlight that momentarily blinded her as she adjusted to the unexpected sight of Rudy. He stood there, visibly uncomfortable, his hands buried deep in his pockets and his posture making evident the tension beneath.

"Hey Rudy." To her own ears she sounded steady, but she felt caution within. She couldn't help but notice his twitchy movements and the way his eyes seemed to avoid meeting hers directly. The air between them was thick with awkwardness, stirring a mix of curiosity and apprehension within her.

"It's been a while," she added, watching Rudy's nervousness with his hands still hidden away. Alexa braced herself, unsure of what to expect from this unexpected encounter.

"I... um... wanted to show you something," Rudy stammered, offering Alexa an earbud. "It's this song, 'Patria y Vida.' Made me think of you. It's got over nine million views on YouTube. It's pretty big, even caused a stir in Cuba. One of the songwriters got detained and all."

Alexa's eyebrows furrowed in confusion and irritation as she accepted the earbud. "Rudy, you're talking about Cuba and politics now? Since when?" She paused. "What are you doing here actually?" She felt a mix of disbelief and discomfort, struggling to connect this new side of him with the person she used to know.

Rudy's eyes met hers, a glimmer of earnestness in them. "It's about this song, 'Patria y Vida,' we talked about yesterday at the Voto Latino meeting. I've been helping them out recently. Thought you'd find the song's message interesting."

Alexa's irritation softened slightly, replaced by a curious skepticism. "Voto Latino, huh? That's... unexpected. But why bring this to me now, Rudy?" Her tone still held an edge, a clear signal that while she was listening, she wasn't entirely convinced.

Rudy stopped and looked intently at Alexa. "Never mind, Alexa. Clearly, it's not a good time. Sorry to bother you."

As Rudy mumbled his goodbyes and turned to leave, Alexa noticed a slump in his shoulders. His usually animated movements were replaced with a defeated slouch, a clear sign of his unhappiness. Alexa watched, a mix of emotions swirling within her as she observed this unexpected side of Rudy.

He walked away quickly, eager to escape the awkward situation. Alexa watched him go, feeling a strange mix of relief and confusion. She hadn't even had a chance to say anything back. Just like that, huh? she thought, a bit stunned by the abrupt end to their interaction. His figure grew smaller in the distance, and Alexa stood at her doorway, trying to make sense of what had just happened.

Voto Latino? Rudy? She typed the words into her cell. The information came up right away. A political advocacy organization empowering Latino vote. Wow, Rudy is doing political work! She found the song and listened to it. She liked it.

A text from Ella interrupted her thoughts and intention to tell Rudy about the song. *Maria Aristigueta, Dean Biden School, University of Delaware, get info. Thks!*

The enticing smell of chicken mole filled the house, making Alexa's mouth water. The perfect blend of chocolate, spices, and tender chicken was calling out to her. She was so ready to jump right into the savory feast, but she wanted to start exploring about the new interviewee. Standing there, with the aroma of mole sauce teasing her taste buds, she pulled up the web search bar. Her fingers flew over the screen as she sent off a text to Ella: *Hey Ella, got a sec? What does a dean actually do?* Her stomach grumbled, craving the delicious dinner. *Better call you after dinner, okay?*

Ella quickly responded. *Tomorrow. Out. Dinner w/hubby.*

Mid-Monday morning, as Alexa was comfortably reclining in bed with her phone, deeply engrossed in researching college options, her phone rang with Ella's name flashing on the screen. Shifting to sit up, tucking a pillow behind her for support, she quickly swiped to answer the call.

"Hi! Just quickly as I have a meeting in five. Regarding Maria, think of her as the CEO of a corporation. She's responsible for one of the ten colleges and schools at the University of Delaware. She's a kinda big shot there."

The cell signal was breaking up and Ella's voice was crackling. "She's coming to the studio in two weeks. Can you research her? Call her if you think it might help prepare the interview better. Let me know. Have a bad signal. She's from Cuba—"

The call abruptly ended.

Alexa texted back. *I'll get info. Cyou!* Then she kept thinking, Cuba? Isn't that where Rudy's song is coming from? What a coincidence.

On the following Saturday morning, Andy dropped by Alexa's house. With a friendly smile, he asked, "Hey, Alexa! Are you interested in going to the school party together tonight? I can swing by your place and pick you up on my way there."

"Thanks, but no thanks, Andy. I have to do some research for *Latinisimo...*"

"So, you're avoiding Rudy, huh? I can tell." Andy's tone held a hint of teasing, but his words were direct. "He mentioned stopping by here recently. Said you seemed pretty thrown off. He's actually doing some decent stuff, you know, trying at least. But hey, it's your call. Catch you later, alright?"

Alexa felt a pang of discomfort at Andy's blunt callout. His words stirred a mix of emotions, a blend of defensiveness and a twinge of guilt. She was caught off guard, not expecting Andy to be so straightforward about her avoidance of Rudy.

After lunch, Alexa googled Maria Aristigueta. It was a great way to put her mind in a different place than the party she was trying to avoid. Alexa found the University of Delaware's webpage. Maria's career had been long and distinguished.

Alexa's eyes caught the name of one of Maria's books: *Civil Society in Cuba: Advancing through Moral Convictions and Public Connectedness.*

After emailing Maria to introduce herself and explain the purpose of her call, rather than calling unexpectedly, Alexa received a prompt reply. Maria suggested they have a call at 7:00 am on Wednesday, given her busy schedule. Alexa was grateful for the arrangement, as it allowed her time to focus on her college-related tasks.

When Wednesday arrived, Alexa was ready for the call. Right on time, Maria's voice came through the phone, lively and welcoming. "¡Hola, Alexa! ¡Buenos días! ¿Cómo estás? How are you doing? ¡Qué gusto oírte! ¿Hablas Español?" Maria's enthusiasm for speaking Spanish was evident and infectious, making Alexa feel at ease immediately.

"¡Si!" Alexa responded. "¡Un gusto hablar contigo! Happy to practice my Spanish when I can. Thanks for your time, Maria. Can I call you that, by the way?"

"Claro mi'ja. Please, call me Maria."

Alexa started by confirming day and time for the interview. "Can I ask you a question, Maria? Why the interest in Cuban Civil Society? I found one of your books with that title in my research for your upcoming interview. It got my attention."

"I'm originally from Cuba. I came to the U.S. with my family in the early sixties when Fidel Castro seized power. I can't tell you how much it affected me as a child to be forced to leave my country." In Alexa's ears, Maria's voice was soothing yet confident, with a gentle Cuban accent that made each word feel welcoming. Listening to her, Alexa felt a sense of warmth and comfort.

"We left our country too, Maria. It hurts. We're originally from Mexico."

"Give me a sec, Alexa." She disconnected briefly. "I'm afraid I have to leave. I'm unexpectedly babysitting today, and my grandkids want breakfast like now. I'll see you at the studio, okay?"

"Not a problem. See you there!"

Andy came to mind and decided to send him a text: *yright! not ready to see Rudy.Enjoy4me!*

In the balmy heat of a July afternoon, Alexa found herself rummaging through racks of clothes at a thrift shop with her cousins. They had decided to spend the day hunting for unique, budget-friendly fashion finds. The shop, bustling with other bargain hunters, was filled with the chatter and laughter of families enjoying their summer together.

As she sifted through the clothing, Alexa's fingers stumbled upon a lightweight, floral summer dress. It was a beautiful mix of vibrant colors, perfect for the season. The fabric felt soft and breezy against her skin as she held it up, imagining how it would look. It had a bohemian vibe, with delicate straps and a flowing skirt that seemed to dance with the slightest movement.

Excited by her find, Alexa couldn't wait to try it on. She headed to the fitting room, and slipped into the dress. It fit her perfectly, hugging her figure in just the right places while allowing enough room for comfort. The mirror reflected a version of her that seemed carefree and joyful, a stark contrast to the tension-filled days of SAT preparation and college planning.

She twirled in front of the mirror, the skirt of the dress fanning out gracefully. The joy of finding such a gem for a great price, combined with the laughter and chatter of her cousins nearby, made for a perfect summer day. *Mom, found nice&cheap dress for summer, mind if I buy it?*

Encouraged by her mom's quick thumbs up emoji, she decided to buy the dress, already picturing herself wearing it to a family barbecue or a casual day out with friends. As she stepped out of the fitting room, her cousins immediately approved of her choice, their faces lighting up with smiles. The simple pleasure of thrift shopping with family, finding a beautiful outfit without breaking the bank, brought a sense of normalcy and happiness to Alexa amidst the whirlwind of her senior year preparations.

A few weeks later, the day of Maria's interview had arrived. The Biden School of Public Administration, where she worked, was conveniently close to WVUD's studios. As Alexa opened the studio door, she spotted Maria approaching. Together, they entered the studio where Ella was already prepping for the interview.

Ella greeted them warmly as she stood up, adjusting her microphone. "Hello there! I'm glad you're both here," she said with a smile. "I was just thinking about the music for today's show. Do either of you have any suggestions?"

"Here, take this," Alexa offered, extending her flash drive towards Ella. "I've got 'Patria y Vida' on here. Rudy, my ex, brought it up, and I thought of adding 'Guantanamera' too, you know, because of Maria's Cuban roots." She observed a flicker of surprise cross Ella's face at the mention of Rudy.

As Maria listened to Alexa, her eyes seemed to glisten, touched by the mention of Cuba. Alexa could relate; she had seen that same emotional depth in her own parents' eyes whenever they spoke of home.

Composing herself, Maria responded, "Excellent selections, Alexa. I couldn't have chosen better songs myself."

Ella looked into Alexa's eyes. "Excellent job, Alexa. One step ahead! Well we're starting in seconds. Now Alexa—"

"Got you, Ella. Mic and system. On it!" Ella didn't finish the sentence as Alexa was practically reading her mind.

Inside the cozy confines of the *Latinisimo* studio, Alexa felt a familiar surge of confidence. She had come to know every inch of this space, from the foam-covered walls that cocooned them in a world of sound, to the comforting hum of the equipment. The studio, with its mix of high-tech gadgets and homey touches, had become a second home to her.

She guided Maria to a chair situated perfectly for the mic setup, her movements fluid and assured. "Just sit here, Maria. Perfect." She directed gently, ensuring Maria was comfortable yet well-positioned for optimal sound quality.

Alexa then glanced over at the Audacity program running on the computer. The green and red lines danced across the screen in response to their movements and voices, indicating everything was set just right. She gave Ella a confident thumbs up, a silent communication they had perfected over their time working together.

"Welcome to *Latinisimo*, Maria!" Ella started in an upbeat tone. "Today we have Dr. Maria Aristigueta, Dean of the Biden School of Public Administration at the University of Delaware. Thanks for your time, Maria!"

"Thanks for inviting me, Ella. It is good to be back to *Latinisimo*."

"Maria, you have had a distinguished academic career, yet you have shared that your research about Cuban Civil Society is perhaps the most rewarding thing you have done. Could you please explain why?"

As Maria spoke, her hands instinctively moved to her heart, her fingers gently pressing against her chest. "In my heart is the fact that I was born a Latina and was raised very much in a Latino household." The tone of Maria's voice changed slightly. It carried a certain warmth and nostalgia, a resonance that spoke of a deep-seated love and respect for her cultural roots. The way Maria's gaze seemed to drift, just for a moment, as if visualizing a distant memory or a cherished moment from her past, didn't go unnoticed by Alexa. In these subtle movements and expressions, Alexa sensed the profound impact of Maria's heritage on her identity. It was a powerful reminder of the strong emotional ties that bind one to their culture and origins, a sentiment Alexa found both moving and relatable.

"I waited until I had accumulated ten years of experience before I started that research. The work on civil society in Cuba was difficult to publish because it was considered outside of mainstream research."

"Outside mainstream research?" Ella repeated. "Can you explain what that means?"

"Mainstream of public administration are things such as organizational behavior, performance management, program evaluation. Topics to avoid include nationality, race, and gender. They are considered controversial. I was advised to always have projects at different stages of development to increase chances for publication. Something like civil society in Cuba narrows your chances for publication, yet it was a very rewarding part of my career. I'm so glad that I did it, and so glad that I was able to publish it."

"Before we continue, let me ask Alexa to share some of your publications for the audience to have a better idea of the scope of your research. Alexa?"

As Alexa shared Maria's publications with the audience, her voice was steady and clear, outlining the depth of Maria's research with precision. She felt a rush of excitement, knowing she was connecting listeners to the significance of Maria's work. And as Alexa smoothly transitioned to introducing 'Patria y Vida' for the musical break, her timing was impeccable.

Ella's approving smile was all the validation Alexa needed. A wave of satisfaction washed over her. She'd managed to not only inform but also engage the audience, bridging the gap between academic research and everyday understanding. Leaning back slightly, she let the music fill the studio, her heart swelling with pride. In that moment, Alexa recognized her own growth at *Latinisimo* and it felt great.

Ella clicked her mic back. "Welcome back, *Latinisimo* friends. We're here with Dr. Maria Aristigueta, Dean of the Biden School of Public Administration. Thanks for your time today, Maria. Can we get a bit personal? Could you tell us about how your family ended up coming to the U.S.?"

"I was nine when we came from Cuba, not speaking a word of English. I think one of the things that differentiates me, as my children like to say, it is my refugee status. This formed my political thought. I am a true believer in democracy.

"It was in October of nineteen sixty-five when the PT boat we came in went into very rough seas and the ninety-mile trip ended up being a day long. People were very, very seasick because the ocean was wild. Dramatic moments are the ones that stick in our heads for years and years.

"When we arrived in Key West, we had to go through a series of vaccinations. I kept asking, as a nine-year-old does, what is this vaccine for? What is this vaccine for? And then I stopped, looked at the nurse, and said, 'I will not ask anymore. If they're against communism, please make sure that I get them all.'" Maria made a pause reflecting on her own words.

As Maria recounted her journey from Cuba, Alexa felt a wave of emotions wash over her. Each word painted a vivid picture in her mind—a small girl on a tumultuous sea, scared and hopeful. Alexa's hands unconsciously gripped the edge of the table, her knuckles whitening as she visualized the stormy waters and the frightened faces.

The story of vaccinations in Key West struck a particularly deep chord. Alexa could almost hear the young Maria's voice, filled with both innocence and a startling clarity, questioning the nurse. Her resolve, even as a child, to fight against what she perceived as wrong, stirred something within Alexa. It was like a spark igniting, filling her with a mix of awe and a newfound understanding of the struggles faced by refugees.

Tears threatened to spill from Alexa's eyes, but she blinked them back, not wanting to break the moment. Maria's narrative wasn't just a tale of the past; it resonated with Alexa as a poignant reminder of the resilience and strength that defined the human spirit. She felt a deep connection to Maria's story, although her life had been much different. This was more than history; it was a testament to courage and hope.

"I really do feel that anyone who's gone through that experience has a very strong dislike for communism. Early in my education in Cuba, I clearly remember the indoctrination that was taking place. I remember memorizing 'Arriba, abajo los yanquis son guanajo.'"

"Give me a minute, Maria. Let me translate for the audience just in case. *Up and down, Americans are turkeys.* Is this more or less a fair translation?"

Maria nodded. "The regime was trying to convince the Cuban people of the merits of the revolution. Children were an easy target for indoctrination."

After hearing Maria's moving recollection of indoctrination in Cuba, Alexa felt a surge of curiosity. She quickly pulled out her phone, her fingers dancing over the screen as she typed in a search for 'communism and indoctrination.' She skimmed through the snippets of information popping up, looking for a concise explanation that could shed light on what Maria experienced.

Alexa found herself reading about the tactics used in communist regimes to shape public opinion and belief systems, especially among the young. The more she read, the more she understood the gravity of what Maria had endured. It wasn't just about politics; it was about a deep-rooted manipulation of thoughts and beliefs from a young age.

So… O'Jete was trying to indoctrinate me? I see it now… No way now that I know what that is! What did Raye say? 'I am the captain of my ship, I am the master of my soul.' I want to be the captain of my own ship!

Alexa's thoughts were interrupted when Maria brought the conversation to more recent events. "I'm really concerned about what happened in this country on January sixth. That's a very negative expression of anger that we do not need, deserve, or should see in this country. That was anti-American in every way. I see all kinds of extremism going on in our country, on both the left and the right. Some are people I socialize with on Facebook or Twitter."

Alexa leaned in closer, absorbing every word remembering the flood of posts on Instagram that day, her feed a wild mix of shock, anger, and disbelief. Friends and classmates were all expressing their feelings. Some sadly posting nasty comments behind the safety of their cell phones. Now, listening to Maria, it all became more tangible, more real. This wasn't just another Instagram story or a trending hashtag; this had been serious stuff, real and unnerving, and way closer to home than she had ever realized. It made her rethink everything she'd seen online, questioning how things in her own country were spiraling into levels of crazy she never imagined possible.

Maria continued after a short pause. "I am so grateful for the opportunities this country's provided. I honestly never thought that I would be a named professor, or that I would be dean of a named school. I didn't think that was in the cards for me. I've never forgotten that I have a responsibility to give back as a result of what I was given."

"I see. Maria, please tell us more about the time you arrived to the U.S. How was it?"

"Miami was very tough. I wasn't able to speak English and was living in a rough neighborhood. We were in Florida for about eight months. We went to Virginia then Maryland. Our lives as Cuban Americans started."

Alexa couldn't help but smile in empathy with Maria's difficulties with the language and navigating a new, not always welcoming place.

"Baltimore was really home for us. That is what I considered home for many years. Elementary, junior, and high school were all in the same area. It was all within walking distance from where we lived. A very, very happy time."

"Tell us about your family, Maria," Ella said.

"My father was a physician. He actually had trained as an OBGYN in Cuba. When he came here, he had to retrain and take the foreign exam. He specialized in psychiatry. Once he finished his internship in Virginia, he went to Baltimore for his residency."

The turn in the conversation made Alexa sit up and pay more attention. There was something about hearing personal stories that always got her. She observed Ella, who seemed genuinely interested in digging deeper.

"Completing a residency and essentially starting a medical career in a different environment speaks volumes to the fortitude of your father. What kind of individual was he, Maria?" As Ella posed the question, Alexa's attention was fully on Maria, wondering what it must have been like for her father.

"He believed that it was important to go to college for a profession. My father always wanted to make sure that whatever we studied, it was going to result in a career. All three of his daughters did get a college education. He did believe that we as human beings needed to do good for society. He thought that anything in the medical field would be the ideal career option. Like other immigrant parents, he believed that education was essential for advancement. He thought that education is the only thing that can never be taken away from you."

As Maria spoke about her father's belief in education, Alexa's mind drifted to her own parents and also what she had heard from *Latinisimo*'s guest. Their hopes and expectations for her shimmered in her thoughts, aligning closely with what Maria described. Mom and dad are just like Maria's dad she mused, a warm feeling spreading through her. Alexa pondered quietly, education really is the one thing that no one can take away, isn't it? Engineering… here I come!

"What about other members of the family, Maria?" Ella asked.

"My mom was a stay-at-home wife. Don and I have been married for a long time. Forty-some years. I have three children, all doing well, all in professional careers, all married. Two of the three have children. I have eight grandchildren, six of which are boys and only two girls."

"How did you combine work and family? Was it difficult for you, Maria?"

"I wanted to make sure that I was close to work to do what was needed both at home and at work. It has been a wonderful career. And now, I have been in Delaware for over twenty-five years. It has become home and the place I have lived the longest in my life."

"What does Delaware mean to you since you mentioned the state, Maria?"

"This is a giving and collaborative community. We all know each other well. We can sit down and have a conversation about the issues that are going on in the area. This is not at all a dictatorial environment that would be found in other places. There is importance and emphasis in building relationships. There is a lot of engagement and collaborations which sometimes is hard for people from the outside to understand or participate in. This is very much the Delaware way."

"Maria, let's delve into what drives you. What motivates you to do the things you do?" Ella inquired.

"I am a spiritual person. Spirituality is something that I hold very close to my heart. I feel God's presence in what I do. However, as somebody that works in government and in a public institution, I have to separate my religion from my workplace. I have a responsibility to give back as a result of what I was given. That has been a tremendous driver for me."

"Very meaningful. Thanks for sharing! Have you served the community in other capacities besides the scope of your work?"

"They are very much interconnected." Maria answered. "As faculty members, we're required to do public service as part of our job. We as a school had always been engaged in the broader community. I have worked with government offices, city councils and boards. In fact, the University of Delaware a few years ago won a very special recognition for community engagement. I am also part of ASPA, the American Society for Public Administration, which is the largest organization in our field. It has about ten thousand members. I have been very, very active there for many years, including serving as President of the organization."

As Alexa listened to Maria, a realization dawned on her. Immigrants like her, they really contribute so much. It's not just about finding a better life; it's about improving things for everyone. And Maria's commitment is just incredible. Wait... isn't Rudy doing something similar? This thought cast Rudy suddenly in a new light.

Maria continued, "I have done community work by helping municipalities develop strategic plans. I was a member of the Hispanic board for many years in Florida. We were helping Hispanics build businesses in the community, explaining to them the process they needed to go through to get a license, to apply, filling out the application and that sort of thing. The most interesting board that I ever served on was with an organization helping abused women. It was a very meaningful board. This was a while ago when I was working in Florida."

Ella introduced the second song, 'Guantanamera', allowing Maria a moment to sip some water. As the familiar lyrics filled the room, Maria's reaction was immediate and heartfelt.

"Mi'ja! That song... that song is Cuba itself! Thanks for including it, Alexa! It means a lot! Do you have something similar in Mexico?"

"Yes, we do! 'Mexico Lindo y Querido' gets mom, dad, Tía María, and pretty much everyone teary-eyed. It speaks of their homeland in a way that's similar to how 'Guantanamera' speaks to you, Maria."

Ella suddenly broke the moment. "Ready? We're back in thirty seconds, guys. Sorry about that!" she said, quickly reopening the session and checking that Audacity was still recording. "Hello, *Latinisimo* friends," she smoothly transitioned back into the show. "We're back with Dr. Maria Aristigueta, Dean of the Biden School of Public Administration. Welcome back, Maria! One final question to close the program. Could you please tell us about what you have accomplished as consequence of your work?"

Maria thought for a minute. "It is not necessarily about my accomplishments and publications but rather the impact that I have been able to have on people's lives. Like, the email I got this week from a student referring to me as a mentor and a friend. It means that I've had an impact on their lives." Maria smiled proudly and paused for a second.

"A couple years ago, we were contacted by IREX, the International Research and Exchanges Board, to assist in selecting Cuban students to the English Language Institute to help them learn English. Some were interested in the nonprofit sector. I became involved because nonprofit management is part of the Biden School of Public Administration. It was just fascinating to see how serious they took the opportunity given. Now several of them are pursuing PhD degrees as consequence."

Alexa was enjoying the interview while reflecting on Maria's past, accomplishments, character, and gratitude for her new country. As Alexa listened to Maria, she felt once again a real connection. There was something about the way Maria talked —her strength and thankfulness for her new life—that really hit home for Alexa. She was more than just impressed; she felt like she understood where Maria was coming from. It made the whole interview feel special, like she was learning from someone who really got what it's like to start fresh and make it count.

"Sadly, Maria, we've come to the end of our time today." Alexa heard Ella wrapping up the program, pulling her out of her reflections. "A huge thank you for joining us, and to our listeners for tuning in. Our series showcasing diverse career paths for young people will continue next month. Exciting news—we'll have JoAnn Balingit, the former Delaware's Poet Laureate, as our next guest. So, be sure to join us then. *Latinisimo* will be back with our regular programming next week. Have a fantastic day!" Ella concluded the show, leaving Alexa feeling a mix of satisfaction and a tinge of disappointment that the conversation had to end.

"Thanks again, Maria. It was a great and meaningful program."

"That was epic, Maria!" Alexa threw her hands up in a playful gesture, emphasizing her words. Her lighthearted remark, paired with her enthusiastic body language, sparked laughter among the three, cutting through the seriousness of the moment with a shared sense of joy.

Still smiling, Maria added, "Thanks to you both! I have to hurry to the last Friday appointment believe it or not!"

Ella turned to Alexa. "Before you go, tell me about the SAT. I'm curious to know how it went."

"Ella, I did it! I absolutely nailed it! I got fifteen hundred, which is great... I think," she exclaimed. "And you know what? I've got to give credit to *Latinisimo*. It played a part in shaping my essay. I drew insights from every interview we've done. You've been such a help, even if you didn't realize it!"

Ella reached out, placing a warm hand on Alexa's shoulder, her touch conveying the happiness and pride she felt. "That's fantastic to hear! I'm really thrilled that *Latinisimo*'s been such a positive influence for you," she said, her eyes sparkling with genuine delight and warmth. Her voice was encouraging, her enthusiasm palpable. Leaning in slightly, Ella's expression turned curious.

"What did you think about Maria's interview? You seemed really into it!"

As they reorganized the studio equipment, Alexa chatted with Ella, her hands moving deftly from one task to another. "I absolutely loved Maria's interview," she said enthusiastically. "She's achieved so much, yet remains so down-to-earth. It's so refreshing to meet someone successful who's also humble. Her story, especially the part about being an immigrant, really hit home for me. The way her parents guided her through the challenges of settling in a new country... it's just like listening to my mom, dad, and Tía María talk about their experiences!"

Alexa stepped out of the studio briefly to return a borrowed cable to the adjacent studio. Upon her return, she picked up the conversation right where she had left off. "What really struck me about Maria was her focus on giving back. You can tell she's grateful for the opportunities she's had here. It made me realize how lucky I am too," Alexa continued, her words blending with the soft clicks and snaps of the equipment as they tidied up.

"People can come from many places, like you and me, yet they're similar at the end. We should be grateful for what life has given us, don't you think?" Ella said, "Or change what we need to change to improve, right? Anyway, I don't want to take too much time from you on a Friday. Go have fun, Alexa! You deserve it!"

"Thanks. I will. Happy weekend!"

As Alexa left the radio station, she made her way through the University of Delaware's open spaces. The campus, bathed in the warm glow of the setting July sun, felt alive with the vibrant energy of student life. She walked past the sprawling green lawns and historic buildings, each step taking her further from the studio and closer to her future.

Boarding the bus, she settled into a seat by the window, her eyes lingering on the university's silhouette. As the bus began to move, Alexa turned her gaze forward, her mind filled with plans for college applications, visits, and the new chapter that awaited her.

CHAPTER 9

A POET BUILDING COMMUNITIES, JOANN BALINGIT

Sitting in the bustling Christiana Mall, Alexa felt the energy of the crowd and the familiar scents from the food court, but there was an awkwardness in the air for her. This was her first summer without Rudy by her side. Surrounded by the lively atmosphere, she couldn't shake off a sense of being alone in a crowd. Being single felt strange, a mix of newfound independence and a quiet longing for the comfort Rudy used to bring to moments like these. Alexa was navigating a new chapter, one filled with freedom and a hint of nostalgia.

The mall's cool, air-conditioned environment offered a much-needed escape from the stifling heat of the last days in August, a stark contrast to Alexa's home, where the absence of air conditioning made the summer days particularly challenging. The relief from the heat at the mall was not just physical but also a mental respite, allowing Alexa to enjoy a moment of comfort and ease with her best friend Andy before senior year started in the next few weeks.

"So, Georgia Tech was impressive, but the costs are daunting," Alexa shared, sipping her frozen green Chai latte. The recent campus visit with her parents had left her with mixed feelings—excitement about the school's potential and apprehension about the financial implications.

Andy nodded in understanding as he bit into his snack. "I'm planning to visit there soon. What should I look out for?"

"The campus is great, and the programs are top-notch. But brace yourself for the financial reality check," Alexa replied with a wry smile.

Their discussion shifted to Andy's college choices. "I'm still thinking about design. I've narrowed it down to three choices: Georgia Institute of Technology School of Industrial Design, Carnegie Mellon University School of Design, and Purdue University."

"That's a tough choice, but I'm sure you'll figure it out," Alexa reassured him. She always appreciated these moments with Andy—their easy conversations and shared anxieties about the future.

Andy glanced at Alexa and smiled. "You know, that outfit really brings out the color in your eyes. The earth tones make your brown eyes stand out more. It's a great look on you," he said, genuinely.

Alexa's smile widened as she responded to Andy's compliment. "Thanks, Andy! I actually got lucky with this outfit," she began, her voice tinged with excitement as she shared with Andy. "I stumbled upon this top in a thrift store just last weekend—it was tucked away on the clearance rack. And guess what? Everything was seventy percent off! I couldn't believe my luck," she exclaimed. "This olive-green crop top caught my eye immediately. It's not every day you find something that feels like it was made for you, especially at a thrift store," she added, her enthusiasm growing.

She gestured to her jeans with a smile. "And these jeans were such find. They fit like a glove, which is a rarity with thrift store buys. It was like they were just waiting there for me!" Alexa's sense of triumph was evident in her voice, thrilled with her successful shopping adventure.

Andy's smile grew as he listened to Alexa's story, his expression one of genuine admiration for his friend's excitement and thrift-shopping prowess. "That's really impressive. You've got an amazing knack for finding these gems," he remarked, clearly impressed by her ability to spot great deals.

As they chatted amidst the lively ambiance of the mall's food court, Alexa's thoughts briefly drifted to Rudy's recent visit to her house. She recounted the moment to Andy. "You know, Rudy stopped by my house unexpectedly the other day," she began, a hint of bewilderment in her voice. "He said he wanted to share some new music, but it felt... off, like he had another reason for coming over."

Andy, absorbing Alexa's words about Rudy, offered a thoughtful nod. "I know… he told me. You know, he's trying to change, or maybe do something different. It's good he's trying, even if it's a bit awkward," he said. Andy was always one to look for the good in people.

After a brief pause, Alexa smoothly steered the conversation back to their college plans. "Speaking of new directions. I've always been a numbers person as you know, but taping *Latinisimo* really opened my eyes. I loved how Lisa Bartoli, the arts healer we interviewed, described the blend of arts and sciences. I've been looking into biomedical engineering, specifically rehabilitation engineering."

"Oh, that's interesting! What's that about?" Andy's curiosity was piqued.

Adjusting her posture and leaning forward, Alexa delved on. "It's about creating devices for people with disabilities, you know? Things that help with mobility, communication... It's so empowering to think I could be part of that change. After talking to Lisa on our show, I'm even more pumped about heading in this direction."

Andy nodded, clearly impressed. "The arts-science mix really got my attention. So, which colleges are you considering for this besides Georgia Tech?"

"I'm looking at colleges like Johns Hopkins, MIT, and Stanford," she said, her mind going back to a vibrant discussion in her STEM high school club months ago.

Then, with a hint of apprehension, she glanced into Andy's eyes, seeking reassurance. "But you know... I kind of know what O'Jete will say. The silver lining? We might both end up at Georgia Tech, based on our lists, right?" Her voice was touched with hope, the prospect of sharing this next chapter with Andy bringing a comforting sense of possibility to her plans.

"That would be awesome! Now, talking about..."

The two friends chatted and laughed, effortlessly transitioning from one topic to another, thoroughly enjoying their time together. The evening was pleasant, filled with the kind of easy camaraderie that comes from years of friendship.

As they talked, Alexa caught the scent of cinnamon from freshly baked pretzels nearby, making her mouth water. She couldn't help but comment to Andy, "Those cinnamon pretzels smell amazing, don't they?'

Andy opened his mouth to respond to Alexa's comment about the pretzels, but before he could speak, his phone buzzed with an incoming text. He quickly glanced at the screen. Alexa observed a subtle yet significant shift in his expression—a blend of urgency and concern flitted across his face, an unspoken worry that he didn't voice.

"Oops, sorry... I've got to rush. I totally forgot I had something to do," Andy said abruptly, his voice laced with a hint of discomfort. "Can I walk you home?" he said as he hastily began gathering his belongings.

"Yeah, sure, no problem!" Alexa replied, a bit bewildered by Andy's sudden change of plans. His rush to leave caught her off guard, and she felt a twinge of curiosity about his abruptness but decided not to ask. "I've got a few things to do myself, like checking out some deals and picking up Abuelita's medicine at the drugstore. You go ahead. The bus stop isn't far from here anyway."

Realizing it wasn't too late and still debating whether to buy the pretzel, Alexa decided to use her extra time at the mall wisely. She quickly texted Ella, hoping she was available for a chat. To her relief, Ella replied that she was indeed available.

"Hi, Ella! So glad you're free. I'm about to start researching JoAnn, but before I dive in, could you explain a bit more about her work?" Alexa asked, her voice slightly raised over the background noise of the mall.

"Sure, but where are you? It sounds busy there,"

"I'm at the mall. Just finished hanging out with Andy. Decided to stay a bit longer," Alexa replied quickly, eager to get back to the topic.

"Okay, so here's the thing about JoAnn," Ella began, her voice animated. "She's all about using poetry to build communities. It's a real passion of hers, you know?"

Alexa listened, intrigued, as she navigated the crowd at the mall.

Ella continued, "She's always pulling young poets into her projects. It's pretty amazing to see."

Alexa could hear the smile in Ella's voice and her inquisitiveness got the best of her. "Why does she do that?"

"I asked her the same thing once," Ella replied. "She told me, as Poet Laureate, she sees it as her duty to uplift the new generation of poets. It's not just a role for her; it's a mission."

"Is that connected to her involvement with Poetry Out Loud?" Alexa interjected, recalling what she knew.

"Exactly!" Ella's voice brightened. "She's all about nurturing and supporting fresh talent in the poetry scene."

Alexa could almost picture Ella's expression of admiration through the phone, her respect for JoAnn's commitment to her craft and community was shining through in her enthusiastic explanation.

"Okay," Alexa replied, her curiosity piqued, "but what exactly is this Poetry Out Loud?"

Ella's voice shifted slightly. "How about you check that out on your own? I just got a text from my sister; it's about her mammogram results. I need to call her back. I'll catch up with you later, okay?"

As the call ended, Alexa sensed the concern in Ella's voice, the abrupt shift in tone not lost on her. Ella opening up about her family made Alexa reflect on the changing nature of their relationship. This is new. Are we becoming friends?

Ella's voice came through the phone, slightly hesitant, breaking the stillness of the late Saturday evening. "Hi, Alexa," she began.

"Hi, Ella! How's your sister doing?" Alexa hoped her voice carried the concern she felt.

There was a brief, heavy silence on the other end before Ella responded. "Not well, Alexa," she said slowly, the weight of her words hanging in the air. "Thanks for asking." Another pause followed, filled with unspoken emotions.

Then, with a noticeable effort to steady her voice, Ella continued, "She... she has breast cancer."

Alexa sensed Ella was realizing the magnitude of the news herself. She felt for her.

"Early stage carcinoma was detected thanks to a routine mammogram. She's not in good shape, and frankly, neither am I. The call was about the results of her biopsy, which confirmed what her doctor suspected. Her operation to remove the tumor is scheduled for a couple of weeks from now. We're a very close family, so news like this affects us all. Sorry to dump this on you."

Hearing the pain in Ella's voice, Alexa felt a strong urge to offer some comfort. "She's going to be okay, Ella," she said gently, her words trying to bridge the distance between them. "You'll see. And if there's anything I can do to help, just let me know, okay?"

"Thanks," Ella replied, her voice softening slightly. "I really appreciate that. Just having someone to talk to helps a lot. Now, about the interview with JoAnn—maybe you could give her a call?" Ella provided JoAnn's contact details, mentioning she had already given JoAnn a heads-up about a potential call from Alexa.

Alexa jotted down JoAnn's number, her mind still partly occupied with Ella's news. Despite the shift back to work-related topics, she couldn't shake off her concern. "Got it, I'll call JoAnn," she said softly. "And Ella, really... I'm here, okay?"

After zipping through the last of her homework emails, Alexa settled into the relaxed, comfy atmosphere of her room, perfect for focusing or just unwinding. Her desk was neatly organized with textbooks and notes spread out. Feeling curious about JoAnn's work, she dialed her number, curious to understand the scope of her work.

"Hi, Alexa!" JoAnn's voice cascaded through the phone, warm and welcoming.

"Hi, JoAnn! I hope I'm not interrupting. Is now a good time to talk?"

"Absolutely," JoAnn replied, her voice effervescing with joyfulness. "I'm just here enjoying some ginger lemon tea. I'm planning to make 'arroz caldo' which is almost a chicken soup for dinner tonight. Filipinos call it Aroskaldo, my Kapampángan family would call it Lelut or 'lelut manuk.' Manuk is chicken, the typical base. But let's put my culinary adventures aside for now. How can I assist you?"

As JoAnn shared her cooking plans, Alexa felt a warm, friendly vibe. Yet, it was JoAnn's next topic that truly sparked Alexa's interest.

"Speaking of warmth," JoAnn smoothly transitioned, her tone hinting at excitement. "I had a fascinating encounter on my walk this morning. As I was strolling by the reservoir near my house, something incredible happened. I saw this majestic buck. And not just any buck—this one had eyes that were so expressive, like deep, dark pools holding the mysteries of the forest. We just stood there, in a moment of silent understanding. It felt like those eyes were weaving a thousand untold stories."

As JoAnn recounted her encounter near the reservoir, Alexa was captivated, feeling as if she were there herself. She visualized the tranquil water, the striking appearance of the buck, and the profound connection JoAnn felt. Through JoAnn's words, the buck's gaze seemed to reach out to Alexa too.

"That's incredible, JoAnn," she said, her voice filled with awe. JoAnn's vivid storytelling not only painted a beautiful scene but also revealed to Alexa the depth of her authenticity. JoAnn had a gift for sharing experiences in a way that deeply resonated with others, and Alexa felt an inexplicable deep connection to that.

Enthralled by JoAnn's storytelling, Alexa's curiosity about her professional journey sparked a question. "JoAnn, could you tell me more about being Delaware's Poet Laureate? What was that experience like for you?"

JoAnn's response flowed with the same eloquence and passion that had captivated Alexa earlier. "When the state of Delaware appointed me Poet Laureate in two thousand eight," she began, her voice blending humility and pride, "I recognized the responsibility I had to support and elevate the writing community. I believed if I had any influence, it should be used to create more opportunities and bring the arts, particularly poetry, more prominently into schools."

Alexa visualized JoAnn, standing before eager students, inspiring young minds with poetry while thinking how poetry could capture them.

JoAnn paused for a moment, perhaps reflecting on those years of service. "But part of the responsibility, I realized, was that I needed to take my own work even more seriously. I did a lot of literary organizing in the state even before I was Poet Laureate. I stepped down in two thousand fifteen, but I'm glad to see that those different programs keep going."

"What kind of programs?"

As JoAnn began to explain, Alexa felt increasingly drawn into the conversation. She grabbed a pencil and notepad, intent on jotting down a few notes. Easing herself from the desk to her bed, she found a cozy spot and curled up comfortably, phone to her ear, snugly nestled under the soft covers.

"The Delaware writers retreat is now every other year. I still participate in the writing contest for K to twelve students, the Poetry Out Loud contest for high school students, and conferences. I also write occasional essays and articles for the newspaper, where I hope to get new and upcoming poets' work published," JoAnn shared, her voice carrying a deep sense of fulfilment.

Alexa recalled what Ella had said about JoAnn's dedication to supporting young poets and realized it went beyond mere support; JoAnn was shaping poetry throughout the state.

Moved by JoAnn's passion, Alexa found herself asking, "Did you always know that you wanted to be a poet? Do you like being a poet? What does it mean to be a poet?"

This reminds me of Lisa Bartoli... she's seems to be doing similar things, but in her own unique way. I need to get JoAnn's poetry and her life! I'm starting to see poetry differently.

"Yes, I do like being a poet." JoAnn paused for a minute. "Why do you ask, Alexa? I feel there's a lot more than the question itself."

JoAnn's interest took Alexa by surprise. "Well, it gets my attention when I find people who are clear on what they want. I am trying to find my way... my calling... my professional future. I think I finally found it."

"Do you think that sharing some of my motivations could help clarify yours, Alexa?"

"It could be. Perhaps confirming my interest in biomedical engineering."

"Wow! That sounds intriguing! When it comes to me, I've always loved writing. I wish I had the diaries I kept with a little lock and key. I used to write when I was eight, nine, and ten-years-old. Poetry has always been part of me."

JoAnn continued, "I write at my desk in the morning. Eventually, some of that may be published, it may speak to somebody, it may move someone. At the same time, I may be learning more about myself that might make me a better organizer, or arts activist. You know, it's all connected."

Alexa didn't know what to make of her last comment when she heard a male voice calling JoAnn from the distance.

JoAnn paused for a minute and put the cell phone on mute to respond. She came back apologizing. "Sorry, Alexa, it's my husband. Do you mind if we continue the conversation later or the day of the interview?"

Alexa gave her day and time for the interview before hanging up. There was something magical about JoAnn. She wasn't sure if it was the tone of her voice, her calmness when talking, or if it was what she'd said. Alexa was curious and found an article from the Delaware Division of the Arts. Her accomplishments were impressive. JoAnn piqued Alexa's curiosity.

Alexa hurried into the studio, feeling the August heat sticking to her skin. After the walk from the bus stop through the quiet, sun-drenched campus, the warmth had penetrated her light denim jacket, urging her to quickly take it off as she entered the cooler radio station. Rolling up her sleeves, she sought relief from the heat, still feeling a bit flustered from the bus's delay.

Upon entering Alexa's gaze was instantly drawn to Ella and JoAnn, who were huddled around a small table just outside the studio. On the table, there was a tempting cake, a thoughtful offering left by one of the evening radio hosts. The cake looked deliciously indulgent, featuring layers of dark, moist sponge covered in thick, glossy icing.

Catching her breath, Alexa approached them, her eyes lighting up at the sight of the cake. "Oh… wow… chocolate cake! Hi JoAnn! It's great to finally meet you in person!"

JoAnn, with a warm smile, invited Alexa to join them. "I'm glad we're talking again. Help yourself, Alexa. It's as delicious as it looks." JoAnn handed her a small plate while holding her own.

Ella chuckled. "It's dangerously good. I had to stop myself from having a second slice! You know what… the heck with it, I'll get another one."

Alexa eagerly took a piece, the rich aroma of chocolate immediately hitting her senses. As she took her first bite, the flavors exploded in her mouth—the cake was perfectly moist, the icing decadently creamy, and there was just a hint of something like coffee, deepening the chocolate taste. She savored each mouthful, feeling the stress of her rushed journey melt away with every bite.

Between bites, Alexa managed to say, "I was thinking that instead of music for JoAnn's program, we should read two of her poems. And, don't worry, I already have them ready." Her voice was a mix of excitement and a bit of relief, her mind already gearing up for the creative session ahead, yet still thoroughly enjoying the moment of indulgence with the cake.

Ella's smile broadened, clearly pleased with Alexa's suggestion. She nodded in agreement, her eyes reflecting approval and anticipation.

JoAnn, too, chimed in with a warm and enthusiastic voice. "That sounds wonderful, Alexa. I have a small request, though. I'd like you to be the one to read them. You see, when a poem resonates with you, it's a unique experience. Not every poem touches everyone the same way. But when it does, it reveals so much about you. I believe in the energy that a poem can transmit. It's that kind of connection that artists strive for."

There was a thoughtful pause as JoAnn's words lingered in the air, highlighting the intimate relationship between a reader and a poem.

Ella turned her attention back to Alexa, her expression a mix of curiosity and encouragement. "Alexa, are you comfortable with JoAnn's request?" she inquired, her tone gentle, ensuring Alexa felt at ease with the task ahead.

Alexa felt a surge of confidence, a stark contrast to the timidity she had experienced in her earlier days with the program. Having been a part of *Latinisimo* for eight months now, she found her comfort zone expanding with each passing day.

"Sure, I can do that. Just need a bit of practice to make sure I'm ready," Alexa replied, her voice carrying a newfound steadiness and confidence. Gone were the days of nervousness overshadowing her excitement. Now, she felt a sense of belonging and capability that had grown steadily over her months with the program.

As they entered the studio, Alexa watched Ella smoothly take on her role as host. She was impressed by how effortlessly Ella managed the controls and started the program. It was a neat balance of technical skill and on-air presence, all flowing seamlessly under Ella's expert touch.

The show kicked off with Ella's warm voice resonating through the studio. "Welcome to *Latinisimo*! Today, we're honored to have JoAnn Balingit, Delaware's former Poet Laureate, with us. Welcome, JoAnn! Joining us too is Alexa Hope, a key member of the *Latinisimo* team since the start of the year. Alexa will be reading two of JoAnn's poems during our show. A warm welcome to you as well, Alexa!"

Feeling a wave of pride wash over her at the introduction, Alexa was brimming with readiness.

"Let's get right to it, folks. What would you say is the most quintessential JoAnn Balingit poem you've written?"

"I can give you some favorite poems that I love, but right now I'm so involved in this self-excavation. I feel that I am in the midst of writing my most important work now. What I've been working on lately is a memoir. Stories about my family, trying to unearth more about my identity and why I became a writer."

"That was truly meaningful, thank you! It actually inspires me to share one of your poems right now. What do you think? Alexa, would you do the honors?" Ella skillfully steered the interview in a new direction. Alexa took note of the smooth transition and prepared to read the poem.

"Of course," Let me share 'Your Heart and How It Works' from JoAnn's book *Words for House Story*, published in two thousand and thirteen.

"Your heart is a steel wrecking ball, glove unbuttoned at the wrist. Slip it off, see your heart dented flat in places."

As Alexa was reading, each line of the poem felt like it was speaking just to her, stirring up memories of Rudy. Her voice started to shake a bit with emotion. She could feel a lump in her throat, showing just how much JoAnn's words hit home. Gripping the microphone tighter, she found some comfort in the physical hold as she navigated the poem's emotional waves.

Glancing to the side, Alexa saw Ella looking surprised, clearly seeing how much the poem was affecting her. She also caught JoAnn's reaction—a gentle, understanding smile, showing she was touched by how deeply Alexa connected with her poem. JoAnn's eyes were full of a kind of thankful and empathetic look, as if she was really glad to see her words come alive in someone else's voice.

"Let's shift to your creative process." Ella smoothly transitioned the topic, giving Alexa a moment to compose herself. "Could you describe it to us?

"When I get really into writing, I find just as much confusion as I find answers," JoAnn explained thoughtfully to the audience. "When you are delving deep into work and memories and ideas that you have been chasing around for—in my case—decades, it's a pretty squirrelly business. You're bound to find just as many questions as resolutions if any resolutions at all."

Sensing a deeper layer in JoAnn's words, Ella leaned in slightly, her eyes reflecting curiosity. "That's fascinating, JoAnn. It sounds like the process is as much about exploration as it is about discovery. How do you think this journey through memories, especially those from childhood, influences your writing?"

JoAnn paused, considering the question. "Well, Ella," she continued, "Home is where we experience our first sense of comfort, and perhaps that is why our thoughts return to the places we grew up. Images of childhood landscapes arise when we are pensive. Writers mine their childhoods."

Seeking clarity from JoAnn, Ella asked, "So, the journey back to our childhood homes and experiences is where writers find their story's basis?"

"You got it Ella! That's exactly right!"

"This is the perfect segue to ask about your childhood. It seems that part of who you are is shaped by your immigrant roots. Would that be a correct assessment?"

Alexa marveled at the conversation. *It's strange how those early years can shape us. Did JoAnn also find it tough balancing between two cultures, kinda like I do? Wait! This is Insta material.* Alexa snapped a candid of JoAnn at the mic and added the hashtag *#writersminetheirownchildhood, #JoAnn Balingit, pastDE'sPoetLaurate.* Then she tagged *@Latinisimo* in the post. Heart emojis began appearing almost immediately.

"When I started writing and researching my family life, I was very focused on my father's experience, of which I knew relatively little, even though I grew up with him until I had just turned sixteen. He immigrated from the Philippines in a twenty five-day journey by cargo ship from Manila to San Francisco. He did not share any family history with us, nor his Kapampángan culture, which is an anomaly among Filipinos who are very much into family and culture, and sticking together. Kapampángans are the indigenous people of central Luzon, who live primarily in the province of Pampanga and other nearby provinces bordering Pampanga. My father was from the town of Macabébe in southern lowland Pampanga. Kapampángans also live in diaspora in the Philippines and abroad."

JoAnn leaned forward, mimicking an excavating motion with her hands, her eyes reflecting the depth of her research. "I've been digging into his past, trying to build a connection with him. Imagine being twenty-six and arriving in San Francisco right before the Great Depression in May nineteen twenty-nine. It was a very different world back then."

Alexa's eyes widened as she visualized a young man from an isolated river village stepping into the bustling, uncertain streets of San Francisco in the late nineteen twenties. The city's vibrancy, contrasted with the looming economic hardships, painted a vivid picture in her mind.

JoAnn sighed. "I now understand some of the reasons why he closed the door on that part of his life, or at least tried to. I've learned about the circumstances surrounding his departure from his first family in San Francisco. He witnessed his own culture being oppressed, overtaken, and shut down. This is a story common to many Kapampángans. Despite his resilience, it must have been tough."

Alexa felt a knot form in her stomach, empathizing with the struggles of someone fighting to maintain their identity in a foreign land. It sounds so like us… so like Havidán… or Yamil for that matter. Not new for immigrants. It must've been really tough!

JoAnn added, "He took whatever jobs he could. First as an elevator operator, then a janitor, and a night watchman. He even worked on a Works Progress Administration project, but I haven't found out which one."

Alexa imagined him in these roles, each a small battle for survival in a city of contrasts.

JoAnn's voice grew softer. "The longest job he held was the night watchman. Then Pearl Harbor was bombed, and everything changed for him."

Alexa was captivated by the story. It wasn't just a series of dates and events; it was a journey of resilience and challenges, a narrative of a real person facing real struggles. JoAnn's dad, he was… just like us.

"What do you mean by a big change, JoAnn?"

JoAnn continued, her voice imbued with the weight of history. "With the war underway, there was a surge in industry and the production of ships and planes. The Japanese internment was happening. Filipinos and Filipino Americans were not implicated in that internment, and what happens is suddenly he is able to get a job in an engineering corporation in his field. He was almost forty."

From her seat, Alexa listened intently, her history classes flashing through her mind—the chaos and the change of that era. She thought about how significant it must have been for JoAnn's dad to finally get a job in his field after such a long struggle.

Ella, catching on to the significance, remarked, "I see, that was indeed a change for him, wasn't it?"

JoAnn nodded. "This is the time when I begin to see photographs. There are older ones, aboard the ship. And then, there are photographs of a man sitting by an engineering table with his instruments, looking really happy. But that was years after his arrival, after years just making ends meet."

Alexa's imagination began to flow. She glanced through the glass partition at the students in the adjacent studio and suddenly, in her mind's eye, one of them transformed into a younger version of JoAnn's father. He might have been just like one of them, starting out tough, she thought.

"By nineteen forty-one, he had been in the state for ten years and had a family and four children whom I didn't know about until about ten years ago. He was a very quiet person. By the time I was eleven, that was only amplified, he was almost silent actually… he had a stroke."

Wow, he had so much happening in his life that was kept hidden. Poor guy. Questions swirled in Alexa's mind: Why did he keep all that to himself? How did JoAnn deal with discovering all this? And how much can someone take before they break? These thoughts lingered, as she tried to understand the complexities of JoAnn's dad's life and the impact it had on her.

Shifting the conversation, Ella inquired further about JoAnn's family. "How about your mom, JoAnn?"

"I've realized that my mother's family was also an immigrant family, though neither she nor her parents emigrated; her grandparents did." JoAnn shared, reflecting a deeper understanding of her family history.

"I began to ask the same questions about my mother's paternal and maternal grandparents, and even her great grandparents. Why did they leave Alsace and Lorraine? What was happening historically in both areas that prompted them to leave?"

JoAnn then connected the dots between her paternal and maternal sides. "In both cases, there's an aftermath of war and violence. In the case of the Philippines, there was U.S. colonization following Spanish colonization. There are some similarities, yet they're two very different backgrounds," JoAnn explained, highlighting the diverse influences that shaped her family's journey.

"I think in my mother's fairly conservative Ohio family and upbringing, she was probably the renegade, eloping with a forty-nine-year-old Kapampángan immigrant when she was just about to turn twenty-one. He had moved from Cleveland, leaving his engineering job to St. Louis for a new opportunity. From there, he likely sent her a bus ticket. She left home alone, under the cover of night."

Wow! Twenty-one and forty-nine? That's close to a thirty-year age difference! That's huge! Aren't mom and dad just like two years apart?

"How did they meet, JoAnn?"

"At McGee Corporation. He was a civil engineer, and she was an apprentice draftsperson," JoAnn began. Alexa pictured the scene in her head, imagining a workplace romance blossoming against the odds.

"My grandparents, according to my uncle, tried to break up that romance, but it didn't work. They eloped." Alexa's eyes widened at the idea of eloping, a secret and daring escape for love. "I think maybe it wasn't legal for them to get married in Ohio, because when they eloped they went to St. Louis."

"She was a high school graduate. An artist who didn't go to college," JoAnn said, and Alexa thought about how different times were back then. "I don't think that was part of my mother's family's culture. They were farmers," JoAnn added. Alexa could almost see the stark contrast between the life her mother led and the one she might have had.

"She raised chickens, rabbits, turkeys, sold guinea pigs and hamsters to pet stores, ran ads for her pedigreed cats. To help our family income, she ran a Persian cattery and was very involved in all this animal husbandry."

Alexa imagined JoAnn's mother amidst all these animals, a picture of rural industriousness and passion.

JoAnn's voice grew thoughtful. "I often ask myself, as smart and talented as my mom and her siblings were, why was college not in the picture? Why was that not a pursuit?" Alexa felt a pang of curiosity and empathy. She wondered about the untold stories and unexplored paths in JoAnn's family, just as in so many others.

The combination of JoAnn's parents' immigrant stories and college pursuit hit Alexa close to home. "Ella, can I ask a question?"

"Of course, please go ahead."

"With your mom and dad coming from different immigrant backgrounds, how do you think this mix of cultures has influenced who you are and your own story?"

JoAnn smiled and answered, linking her parents' narrative to her distinctive heritage. "I identify as Kapampángan German American. My mother grew up in a household where German was spoken. In trying to piece together their family histories, I often rely on my imagination, as there are few factual trails to follow."

A prolonged pause made Alexa aware of the difficulty JoAnn was facing as she prepared to share the next part of her story. "The watershed event in my life, biographically, would be the death of my parents. They both tragically died when I was sixteen years old." Ella and Alexa exchanged a look of shock, unsure how to respond to JoAnn's comment.

"Do you need a moment?" Ella offered, suggesting a brief respite. Yet, JoAnn pressed on with her story.

"It changed my life. Part of what I focus on in my writing is describing how that event transformed me. It led to our family separating. Much of the longing I describe in my work stems from that separation. Would I be a writer if it hadn't happened? Would I feel differently about my connection to the arts, or my Kapampángan and German roots? Would I have embarked on this quest to understand how it affected my identity, and what my identity really is?"

Hearing JoAnn's childhood memories and her painful reflections, Alexa felt a deep connection. She was captivated, finding parts of JoAnn's story that resonated with her own experiences and emotions. I see now... that's what she meant by poets mining their childhoods.

"It wasn't just the aftermath of what happened to my parents or the difficult realizations that my mother's family was not going to be involved in these brown kids' lives, which is how I really see it now. Although there was a lot of atonement in later years. A couple decades went by. We eventually reached out to my mom's side of the family when we were middle-aged adults."

Gosh! Is she saying that her own family discriminated against her and her siblings? Who does that to a kid? I can't believe this! How awful!

"My birth family is a big family. I am the third of twelve children. I have four siblings in and around Indianapolis, three in Central Florida, one in Tallahassee, Florida, one in Texas, and one in South Carolina. My eight younger siblings grew up adopted or in foster care."

As JoAnn shared her story, Alexa felt a sharp sting in her eyes. The idea of such a large family being torn apart, with siblings growing up separately, was heart-wrenching. Tears silently started to form, and she instinctively reached into her backpack for a tissue, swallowing hard to compose herself.

"Our childhood ended so suddenly that when we get together, there's a lot of joy because we had been separated for so long. I didn't think I would get to see everyone again," JoAnn continued.

Ella, noticing the tears in Alexa's eyes, gave her a look of concern, silently offering support while smoothly shifting gears. "How about another artistic break? Alexa, would you mind reading JoAnn's poem?"

Reading 'Aubade' allowed Alexa to regain her composure by shifting her focus from the emotional intensity of JoAnn's story to the task at hand. She read with unexpected skill, finding stability in the rhythm of the poem. After taking a deep breath and wiping her eyes, Alexa confidently concluded the reading and passed the conversation back to Ella with a composed and steady voice. "And now, back to you Ella."

Ella smoothly transitioned to a new topic. "JoAnn, what about your education?" She took a different angle and shifting the focus to another aspect of JoAnn's life. Alexa, back to normal, leaned in, interested in hearing about this new facet of JoAnn's story.

"I was aware of being different because my classmates would always ask, 'Where do you come from?' Some classmates would make what they thought were Chinese sounds behind my back and stuff like that which I tried to ignore. In junior high school you want to belong, and I thought I belonged just as well as anyone that was white, even though I was always aware that some people considered me 'different.'"

Alexa inhaled. I still feel that way... different. Oh, JoAnn, I see so much of myself in you!

"I've always had the sense of not quite belonging, because there were never any Asian families or kids in my community, my surroundings, in my classrooms, in my church, even on television. They usually only play characters on TV like the sinister butler walking across the room with trays or something. That is why I became a huge fan of *Star Trek* when it started around nineteen sixty-seven because Mr. Sulu was Asian."

Oh, that show! Dad still watches the reruns... it's an oldie but interesting TV show, Alexa recalled, as memories of the program came to mind.

JoAnn pressed on describing a world not made for somebody with her background. "As an English grad student, it was all about novels and poems that were written by white men. I didn't see anything like my experience reflected. My Filipino community also has literature that I didn't have access to when I was growing up."

JoAnn took a moment to have a mint, refreshing her throat. "I'm trying to figure out what kinds of reading I have been taught in that I need to break out of in order to decolonize my writing. It took me a long time to understand that reflecting my experience in words could be interesting to someone else. My education was very much made in the eyes of the white supremacist."

"While the topic of white supremacy and poetry is really intriguing, let's shift focus a bit," Ella smoothly interjected. "I'm curious, JoAnn. What inspires the poems you write? How do you find your muse?"

"They arise from a struggle within myself. It's like heat: when a poem is great, we feel its burn of emotion, its struggle, and we respond to that intense energy with emotion, perhaps the same emotions the poet intended to express in thoughts and words. Heat means the poem, or that part of the poem, works. It's when language's power has been unlocked."

This description reminded Alexa of her own experience reading JoAnn's first poem. She recalled how the words had stirred something deep inside her, evoking emotions she hadn't fully understood but had felt intensely.

"When I 'feel the heat' in a poem, it communicates to me emotionally, even before, or beyond, understanding. I hurt or delight, or I cry out. The poem unleashes feelings in the reader that they can't shake, that they recognize, maybe with dread, maybe with joy. I've heard poets describe this as when the poem pops."

Ella asked, "And how does JoAnn the poet describe herself? How do you make the poems pop? How do you make us 'feel the heat'?"

"We all have the ability to connect and plug into each other. It's really about chemistry and alchemy, and the imaginative way of putting the right words together. Poetry is a resource for understanding yourself and others."

As Alexa listened to JoAnn, she was deeply captivated, her thoughts drifting back to when she had read JoAnn's poem. Indeed, the poem *popped*, she remembered, reflecting on the intense emotions it had stirred within her. In that moment, a new understanding of poetry's power dawned on her. She then realized that poetry is a bridge, connecting the poet's heart directly to the reader's soul, a profound connection she had just personally experienced with JoAnn's words.

"My language is often lush and woodsy. I am not an urban poet, not a hip poet. I create poems to open myself. And I write for my loved ones. There is beauty in language."

Ella agreed with JoAnn. "There is indeed beauty in language, but even more beauty in its intrinsic capacity to reveal the person inside JoAnn. What is poetry for you? What is the meaning of being an artist?"

As Alexa thought about the first question Ella had asked JoAnn, Alexa felt a strange sense of validation regarding her growing, yet unspoken, connection with Ella. We're thinking similarly. That's weird... Is this what happens when you start working closely with people? she pondered.

"It is a form of communication and self-questioning, trying to process things that you naturally want to. That has been a constant. Right now, there's an opening that is really dynamic and full of energy. Looking back, I can see that I didn't have this in my twenties, thirties, or even forties, but I have it now. I'm trying to make my voice heard."

So, Alexa mused, finding your voice is something that grows stronger over time. She felt inspired by how JoAnn had gained a more powerful voice as she aged. I'm finding my own voice bit by bit... and it feels great!

"And what are you trying to make us hear, JoAnn?" Ella asked.

"The desire to belong that everybody has. I didn't have a place to put that sense that was completely satisfying. Some of the issues I am dealing with are reckoning with my own self of a sense of identity, having grown up as a kid in a completely white community."

JoAnn tried to reconcile with her past. "I identified with my mom, my white classmates, teachers, and their culture, not really knowing how to understand or connect with my father because he didn't share anything about his culture. It took me a long time to feel that my writings could interest others. I didn't publish a poem until my late twenties."

Alexa thought about her own doubts and fears, admitting to herself, it takes real courage to find your voice and share your work with the world. I get what you're saying, JoAnn!

"I imagine that we all have our unique struggles and triumphs expressing ourselves, don't we JoAnn? Believe it or not, we're reaching the end of the interview, but one final question if I may," Ella ventured. "If you were to describe JoAnn Balingit to somebody else twenty years from now, what would you say?"

Alexa made herself the same question, how would I describe myself twenty years from now? Would I be proud of myself? I certainly hope so!

JoAnn smiled, took a moment to think, and then said, "That she tried to share with people the love of poetry, because poetry and literature really saved her life."

Alexa noticed a shift in JoAnn's tone as she continued. "Poetry gave me a better understanding of myself. It connected me to a larger world and a community when I could have become very isolated, and vulnerable to the trauma that I went through and then constant healing. Actually, if you're an artist, you're always looking at yourself and your motivations."

As Alexa absorbed JoAnn's words about the transformative power of poetry, she felt a deep connection to the idea of art as a tool for self-discovery and healing. JoAnn's experiences struck a chord within her, reshaping her view of poetry from mere words to a vital lifeline and a means of understanding oneself.

Despite her desire to continue the interview, Alexa realized time was running out. She listened as Ella thanked JoAnn, and with a sense of reluctance, Alexa echoed her thanks. Watching JoAnn close the studio's door, Alexa felt gratitude for the insightful discussion.

"Wow, that interview was amazing!" Alexa exclaimed with a smile. "I might not be on my way to becoming a poet, but I really felt a connection with JoAnn. There's something special about her, isn't there?"

Ella nodded in agreement, her voice warm. "Absolutely, and I could see it in your reactions. She really resonated with you, didn't she? JoAnn always has this way of making me feel and think simultaneously. Hey, it's already Friday night. Let me drive you home, it's late and you shouldn't be going back alone. What do you say to dinner on me?"

Alexa's face lit up at the suggestion, realizing how hungry she was. "That sounds great!

"How about Italian?" Ella suggested. "I know this cozy place here in Newark. Why don't you call your parents to let them know where we are and that I'm driving you home afterwards?"

The drive to the restaurant was short and pleasant. As they neared their destination, Alexa casually asked, "By the way, Ella, how's your sister doing?"

Ella, finding a parking spot right in front of the eatery, turned to Alexa with a relieved expression. "She's actually doing better now. They removed the tumor, and she had chemotherapy during the surgery. It looks like her breast cancer will be manageable with medication for a while. Early detection really was key. But let's focus on enjoying our dinner tonight, shall we?"

Over plates of delicious pasta, Alexa and Ella engaged in a friendly, relaxed conversation. It was a simple yet meaningful evening, just two friends sharing a meal on a Friday night.

CHAPTER 10

A YOUTH SPEAKER, JANE RUBINI

As the first light of dawn filtered through the bus window, Alexa felt the soft warmth on her face and savored a soothing sip of her hot green Chai latte. The brisk chill of the September morning made the drink especially comforting. Each sip was a delightful harmony of cinnamon, ginger, cardamom, and the distinct, earthy undertone of green tea, wrapping her in a cocoon of balminess that complemented the calm morning ambiance. Is this perfection or what? Exactly what I needed to help with the school comeback, she thought, inhaling the rich, spicy aroma and finding solace in the heat of the cup cradled in her hands.

As the bus hissed to a stop at the school, the doors opened to the vibrant energy of senior year. Stepping off, Alexa was immediately enveloped in the excited chatter of her peers. The school entrance, adorned with a 'Welcome Back!' banner, was alive with students sharing summer stories and reunions. Inside, the hall was alive with the energetic buzz of students chatting and laughing.

Navigating through the crowd, Alexa shared a laugh with Andy, when a soft 'hello' caught her attention. She turned to see Rudy, their eyes briefly meeting in a silent, intense exchange before he disappeared into the crowd, leaving her momentarily lost in thought.

"Hey, Aleeexaaa! You okay?" Andy asked, waving his hands to regain her attention.

"What? Yeah, just saw Rudy," Alexa replied, shaking off her daze. "Took me by surprise."

Andy paused for a moment, seeming to weigh his words carefully before speaking. "You know, Rudy misses you," he finally said, his tone tentative yet sincere. "He's been doing a lot of thinking about his future since you two broke up."

Alexa took a brief moment, collecting her thoughts. "I'm glad for him, really, but I've moved on."

The first day back at school buzzed with the excitement of new classes and sharing summer stories. Alexa found herself especially engaged in social studies class, where her team was assigned to research Greta Thunberg, the young Swedish activist advocating for urgent climate action. As she delved into Greta's work, Alexa couldn't help but draw parallels to Rudy's efforts in rallying Latino voters. Throughout the day, thoughts of Rudy subtly weaved into her mind, his presence lingering in unexpected ways.

Towards the end of the day, Alexa received a mysterious text from Ella. *Yready for a youth megaphone?* Curious, she called Ella to clarify. "So, what exactly is a 'youth megaphone'?"

Ella's warm and infectious laughter rang through the phone. "I knew you'd be curious. How was the first day back at school? Anyway, our next guest is Jane Rubini, the founder of MLK VOICE 4 YOUTH®, a spoken word contest for youth. I interviewed her some time ago, and the contest has really taken off since then. She's currently with Christ Church Christiana Hundred. Her activism comes from a very personal place. Want to look her up?"

As they waited for the bus, Alexa and Andy stood close, engrossed in her phone. Together, they delved into searching for information about Jane Rubini. When the bus arrived and they found their seats, the background chatter of their schoolmates filled the space, but their attention stayed fixed on the phone screen.

"Find anything interesting?" Andy asked, peering into the screen as they scrolled.

"Yeah, this Martin Luther King contest sounds really intriguing."

Just then, for a bit of fun, Andy grabbed Alexa's light jacket—the same one she had worn during their mall trip weeks ago—and attempted to put it on, stumbling as the bus took a sharp turn. The two burst into laughter as the jacket, clearly too small, barely fit over Andy's thin, taller frame, with the sleeves ending comically short on his arms.

Alexa chuckled as she watched Andy struggle with the jacket. "Oh yeah, that's definitely your look—very sexy on you!" She joked, her laughter echoing through the bus.

The bus neared her stop, and an idea struck her. "Hey, Andy, want to come over for dinner? Mom's making her famous green enchiladas tonight. Your favorite, right?" She knew he rarely passed up an opportunity to enjoy her mom's cooking.

As Alexa made her way to the studio on the day of Jane's interview, she found herself immediately captivated by the dynamic scene outside WVUD's entrance. Spread across the area, and in front of the cafeteria's windows, were several tents and tables, each overflowing with its own unique charm, contributing to a vibrant and casual atmosphere. The tables, adorned with handmade posters rich in personal flair and an assortment of intriguing gadgets, showcased the diverse talents and interests of the student body.

The atmosphere resembled a mini-festival right on the campus grounds, favored by pleasant September weather. Background music, a harmonious blend of current hits and nostalgic classics, further enhanced the ambiance, transforming the university space into something more akin to a weekend social hub than a traditional academic environment.

Amidst this lively backdrop, Alexa recognized Jane from a picture she had seen with Andy before. Jane stood near a tent, her posture hinting at a sense of being slightly overwhelmed by the surrounding activity.

"Hi, Jane! I'm Alexa Hope from *Latinisimo*. Glad I saw you. You looked a bit lost."

"Hello, Alexa. Nice to meet you," Jane replied with a warm smile. "And… you were right, I wasn't sure where to go actually."

"The studio is downstairs in the basement," Alexa said, gesturing towards the building and leading the way.

As they navigated through the bustling crowd outside, Alexa's eyes inadvertently caught sight of Rudy amidst the sea of faces. What is he doing here? Turning to Jane, she said, "I'm just going to text Ella to let her know you're here. Could you tell her I'll join you both in a couple of minutes? There's something I need to take care of."

"Of course, no problem," Jane replied, offering a nod of understanding. Alexa quickly directed Jane where to go, then Alexa excused herself and navigated through the crowd.

With her curiosity mounting, Alexa approached Rudy.

"Hi Rudy!" Alexa realized her voice was laced with a mix of curiosity and a hint of hesitation. "This is a surprise! I didn't expect to see you here. So, what brings you around?" Her words, carefully chosen, conveyed an inquisitiveness, reflecting her eagerness yet uncertainty about how to broach the subject of his unexpected presence.

"Hi Alexa!" Rudy's voice was calm, unfazed by Alexa's curious tone. "I'm here with Voto Latino for one of our new digital campaigns. Today's Voter Registration Day, and our team is covering the campus in two different spots. I got this one." There was a subtle awareness in his expression, a look that suggested he wasn't entirely surprised to run into Alexa, given that he had dropped her off and picked her up from this location before.

Alexa paused, taken aback. The sudden realization that Rudy was there for reasons entirely his own, unrelated to her, struck Alexa unexpectedly. This time his presence and enthusiasm were now rooted in his personal journey, separate and distinct from their shared past. Watching him speak with such passion about his work, she saw a side of Rudy that felt new to her, almost like he was a different person.

"I see. Good for you, Rudy," she managed to say. "It sounds like a great cause."

Feeling a bit awkward and needing to exit the conversation gracefully, she quickly added, "Well, great seeing you, Rudy! I have to go. We're about to tape *Latinisimo*, and our guest's already here." She gestured vaguely towards the direction where she'd left Jane.

"No worries, Alexa. I can follow up later to help you register to vote, or even some radio friends if you want. You're close to being able to vote, right? Isn't your birthday in November?" Rudy offered, his tone easy and helpful.

With a slight nod and a hurried smile, Alexa turned toward the door. "I'll keep that in mind. Thanks, Rudy!" she called out over her shoulder as she rushed away, feeling a mix of relief and eagerness to distance herself from the situation.

Don't sweat it, Alexa! He's over you! But are you really over him? Alexa's mind was clouded with doubt. She wondered if Rudy had truly moved on as it appeared, or if there were still lingering feelings on his part.

"Sorry I'm late." Alexa rushed into the studio, a hint of breathlessness in her voice. "Voto Latino is conducting a Voter Registration Day right on campus. They've set up one of their spots just outside WVUD, almost blocking the entrance to the studio. And, well, one of the organizers happens to be Rudy, my ex-boyfriend."

Upon hearing the news, Ella's eyes widened briefly in surprise before softening with empathy. She leaned in slightly towards Alexa. "Are you okay?"

Alexa let out a small sigh and gave a half-hearted shrug, her hand gesturing in the air as if to weigh her feelings. "Kinda," she responded briefly.

"Got it." Ella changed subjects. "Well, ladies, we have a program to tape. Are you ready?"

"Sure, but may I suggest something?" Jane requested. "Any chances that we showcase some MLK VOICE 4 YOUTH® material?"

"Of course!" Ella responded. "What do you have in mind?"

"How about we feature Neha Das's 'Pretty for a Brown Girl'?" Jane suggested. "It was the winning speech from our last contest. Neha brilliantly challenged Euro-centric beauty standards, drawing parallels with Dr. King's speech, 'The Other America.'"

"That sounds like a powerful and impactful piece." Ella's eyes lit up at the suggestion.

"Glad you like the idea. It's a thought-provoking piece. I believe your audience will like it."

"Sounds like a plan." Ella's expression was thoughtful as she mulled over the suggestion. "Now we just need to figure out the best way to seamlessly integrate it into our program from the internet."

Without hesitation, Jane reached into her bag, pulling out a flash drive. She extended it towards Ella with a confident smile. "There you go!" she said, offering a simple solution to the dilemma.

Ella's face brightened at the prospect of adding a unique element to the program. She turned to Alexa, who shared her excitement. "Excellent!" Ella exclaimed. "Good to go!"

Alexa chimed in while she started working to set the studio system up. "I'm liking this changing things on-the-spot, Ella. It reminds me of the program last month. Nice! Now, let me get things set up." A swift system check—every light and indicator seemed on point. Now... adjusting the settings... over the headphones. Let's give the mic one final, thorough check. Let me see if Jane's mic is at the right distance. Great! Okay... good to go. Alexa looked into Ella's eyes, offering a smile and two thumbs up.

"Hello!" Ella greeted with a playful wink towards Alexa, then turned her attention to the audience. "Welcome to *Latinisimo*. Today, we're thrilled to have Jane Rubini with us, the creative force behind the MLK VOICE 4 YOUTH® a spoken word contest. Now, I'd like to turn it over to Alexa, who will give us an insider's view of what this contest is all about. Alexa, could you share with us?"

"Thanks, Ella, and a big welcome to Jane! Now, let me tell *Latinisimo*'s audience about this amazing contest. It gives Delaware students a megaphone, offering them a platform to express what's really on their minds. They get creative with speeches and poems, drawing inspiration from Dr. Martin Luther King Jr.'s legacy. But here's the coolest part—they're addressing today's hot topics in their own way. It's inspiring to see these young talents step up and make their voices heard!" Alexa's voice brimmed with enthusiasm. She pressed on without even thinking. "After watching videos of past winners, who are actually around my age, I was blown away. Each performance is so powerful. If I may ask—" Alexa glanced briefly at Ella for affirmation. "What inspired you to create the MLK VOICE 4 YOUTH®? We're really curious about how it started." Catching Ella's approving smile, Alexa responded with a smile full of pride.

"You did a great job summarizing Alexa. Let me just add that I'm trying to provide a space for people your age to speak up and use their voice to push for the changes they want to see in the world. Your words have power. They can hurt and wound, but they can inspire and motivate as well."

Ella transitioned to take the lead in the program. "Thanks for that fantastic summary and insightful question, Alexa," she said. Turning her focus to Jane, Ella continued. "Now, let's introduce our audience to Jane Rubini, the person behind MLK VOICE 4 YOUTH®. Jane, you emigrated from Canada, isn't that right?"

"Yes, my entire family and my husband's are from Canada. I grew up in a small town just east of Toronto, lived there for years. It's been twenty years since we moved to the U.S., twenty-one this June. My husband and I had a couple of relocations within Ontario before he transferred to Delaware to work on the Y2K, or Year Two Thousand, project with DuPont. That brought us here, and we never returned. While I don't have any relatives in Wilmington, I've managed to create a family of my own here—a chosen family, you might say."

"That sounds like you've found a close-knit community here. People you choose to be with, like a local family, right?" Ella clarified.

"Exactly! They're like family now," Jane agreed, nodding.

"Do you have any interesting stories about moving here from Canada—any cultural mix-ups or surprises?" Ella asked, intrigued.

Jane chuckled lightly before responding, "Oh, definitely! For instance, I remember how some Americans used to view Canada as a socialist country, and by extension, thought I was a socialist."

"That's intriguing. What do you think led to that assumption?" Ella probed further.

"Well, in Canada, we view health care and education as universal rights, not privileges," Jane explained. "It's funny because I never thought of myself as a socialist just for being Canadian!" Her voice carried a mix of humor and reflection, highlighting the nuances of her immigration experience.

Alexa was totally baffled, and all she could muster was a quiet "What?" Her eyes darted back and forth between Ella and Jane, seeking some sort of confirmation or explanation for the unexpected comment.

"Canadians generally hold the view that quality health care and education are essential rights for everyone. In the U.S., there's often a belief that health coverage is sufficient. However, sometimes, when a major health crisis hits, people suddenly realize that their coverage isn't as comprehensive as they thought. It's unfortunate that it often takes a catastrophe to reveal the gaps in their health insurance, and by then, it's usually too late to change anything." Jane paused to take a sip of water, composing her thoughts before delving deeper into the topic.

"Some people are often surprised when I mention that education and healthcare is not free in Canada. Yes, we do have a robust public healthcare system, but it's funded through taxes, and when it comes to higher education, there are tuition fees.

They're generally more affordable though, not something that would necessitate taking out a second mortgage on your home. I also recall someone being taken aback by my fluency in English; they assumed most Canadians primarily spoke French. In reality, about eighty percent of Canadians are first-language English speakers. However, the country has been embracing bilingualism more and more, especially since the implementation of Bill One-Oh-One and the recognition of two official languages."

Alexa, aware of the need to keep the show moving, subtly gestured to Ella with a circular motion of her hand, signaling to pick up the pace. This was a quiet but clear cue to maintain the engaging rhythm of the program. Observing Ella's quick response and smooth topic shift, Alexa realized she was starting to master this skill herself, ensuring the conversation remained dynamic and engaging.

Ella asked Alexa to introduce the material Jane offered. "The MLK VOICE 4 YOUTH® celebrates Dr. King's legacy. He was recognized as the leader of the American civil rights movement until his assassination in nineteen sixty-eight. I thought that before we share material from the contest we could hear Marvin Gaye's 'What's Going On' song from nineteen seventy-one that captures the spirit of the times."

Ella turned off the mics to let the music take center stage and congratulated Alexa. "Super, Alexa! The song is right on! We'll play the contest material a bit later."

Jane patted Alexa on the back while saying, "What a wonderful job you did! I still remember how that song made me feel the first time I heard it. Indeed, so relevant today. Perfect choice!"

Ella brought them back to *Latinisimo*. "Jane, the creation of a contest like the MLK VOICE 4 YOUTH® opens up a space for dialogue for youngsters. Why did you decide to start the contest?"

"What started it?" Jane slowly repeated the question as if thinking to herself. "There was a combination of things. November was the first major change. I don't usually share this whole story in one sitting because it's a bit overwhelming. The first change involved my son. I have to give him credit to being the catalyst behind it."

"How so?" Ella asked.

"Nine years ago, in November, my son died. He was nineteen." Jane breathed deep. "He took his life."

As Jane's words echoed through the room, a profound stillness took hold. Alexa, caught in the emotional gravity of the moment, instinctively held her breath. The studio, usually a place of lively conversation and energy, felt unbearably still, as if time itself had paused in honor of Jane's loss. Alexa's own reaction, a mix of shock, empathy, and a deep sense of sorrow, mirrored what she imagined many in the audience were feeling.

"I'm so sorry to hear this," Ella said. "Please feel free to share whatever you're comfortable with."

Jane was able to continue. "Time helps. And the fact that it has been nine years. He had his issues and troubles but that night, I was not worried about him. That day was the perfect storm for him. That was… that was something. Obviously, you're never the same after that."

"You cannot possibly be the same. Would you like to take a moment?"

Looks like she really needs to talk about it… like she needed to let out all the heavy stuff she's been holding onto. Is this her therapy? I had no idea! Gosh… poor Jane! Alexa thought, shifting uncomfortably in her seat.

"It was very hard for us. When I moved here, I was a wife, a mother, an immigrant, a daughter, a sister, and then nine years ago everything changed. I was very fortunate that we had many good people around us. As said, I don't have much family here." Jane paused and then continued, "My husband didn't do so well. He really struggled. And three months later, there was an accident and he passed."

Alexa and Ella gasped in disbelief. Oh no, it can't be… one tragedy after another!

Ella, at a loss for words, could only exclaim, "Oh, Jane!" her voice filled with empathy.

"I was very fortunate that all these good people were still around and able to help me through it. But when you go through it… like one day you wake up? You're not a mother. You're not a wife. Everything you thought you were, you weren't."

Alexa was deeply struck by the sheer composure Jane maintained despite her painful experiences.

"Jane, your courage in sharing your personal journey is deeply touching. The transformation you've undergone, especially in redefining yourself beyond the roles of mother and wife, is profound. How did you muster the strength to channel these experiences into new endeavors? Your resilience and ability to transform grief into positive change is truly inspiring."

Jane, bathed in the gentle, serene light emanating from the system's console, listened with intent. Her silhouette, a blend of tranquility and strength, was softly illuminated. When she spoke, her voice was calm but laden with unspoken emotions, resonating deeply in the quiet room. "You can't go through all that and not learn something," she started, her eyes reflecting a profound depth of experience. "I always say, without learning from those experiences, it would have been a complete tragedy."

As Jane's story unfolded, Alexa's hands were clasped tightly in her lap. Oh, my goodness, how can you possibly move on after that? This reflection caused a slight, almost imperceptible shake of her head as she grappled with the magnitude of Jane's experiences.

The air around her seemed to shift as she delved deeper into her journey. "I had so many different emotions," she confessed, her voice tinged with raw honesty. "Anger being one of them, let me tell you… yeah, I was angry." Her hands clenched slightly, releasing a tension she held within. "I was happy to be angry. That anger kept me going, kept me motivated, and kept me on my feet."

She glanced towards the window, where the light from the adjacent studio cast a warm, comforting glow. "Plus," she added with tenderness. "I had two dogs to take care of. I had to get out of bed in the morning." Her gaze returned to Alexa then Ella. "All those things, even those you think are involuntary, become voluntary. Every day, you have to make decisions."

"How so, Jane? Please explain."

"I learned I was stronger than I thought." As she spoke, her hand gestured the number three. "Three things really allowed me to continue: family, friends, and faith. Faith provides hope, and I find all three to be interconnected."

Goodness… this is an emotional roller coaster! Is there more? How much can one person actually take?

"Now, please help us understand how you translate such unspeakable tragedies into something so positive like the MLK VOICE 4 YOUTH® contest?" Ella queried.

Alexa noted Ella's efforts to keep the discussion balanced and focused while navigating the emotionally charged conversation. Good for Ella! Putting a positive spin on difficult times helps the program flow.

"Perhaps if I had listened more… if I had been more sensitive, yelled less, and listened more, maybe he would still be here,"

Jane pondered, her voice trailing off. This confession stirred a sense of disquiet in Alexa. She sensed that despite Ella's probing question, Jane was still grappling with unresolved feelings, a sign that moving on was still a work in progress for her.

A profound silence enveloped the room once again, lingering for what felt like an eternity. Alexa observed a subtle transformation in Jane's expression. Gradually, a faint, almost hesitant smile began to form on her face.

"My son's loss gave me a sense of purpose that has really driven me forward. I needed that purpose. Three years later on Martin Luther King Day, I attended a panel discussion with a colleague about work done in the community. At the end of the session, the host asked, "What will you do?""

"And… what happened?" Ella inquired.

"Fast forward to twenty fourteen. Then there's the issue with Michael Brown, Ferguson, the shootings, the protests, the chaos, people yelling and screaming. So, I'm getting this idea in my head. I'm thinking, have we forgotten about everything Dr. King did?" The frustration was evident in her voice.

As Jane spoke, Alexa noticed her wide, animated eyes reflecting agitation and disbelief, a slight head shake, and hands clenched slightly—all gestures underscoring her passion and dismay.

"I thought, is somebody listening?" Jane concluded, her tone dropping to almost a whisper. Alexa leaned forward slightly, an unconscious movement that conveyed her deep involvement in the story.

"The idea to create the contest began to solidify. I first shared my idea with a colleague who thought it was a good idea. So, I formed a committee. We exchanged ideas and one was to solicit feedback from educators to determine if there would be interest in a public speaking contest."

"Feedback from teachers?" Ella explored.

"Yes, teachers told us youth would be more interested if it was poetry, like slam poetry, not just public speaking. That made us think about giving them creative freedom and letting their message be the most important thing. I even suggested to consider rap. I had a bit of pushback because of its reputation. Rules were set and with everyone's help and support, it came together pretty quickly and now we will celebrate eight years providing a platform for youth voices."

The moment was perfect for sharing the video of last year's winner. Ella smoothly transitioned and adjusted the settings on the console. Her hand gesture indicated it was time for Jane to take the lead. Jane leaned slightly toward the microphone and began introducing last year's winner, Neha Das, and her work, 'Pretty for a Brown Girl.'

As Neha's voice resonated through the studio, Alexa was instantly captivated again. Each word seemed to speak directly to her, its meaning deep and relatable. She was completely drawn in by the powerful delivery.

When the poem ended, Ella brought the discussion back, signaling Jane to explain its deeper meaning. The microphones went live, and Jane started, "Neha's poem is more than about looks. It's about facing racism and classism, about challenging a system that judges you by your skin color. It's a strong message from a young, brown-skinned girl about to start her college life."

Hearing Jane's explanation about the poem's take on racism and classism, Alexa couldn't help but relate. That's spot on, she mused, seeing clear parallels between its themes and the upcoming challenges of her own college life.

"A program like MLK VOICE 4 YOUTH® gives youth the opportunity to be heard. It helps students develop communication skills, enhance social awareness, and build confidence, self-esteem, and leadership skills. Perhaps most importantly, it gives them a platform to express themselves and the priority is their message. If ever we needed to be reminded of Dr. King's work and legacy, it is today."

"The contest is gaining momentum and recognition," Ella observed. "Each year, we're seeing more sponsors coming on board to support the event. In your opinion, what's driving this growth?"

"I've always viewed the contestants as change makers. They started speaking out years before the Parkland incident. Their anger and frustration have been a barometer for me. In the first year, they were very angry, and that anger continued until recently; there has been a small shift away from anger. They're saying 'enough is enough!' It's encouraging. There are so many incredible young people out there doing remarkable things." Jane made a deliberate pause.

"We don't hear enough of all the really good stuff. Let's give them freedom. Let's give them a platform and hear what they have to say. If we are smart, we'll listen."

"And there you are providing a platform for them to speak up and for us to listen. What's next for the contest?" Ella asked.

"After our first year, we learned quite a bit," Jane explained. "The kids expressed a strong desire for help with writing. So, in response, we introduced writing workshops the following year. We've also added presentation workshops to help them prepare for the competition. Plus, we've made efforts to keep past participants involved."

"What do you mean by keeping participants involved?"

"Several of our past contestants are now involved in helping with workshops and have even taken on roles as judges in the semifinals. This peer involvement has a powerful effect; the youth really connect with their peers, showing respect and maintaining focus during these sessions. Having discussions led by their peers and hearing shared experiences adds a uniquely impactful element. Moving forward, I'm thinking about further developing the mentoring side of our program to enhance this peer-to-peer dynamic."

"Expanding the mentoring program sounds like a fantastic initiative. We wish you the very best! To close the program, Alexa and I want to express our gratitude for your openness and honesty. Your insights have really illuminated the significance of the MLK VOICE 4 YOUTH®. Could you please share details about the upcoming contest with our audience? Many are likely interested after this inspiring conversation."

Jane provided comprehensive information about the next contest, including details on participation and the prizes for winners.

"Thanks again for your time, Jane! Thanks to our audience for taking the time to listen to another *Latinisimo*. Until next time!"

As the program concluded and the microphones switched off, Ella moved towards Jane with a warmth that went beyond professional courtesy. She gently embraced her, a gesture of support and care. "Are you okay, Jane?" Ella's soft and empathetic voice showed her genuine concern. "The interview took some unexpected turns. I just want to make sure that it didn't bring you any discomfort or harm." Her eyes searched Jane's, looking for any sign of distress, ready to offer further support if needed.

"I am okay, Ella. I can talk about things now. Thanks for the opportunity to explain what the contest is all about. Now you know why it's very close to my heart."

Ella turned towards Alexa, her expression thoughtful. She paused for a moment, considering her words, then said, "Do you mind taking care of the interview editing? I'd like to walk Jane to her car, just to make sure she's okay after all this. Is that alright with you?"

"Of course, Ella." Alexa wasn't sure about Jane's well-being, either.

Ella stopped by the door before leaving and turned her head to Alexa. "Are you okay?"

Alexa quietly nodded. She knew that editing a radio program was laborious. She started by checking that the volume was at a good level. She then saved the program to the system. She found the pre-recorded intro and ending and added it to Jane's interview to complete the thirty-minute time each program had to last. She saved the program again and indicated to the system when it needed to air by selecting day and time. She checked the sequence of all programs for the month and verified that everything was in place. It was late by the time she left the radio station. A familiar figure approached.

"Hi, Alexa. You okay? I realized you were still working on the interview when I saw Ella leaving the station with the other lady. I finished wrapping things up for the voter registration drive and decided to wait for you. Is that okay? Can I drive you home?"

"Hey, Rudy! I didn't expect to see you here. It's kind of late, isn't it? Are you sure you have the time?" Alexa asked, peering into the dark night outside WVUD. The darkness was so dense that she couldn't make out anything beyond the station's lights. "Yeah, a ride home would be really helpful, especially with how dark it's gotten," Alexa replied, her voice wavering slightly. She found herself nervously twisting a strand of her hair around her finger, a habit she fell into when unsure. It had indeed been a long time since she and Rudy had spent any significant time together. Their paths had gradually split, each becoming engrossed in their own school activities and personal pursuits.

As they settled into the car, a sense of unease hung between them, a silent acknowledgment of the distance that had grown. The initial conversation felt stilted, each comment punctuated by brief, awkward pauses. Alexa kept glancing out the window, taking in the deepening darkness outside as a way to steady her nerves.

Gradually, as they drove through the night, the conversation began to flow naturally. They talked about friends they both knew, shared recent music favorites, exchanged family stories, and discussed their college visit experiences. With each shared memory and laugh, Alexa felt the stiffness in her demeanor begin to soften. The comfort of their old friendship slowly seeped back, easing her initial discomfort and reminding her of the connection they once shared.

The conversation deepened when Rudy expressed his frustrations with college applications and his experiences with O'Jete. Alexa's concerns increased. "It's like he has issues with certain people, you know?" Rudy admitted.

Feeling a surge of shared frustration, Alexa responded, "I totally get what you mean. Every time I talked to him, I feel put down. I thought I was the only one, but hearing this from you, it's not just me." Their shared grievances created a sense of unity.

With growing resolve, Alexa stated, "We have to do something about this. Think about it—thirty percent of our school is black and Latino. We can't be the only ones feeling this way. It's just not fair."

"What do you think we should do?" Rudy asked, picking up on Alexa's determination.

Engrossed in their discussion, they brainstormed potential ways to tackle the O'Jete issue. The car became a space for planning and solidarity, a stark contrast to the darkness outside. By the time Rudy dropped Alexa off, the plan was taking shape. Somebody was going to get an unexpected surprise.

CHAPTER 11

A NONPROFIT HEALTHCARE CEO, ROSA RIVERA

As October rolled in, Alexa, along with her classmates, dove into the hectic world of college preparations, a common ritual in Delaware's high schools. Conversations buzzed with talks of college visits and favorite university picks.

Facing financial limitations at home and navigating the aftermath and lingering effects of the pandemic, Alexa pivoted to exploring colleges through virtual tours when possible. She kept a steady focus on the list of universities she had previously discussed with Andy, with a special emphasis on MIT. As she delved deeper into what MIT offered, her interest grew—the institution aligned perfectly with her aspirations. However, Alexa was aware that securing a scholarship was crucial for her dream to materialize. Additionally, MIT's supportive approach towards dreamers further heightened its appeal, making it an increasingly attractive option for her.

Imagine being at MIT! It'll be a dream coming true! For that college campus visit… maybe mom and dad want to go. Driving of course… we can't afford to stay.

To bolster her chances, Alexa spent increasing amounts of time at the public library, immersing herself in her studies and college applications. One day, upon returning home, she was surprised to find Andy waiting at her doorstep. His unannounced visit was out of the ordinary, and Alexa immediately sensed something was amiss. "Hi, Andy, I didn't know you were coming. Did I miss we were going to get together? Something happened? Did Rudy call you?"

"No, he didn't call me. I just really wanted to talk to you. Can we walk a bit?

The sidewalk by Alexa's house was modest, a simple concrete path lined with the occasional weed poking through the cracks, mirroring the unpretentious nature of the neighborhood. As they strolled along, Andy's steps were kind of jittery, his gaze often dropping to the cracked sidewalk. Alexa noticed how he kept messing with his hands, and his voice sometimes got all shaky. It hit her then—this wasn't just some casual chat.

"I've been meaning to have this conversation with you for so long, and it just feels like today's the right day. I needed to talk to my best friend," Andy said, his voice tinged with a mix of earnestness and apprehension.

Alexa felt a knot of worry form in her stomach. "Of course. What's on your mind?"

Andy offered a tentative half-smile, his usual confidence momentarily eclipsed by hesitance. "You know, Alexa, we pretty much share everything." His voice wavered slightly. After a brief pause, filled with a deep, steadying breath, he continued, "But I've been keeping something from you. I'm actually in a serious relationship... with a guy. His name is Simon." It was evident that Andy was grappling with a significant internal battle, mustering all his courage to reveal a deeply personal aspect of his life that he had kept hidden away.

Alexa searched for the right words, understanding the significance of Andy coming out to her. She could see the vulnerability in his eyes. Without a word, she reached out and gave him a long, supportive hug.

Breaking the embrace, she looked into his eyes. "Andy, I love you just the way you are. Our friendship means everything to me, and it has nothing to do with who you're dating. It's about who you are, and I'm so glad you told me this."

Andy's shoulders visibly relaxed. "I was worried, you know, with you being Catholic and all... the church's views on this..."

Alexa's response was immediate and heartfelt. "Andy, I might be Catholic, but I don't agree with everything the church says, especially on this. Love is about acceptance, and being gay doesn't change who you are, not one bit. I'm not one to judge, least of all you."

They embraced again, a silent affirmation of their deep bond. Andy then mentioned a class gathering where Simon would be, and Alexa quickly said, "I'd love to meet him, Andy. Just let me know when."

As the day came to an end, Alexa found herself reflecting on the events that had unfolded. She realized that she hadn't opened up about her own challenges, having chosen to prioritize Andy's needs over her own. This choice spoke volumes about the strength and depth of their friendship, a bond that had only deepened with every heartfelt conversation and shared experience. She picked up her cellphone and sent a quick text to Andy, typing *AndyILY!* With a contented smile, she then snuggled into bed, the comfort of their strengthened friendship soothing her into a peaceful sleep almost immediately.

Monday dawned, and Alexa was immediately swept up in the whirlwind of school assignments. Time seemed to be slipping through her fingers as the semester raced towards its end, coming much quicker than she would have liked. By midday, Pete O'Jete had mentioned that all students were scheduled for conversations with him to follow up on college applications. Alexa cringed at the prospect of talking to him. She wasn't the only one feeling that way.

Pete O'Jete mentioned that people from Aspira Delaware were going to come to help students with college applications in the next few days. A time slot sheet began circulating. Alexa saw Lourdes Puig's name and made sure to a select time with her.

It was during the last class on Monday that she got Ella's cryptic text. *Rosa Rivera/La Red.* Taking advantage of the ride home in the school bus, she began her research.

The organization's website was useful. It said that Rosa was the Chief Operations officer at La Red Health Center in Sussex County, Delaware. Alexa took advantage of the last minutes of the school bus ride and quickly texted Ella. *Hi! Superbusy@school, getting music, talk soon.*

A few days later, when Alexa's bus pulled up, she caught sight of Lourdes Puig navigating her car through the school's packed parking lot. The area was bustling with activity, and part of it seemed to be taken over by some ongoing construction, making parking spots even more of a rare find. Alexa felt a surge of hope at the prospect of catching some time with Lourdes to discuss her college and scholarship applications further. As she walked past O'Jete's office, engrossed in these thoughts, she was pulled back to the present by the sound of her name being called.

"Alexa, can you step into my office for a moment?" O'Jete called out, his tone lacking cordiality, something Alexa had grown accustomed to.

"Good morning, Mr. O'Jete," Alexa maintained her politeness despite the chilly reception.

Walking into O'Jete's office was like stepping into a hurricane's aftermath. Papers everywhere, total chaos—a perfect reflection of him. He barely glanced up, too busy digging through the mess on his desk.

"Alexa, you're meeting with Lourdes Puig today, right? Let's meet up tomorrow to go over what you guys talk about. I've already scheduled a time for you—it's on the list. Check your slot and I'll see you then," O'Jete said in a tone that brooked no argument.

"Um, sure, okay. Thanks," Alexa replied hesitantly.

Without warning, O'Jete's tone turned sharp. "Alexa, save the attitude, please!"

"I'm sorry, Mr. O'Jete. What are you talking about? I'm confused…"

"People like you come to this country expecting that we pick up the tab for you." O'Jete barely contained his anger. "And then you have the nerve to even think… You should be grateful that we're even giving you a high school education, if you ask me."

Stunned by his vitriol, Alexa could only watch as Rudy passed by in the corridor. Her eyes felt hot with unshed tears. O'Jete's prejudice was nothing new, but this confrontation was beyond anything she had experienced before.

"Now go. We'll continue this tomorrow, Alexa," O'Jete dismissed her.

Regaining her composure, she made her way towards Rudy, her resolve strengthening. "Rudy, it's time to do something!" Alexa knew that Rudy had been investigating O'Jete's online activities for Voto Latino and had stumbled upon a video of O'Jete ranting about immigrants on a radical website. She was sure that once they exposed this video to the school administration, O'Jete was in for quite a surprise.

Chatting with Lourdes later in the day was not only positive but very encouraging. Lourdes helped Alexa complete her paperwork and scholarship information and even offered to write a recommendation letter. Alexa had a very solid shot, in Lourdes' opinion, and aiming high was the way to go.

"How can somebody be so cruel Lourdes?" Alexa shared what had happened with Pete O'Jete.

"Told you before, never let anyone define your capabilities, him included. He doesn't have the power… you have it!"

"You know what… you're absolutely right! Thanks for the reminder—I really needed that!" Alexa responded with renewed conviction.

Still, it took Alexa a few days to recover from the meeting with O'Jete, but somehow, she managed to get through the weekend. She had promised Andy she would be at the party to meet Simon, who turned out to be an unassuming yet talented musician. At one point, someone in the crowd, recognizing him from the local music scene, requested a song. Simon obliged, transforming the gathering into a charming, bohemian musical night. From across the room, Alexa caught Andy's eye and shot him a thumbs up, silently telling him, *Way to go, Andy!* She couldn't help but notice Rudy's absence, and a surprising sense of longing for him crept up on her. *Can't be… am I missing him?*

Despite her best efforts, Alexa found herself struggling to carve out enough time for in-depth research on Rosa. She managed to select a couple of songs that would go well with the interview's theme. Time seemed to slip through her fingers, as college preparation took precedence, much like it did for the rest of her peers.

Alexa and Ella reached the radio station just moments before Rosa Rivera's arrival. With no time for a detailed pre-interview discussion, they were set for an impromptu, on-the-spot interview. Ella quickly asked Alexa to come up with a few questions for the interview. Alexa pulled out the flash drive containing the music she had selected for the show. Ella nodded.

"Rosa, thank you for coming. We'll start in a minute. How are you?" Ella took her seat and motioned for Rosa to do the same. "Alexa, are we ready to start?"

"We're good, Ella. We can start when you say so," Alexa said.

"Great! Here we go! Ella opened mics. "Welcome, *Latinisimo* friends! As many of you know, we've been diving into conversations with inspiring individuals who are shaping the paths for new generations to explore diverse professional careers. Today, we're thrilled to have Rosa Rivera with us. She's the Chief Operations Officer at La Red Health Center in Sussex County, Delaware.

Prior to this role, Rosa was the CEO of the Henrietta Johnson Medical Center, dedicating nearly three decades of service there. Welcome, Rosa!" Ella warmly introduced Alexa as well.

Rosa smiled. "Happy to be here. Thanks for the invitation!"

Ella started the interview. "Health care careers are very much in demand these days, Rosa, particularly for bilingual people like you. But some time ago that was not necessarily the case. What made you decide to select this career path?"

"Well, actually when I was in high school, I wanted to be an accountant because I liked numbers. It just so happened that I ended up in healthcare."

"That's a change! Landing in healthcare by default isn't common, is it?

"No, it's not, yet I actually love working in this field. You don't need to be a doctor or a nurse. Healthcare is so vast, and there's so much you can do. I love it! I don't think I would want to do anything else."

Ella smiled. "I know, but how did you get there?"

As Rosa recounted her vivid memory, her expression was a mix of reflection and resilience. "I remember going to the community clinic to see a dentist because we didn't know where else to go," she began, her eyes momentarily drifting as if visualizing the past. "I remember someone there pulling out one of my teeth. I was in so much pain!" As she spoke these words, her face briefly tensed as if reliving the discomfort of that moment.

Rosa's hands gestured slightly, illustrating her story. "I didn't know how to tell the person that I was in pain. That visit was so traumatic that it left me terrified of dentists," she continued, her voice conveying the lingering impact of the experience. "I avoided seeing a dentist for about fifteen years after that." She looked earnestly at Alexa then Ella. "I don't want others to endure what I went through. Those experiences inspired me to make a difference in healthcare." Her determination was evident, not only in her words but also in the firm set of her jaw and the passionate gleam in her eyes.

"Wait, what do you mean by you couldn't tell that you were in pain?" Alexa blurted out, her curiosity getting the better of her without checking for Ella's approval first. Oh gosh, I hope she's okay with me jumping in like that. But Ella, understanding Alexa's impulsiveness, nodded with approval and offered her the biggest, most reassuring smile.

"That's a great question Alexa." Rosa responded. "In short, it was about the lack of English but to answer that, I probably need to explain how we got to Delaware if okay with you?"

"Sure, please go ahead." Alexa prompted Rosa to continue.

"We landed in Delaware because my parents wanted better education opportunities for us," Rosa began, her voice steady but tinged with gratitude. "I was fifteen when we arrived. We were six, living in a one-bedroom apartment. It was tough finding a decent, clean place to rent, and we had difficult landlords."

Rosa inhaled, and Alexa observed a distant look in her eyes, as if she were recreating those challenging times.

"Going to school was another hurdle. I couldn't speak English, which was incredibly challenging." Rosa's hands gestured subtly, emphasizing her points. "If it hadn't been for the bilingual program in my high school, I think I would've been so frustrated that I might have dropped out."

"Based on your upward career trend, you overcame that rough start, didn't you?" Ella retook the lead in the program.

"I guess so," Rosa responded modestly, a hint of a smile playing at the corners of her mouth. "Despite my struggles with English, I managed to graduate in the top ten of my high school class." Alexa could see a glimmer of pride in Rosa's eyes as she recounted her achievements.

"I studied business management while working full-time. The Henrietta Johnson board encouraged me to pursue my bachelor's degree." Rosa continued, her voice reflecting a journey of hard-earned success. "I ended up attending Wilmington University. The experience was enriching, as I could directly apply what I was learning to my daily work."

As Rosa spoke, Alexa observed the subtle changes in her expression—the way her eyes lit up when discussing her education, and the satisfied nod when mentioning her work. It was clear to Alexa that Rosa's journey, though filled with challenges, was also marked by significant triumphs and personal growth.

Alexa's gaze drifted to the studio next door. Her eyes, fixed and unblinking, seemed to look beyond its walls, lost in a sea of thoughts. She absorbed Rosa's words, feeling them intertwine with her own life experiences. Memories of her time at *Latinisimo* cascaded through her mind, each story, each voice, including Yamil, María, Havidán, Raye, JoAnn, and all others bringing with them moments of profound realization.

In these fleeting seconds, Alexa was struck by the magnitude of her personal growth, fueled by the authentic stories she had helped to share. These weren't just interviews; they were life lessons, each person's journey adding a layer to her own understanding of the world. Her eyes, though staring at the studio, were seeing the faces and hearing the voices of those who had left an indelible mark on her. I get it now, she thought, a sense of clarity washing over her. All of them, they are the people who make us… me pause!

"I see, Rosa. This seems like the perfect moment for our first song. Alexa has chosen two songs especially for you," Ella said. "Alexa, do you mind?"

Startled back to reality, Alexa quickly shifted in her chair, adjusting her posture as she returned her focus to the here and now. She moved closer to the microphone, her hands instinctively checking its position and her headphones. Regaining her composure, she nodded at Ella, ready to introduce the first song she had selected for Rosa.

"Sure, Ella," Alexa inserted the flash drive and began commenting on her choice of Camila Cabello's 'Havana' for Rosa. While the song played, Ella quickly turned off the mics for a brief interlude. She leaned towards Rosa. "How are you finding the conversation so far?"

Rosa, smiling, expressed her enjoyment of the interview, clearly engaged in the conversation. As the song began to wind down, Ella caught Alexa's eye and pointed towards the mic, signaling that it was almost time to resume the interview, with her taking the lead again. Understanding the cue, Alexa adjusted her headphones and prepared herself to continue the dialogue as 'Havana' neared its end.

"Welcome back, *Latinisimo* friends! I'm your host, Alexa Hope. Today, we're honored to have Rosa Rivera, the COO of La Red Medical Center, with us. Welcome back to the show!" Alexa continued right where Ella had left the interview before the break. "So, Rosa, can you tell us about your journey with the Henrietta Johnson Medical Center? It appears to be where you've had your longest tenure. How did that opportunity come about?"

"Henrietta Johnson Medical Center was indeed my longest tenure, at least so far," Rosa began, her eyes lighting up with the memory. "I landed at Henrietta Johnson Medical Center because of a newly hired doctor from Puerto Rico. As soon as word got out that there was a Spanish-speaking doctor available, it naturally started attracting a lot of attention from the Latino community. The challenge was that she was the only one who could communicate with the patients in Spanish. Rosa's expression became animated as she continued, "She invited me to join the team, even though I confessed to her that I knew nothing about healthcare. Her response? 'Don't worry, I'll teach you.' I figured, if she was willing to take the time to teach me, then I was willing to learn."

Pausing for a moment, Rosa reflected. "It wasn't like I had a sudden revelation or a moment where I thought, 'This is what I want to do forever.' But over time, I started feeling this deep internal satisfaction, a sense that I was really making a difference. And that's why I stayed."

Ella followed up with a related question. "You certainly accomplished a lot. The respect you've garnered in the medical field and within the community speaks for itself. You were asked to be the CEO for a reason. As far as I remember, you initially didn't want the position but eventually said yes. Is it true that both the Board of Directors and the staff asked you to lead the organization?"

"I was humbled and honored because I didn't think I could do the job and they thought that I could." As Rosa recalled her journey, Alexa noticed a thoughtful expression on Rosa's face.

"When I was at Henrietta, I did a bit of everything—from running the front desk to handling bills and learning about computers. I was all over the place. Eventually, the CEO left, and the Board was in a bit of a bind. They told me they had hired a company for an operational assessment but in the meantime, they thought I was the best person for the job. I couldn't believe it."

Rosa's expression became more expressive as she continued, "They asked me to step in temporarily, and my first reaction was, 'Absolutely not.' I remember having a conversation with my medical director. He said, 'Rosa, you can do this job. But if you don't take it, you'll have to work with whoever comes next, and they might not be the best fit for it, let alone able to handle it.' That conversation really changed my perspective."

"The next day, I accepted the position, but I made it clear it was only temporary, just to help the organization," Rosa said, pausing as she reflected on that pivotal moment.

Listening to Rosa's shift from doubt to being a boss, Alexa realized it was more than just climbing the career ladder. It was a journey of finding yourself and stepping up when it counts. Rosa's story wasn't just about getting ahead at work; it was about figuring out who you are and owning it.

Whoa! Rosa turning down a boss job at first? Who does that? She quietly stood up, carefully positioning her phone to capture the perfect shot. After framing Rosa, she quickly sat back down and began crafting an Instagram post. Picture done. Now, *#whorejectsabossjob? #realLeadership @Latinisimo #RosaRiveraLaRed.* Her eyes sparkled with enthusiasm as she anticipated the reactions the post would garner. It didn't take long for thumbs up emojis to start flooding in.

"And naturally, that temporary position eventually became a permanent one, right?" Ella led the conversation forward.

"They said they had little money, some issues, and needed a lot of help." Rosa began, recounting her journey with a hint of reflection in her voice. "We managed to turn the place around in less than a year. Being familiar with nearly every aspect of the organization definitely played a part. I brought in new staff, set up a dental department, among other initiatives."

As she spoke, Alexa noticed the blend of humility and pride in Rosa's demeanor. It was evident how deeply she cared about her work and the impact she had made.

"Eventually, the staff themselves asked me to take on the CEO role permanently. I decided to go through the formal interview process, and, well… I was hired." Rosa's expression showed a mix of surprise and satisfaction at her own career trajectory.

Alexa caught Ella's eye and subtly waved her hand to signal her readiness to ask a question. Understanding the cue, Ella smoothly transitioned. "Rosa, Alexa has a question for you."

With a nod from Ella, Alexa leaned in. "Rosa, you mentioned earlier that your agreement to be CEO at Henrietta Johnson was supposed to be only temporary. However, you ended up staying in that role for about ten years, which is quite a long time for a temporary position. What were some of the challenges you faced as a CEO, or aspects of the role that you didn't particularly enjoy?"

Rosa responded with a reflective tone, "I am very hands-on." As she spoke, she raised her hand slightly, illustrating her point. Rosa's hand contrasted against the dimly lit backdrop of the studio, creating a beautiful striking visual.

"I enjoy answering the phone, interacting directly with patients, and working closely with the staff. But in a CEO role, your responsibilities shift significantly. It involves attending numerous meetings, being present at various events, and unfortunately, it means less time spent with patients, which is what I truly love doing. Even though I deeply cared for the organization, during my ten years as CEO, I kept feeling that the role didn't align entirely with what I wanted to do."

"What happened after the realization that being a CEO wasn't for you?" Ella inquired while giving Alexa a thumbs up.

"I really wanted to get back to what I was doing before," Rosa explained. "Eventually, the Board and I reached an agreement." She paused for a moment, reflecting on the transition. "They began the search for a new CEO, and around the same time, La

Red needed a new COO. The position had been open for about a year or so. After some discussions, they offered me the job, and I accepted. It's been six years since I made that switch."

Alexa noticed the subtle shifts in Rosa's demeanor—a mix of relief and contentment that came with discussing her current role. It was clear that she had found a balance between her hands-on approach and leadership responsibilities at La Red.

"The time seems right for a break, don't you think? Alexa, why don't you cue up our next music segment?" Ella suggested, glancing over at Alexa for her input.

"Absolutely, I have the perfect song in mind for our listeners," Alexa's voice brimming with excitement as she introduced the chosen track. The music break offered a welcome respite, allowing the trio in the studio to engage in casual off-air chat and grab a quick sip of water.

As the song concluded and the atmosphere in the studio shifted back to the interview, Ella turned the conversation over to Alexa. "Welcome back to *Latinisimo*, folks. We're here with Rosa Rivera, COO of La Red. Alexa, why don't you take the next question?"

Alexa had grown accustomed and happy in the interviewer's seat. "We're eager to know, what do you consider your proudest achievement?"

"My proudest achievement? Undoubtedly my staff, my managers, and my supervisors," Rosa responded with confidence, her voice resonating with a sense of fulfillment. "I've invested considerable time and effort into their development. My primary objective has always been to inspire them to reach their full potential and excel in their respective roles."

"Great question, Alexa. Thanks!" Ella said, appreciatively turning her attention back to Rosa. "That was a terrific answer.

Now, Rosa, as a successful professional and a Latina, we're curious about your journey. Has it been an easy path for you?" Ella's question opened the door for Rosa to delve into the more personal and nuanced aspects of her professional life.

Rosa's smile was tinged with a hint of irony as she began to speak. "It hasn't always been easy. Being Latina and having a heavy accent... it didn't exactly open doors for me at first. I didn't feel welcome initially."

Alexa noticed a certain uneasiness in Rosa's eyes.

"Now, it seems like I'm often pulled into the same circle, representing Latinos," Rosa said, making the quote and quote mark with her fingers as she spoke. "But there are so many other Latinos out there doing incredible work who deserve recognition too."

Ella, seizing the opportunity to delve deeper, asked, "Could you explain to our audience what you mean by that?" Her question aimed to clarify Rosa's point for the listeners.

Alexa felt Rosa's exasperation as she discussed being pigeonholed as the 'Latina representative' in various committees. "Just recently, someone asked me about the 'issues in the Hispanic community.' These kinds of questions frustrate me. The issues are the same across all communities." Rosa's tone grew firmer, more impassioned. "I asked them back, 'What are the issues in the African American or Caucasian communities?' We all want the same things—good jobs, quality education, access to healthcare. Latinos aren't any different. We deserve the same respect and services as everyone else."

Of course, we do! Alexa recognized the exhaustion in Rosa's voice, the tiredness of constantly being the token Latina in rooms where diversity was more a checkbox than a reality. It's so unfair, like she's gotta speak for all Latinos or something. Why?

"Rosa, that's an excellent point. It's too common to generalize Latinos, when in fact there's a rich diversity among the more than twenty nationalities in Latin America," Ella said thoughtfully. "But look at the time—it's flown by, hasn't it? Unfortunately, we're at the end of our segment. On behalf of our listeners, Alexa, and myself, we want to extend a huge thank you for being with us today and sharing your inspiring story," Ella warmly concluded the interview.

As Alexa switched off the mics, she found herself still absorbed in the depths of the interview. The parallels she drew between her life and Rosa's experiences lingered in her mind. It was Ella's voice, soft yet clear, that brought her back to the moment.

Looking up, Alexa noticed Rosa had already left. Ella's next words filled her with a sense of accomplishment. "Alexa, you were outstanding today. I'm genuinely proud of the progress you've made since joining us. It's hard to believe, but your time with *Latinisimo* is drawing to a close. Your final program is just around the corner."

Upon hearing Ella's words, Alexa experienced surprise mixed with a twinge of sorrow. The thought that her time with *Latinisimo* was drawing to a close hit her more deeply than she had expected. "Gosh… really! Has it been a year already?"

Ella continued speaking, her eyes a mix of excitement and a touch of sadness. Alexa, observing this, felt a pang of hope that their friendship would endure beyond these moments.

"And for your final show, you'll be leading the interview. I want you to prepare for a session with Sheila Smith, the former Executive Director of Minnesota Citizens for the Arts. She's a dear friend and a powerhouse in arts advocacy. Based on your performance today, I know you're more than ready."

The prospect of conducting a full interview thrilled Alexa. "Yes, I'm ready! I'll do my best. Thanks for the opportunity!"

"Just remember to let the conversation flow naturally. We'll review your questions beforehand. It'll be virtual, like our session with Havidán Rodríguez. Don't worry, I'll be there to support you. And, of course, choose a couple of songs for the segment. Sheila's looking forward to speaking with you already. And today, leave the editing to me. You've earned a relaxing weekend."

As Alexa stepped out WVUD, she was immediately embraced by the crisp, cool air of an October evening. The sky above the University of Delaware campus was transforming, with shades of blues and purples blending into the coming night. A light breeze, touched with the smell of autumn leaves, brushed against her face.

The campus was lively with students kickstarting their weekend. Some strolled leisurely after a day of classes, while others gathered in chatty groups, making the most of the serene evening. The trees, dressed in their autumn best, showcased a vibrant array of oranges, reds, and yellows, adding a splash of color to her walk.

Amidst the casual chatter, bursts of laughter from students, and the soft sound of leaves crunching underfoot, Alexa sensed a comforting familiarity. Yet, there was a bittersweet undertone, a realization that these everyday campus scenes would soon be memories. Her walk through the campus to the bus stop was a pleasant journey, surrounded by the simple yet profound beauty of fall. It grounded her, leaving her invigorated and ready to face whatever challenges lay ahead with renewed anticipation and determination.

AN ACTIVIST AND ARTS ADVOCATE LEADER, SHEILA SMITH

On this brisk late November morning, the high school was enveloped in a frosty air, the kind that turned breath into mist and had everyone cocooned in layers of warmth. Alexa, zipped up in the same jacket she had last season, walked through the school grounds. She was keenly aware of her family's financial situation, with college visits and application fees tightening their budget. Wearing her old jacket was her subtle way of contributing, a small sacrifice for the bigger picture.

As she walked, Alexa pondered over how to make the holidays special despite their tight finances. She wanted to give her parents something meaningful, a gesture to show her appreciation. Lost in thought, she had a spark of inspiration. You know what... I should bake some cookies for them, she mused. The idea brought a small, contented smile to her face. It wasn't just about saving money; it was about giving something personal, a token of love and gratitude.

Despite the cold, there was a buzz of activity and excitement among the students. Whispers and rumors were spreading like wildfire through the crowded hallways, with groups of students gathered in animated discussions.

Engulfed in her thoughts about the imminent *Latinisimo* interview, Alexa scarcely noticed the noise around her. She marveled at how swiftly the year had passed, a time brimming with learning and personal development at *Latinisimo*. I really am ready for this! A sense of readiness and excitement bubbled within her.

Pulling out her cell phone before the mid-day digital media elective class, she sent a message to Ella. *Hi! About Sheila Smith…?*

Ella's call came through almost instantly, her voice brisk but friendly. "Hi there! You doing okay? It's freezing out there! I've got a meeting in five minutes. Sheila is a big name in arts advocacy, particularly famous for what she's done in Minnesota. She's just retired, and it made quite the splash in the local news."

Alexa could sense the hurried tone in Ella's voice, a clear indication of her pre-meeting rush. "Please let Sheila know I'll be calling her soon. And I'll get back to you if I need anything."

As Alexa was about to start her media elective class, with plans to call Sheila afterward using the contact info she had received from Ella, Andy rushed up to her, barely containing his excitement.

"Alexa, have you heard? O'Jete is stepping down! Can you believe it? He's actually leaving!" Before Alexa could respond, someone else grabbed Andy's attention, pulling him away to hear more.

Standing there, amid the bustling, chattering students Alexa felt a mix of surprise and intrigue. The plan she and Rudy had been designing was unfolding faster than she expected, stirring the pot in ways she hadn't fully anticipated.

Conversations across the high school continued unraveling. TikTok and Instagram with the hashtag *#realOJete* sharing stories about abuses and patterns of discrimination against students of color were proliferating. He was the talk of the town all day long.

Alexa was nearing the modest, well-kept entrance of her home on the same chilly November evening just as the day's light began to fade. The clean, unassuming doorstep, dusted with a thin layer of frost, reflected her family's simple yet attentive care. A few hardy potted plants, resilient against the cold, added a welcoming touch of greenery to the scene.

Just as Alexa was about to open her door, she was startled by the sound of Rudy's voice calling out to her. "Hey, Alexa! Did you catch the latest on O'Jete?" he asked. His voice echoed in the crisp evening air, visible puffs of breath accompanying each word.

Alexa turned, a mix of surprise and intrigue on her face. "Rudy! Yeah, I've heard. It's all over the place, isn't it? Everyone's talking about O'Jete maybe shifting roles or jumping ship for something new. The rumors are just non-stop. What have you heard?"

They lingered outside Alexa's house, engaging in animated conversation amidst the chilly air of the evening, dissecting every piece of the school's hottest news.

Rudy responded, his words accompanied by puffs of vapor in the cold. "It's all over TikTok and Insta, just loads of guessing games and speculation. But I've got to head out now, off to a Voto Latino meeting. Guess we'll find out what's really going on at school tomorrow, huh?" After a quick wave, Rudy took off, leaving Alexa alone with her thoughts and the swirling cloud of rumors about O'Jete.

As Rudy hurried away, Alexa leaned back against the door, tilting her head slightly, lost in thought over the swirling rumors. She couldn't help but smile at how much Rudy had changed.

Once merely the laid-back guy obsessed with video games, he was now evolving into a passionate advocate right before her eyes. Gosh, who knew?

The week finally slowed down, and with her team's science fair project wrapped up, Alexa seized the chance to research Sheila Smith. Browsing through articles and photos, she was struck by Sheila's warmth and confidence, which shone through in every image. Sheila's smile was particularly captivating, full of life and energy, making the idea of her 'retirement' seemed almost mismatched.

Alexa was buzzing with excitement as she gathered information. She planned to organize her notes and send them to Ella before bed. But the fatigue from a week packed with activities soon took over, and she unintentionally drifted off to sleep, her laptop still open on her desk, displaying her unfinished work.

Over the weekend, Alexa video-called Sheila on WhatsApp and was greeted with the surprising sight of her canoeing near her cabin, on a serene lake in Minnesota that was just beginning to feel the touch of winter. The shores were dusted with an early snowfall, creating a tranquil, almost magical atmosphere. Through her screen, Alexa watched as Sheila paddled gently, surrounded by the quiet beauty of the landscape transitioning into winter, where the first snow softened the sounds of nature around her.

"Hi Sheila! Wow... this is beautif...u...l! Bad connection..." Alexa tried to speak through the choppy connection.

"Hey Alexa! How are you? Alexaaa... you're in and out... it's really..." Sheila's face froze on Alexa's screen. "But I'm enjoying the..."

"Sheila, can you hear me? You're breaking up a bit."

"...not too bad, caught a couple of..." Sheila's voice came through in patches.

Seeing the screen freeze again, this time on an image of trees, Alexa continued, "I guess the signal's pretty weak out there, huh?"

"Yeah, it's pretty remote here," Sheila's voice stuttered, "...nice to get away though."

"Listen, about the interview..." Alexa then tried to steer the conversation back on track.

Despite the patchy internet connection, Alexa managed to coordinate a time for the Zoom interview while Sheila mentioned she needed Alexa's help picking out some Latin music for the segment. Alexa responded enthusiastically, but then, unexpectedly, the call dropped. Alexa's excitement about the upcoming interview wasn't dampened. She's got the nicest smile!

On the day of her first solo interview, Alexa was a mix of nerves and excitement. She logged in thirty minutes early to run through the final preparations with Ella. Upon connecting to Zoom, Alexa was greeted by the inviting view of Ella's background. Her apartment radiated warmth and comfort, decorated in soothing earthy tones and softly lit, creating a cozy and serene atmosphere.

They meticulously went through the research material, carefully discussed the planned questions, and reviewed the music selections Alexa had chosen.

Ella, with an encouraging tone, said, "This is great, Alexa! Everything is on point. You're all set for the interview."

Alexa, feeling reassured, responded with a relieved smile, "Great! Thanks! I'm good to go!"

As the interview neared, Sheila Smith's image smoothly entered the Zoom frame, her backdrop revealing a serene lakeside, a slice of Minnesota's natural splendor. Ella, with a friendly yet professional tone, greeted her. "Sheila, it's wonderful to have you. Alexa's in charge of the interview, and I'll be here just in case," she said, then muted her mic with a supportive glance towards Alexa.

The room around Alexa was calm, only the quiet whirr of her computer filling the air. She took a deep, centering breath and confidently clicked the record button.

"Hey there, *Latinisimo* listeners, I'm your host Alexa Hope," she started, her voice steady and inviting. "We're honored to have Sheila Smith with us today, a legend in the world of arts advocacy. Thanks for joining us, Sheila!"

On the screen, Sheila, set against her picturesque, tranquil lakeside background, smiled warmly, her eyes twinkling with eagerness. Alexa, feeling empowered by Ella's silent encouragement, prepared to steer the conversation into a meaningful and engaging dialogue.

Sheila responded with a bright smile. "Thank you, Alexa. I'm delighted to be here with you and your listeners."

"Sheila, your career is incredibly inspiring. But what really intrigues me is the beginning of your journey. Could you share with us what initially sparked your passion for arts advocacy?"

"My mom and dad were politically active," Sheila began, a note of fondness in her voice. "They were deeply involved in our church, and Dad, being a city planner, also chaired campaigns for Republican candidates. My mom, a realtor by profession, was the social cornerstone of our family. She often took me along to Republican state conventions, where she was a delegate. So, growing up, political activism was not just encouraged, it was expected from you."

"So, it's fair to say activism runs in the family, right?" Alexa remarked smiling. "Your achievements in arts advocacy are amazing. You've been instrumental in securing funding for the arts and collaborating with a lot of advocates and organizations. Could you elaborate on that for our audience?"

As Sheila started to respond, Alexa's phone buzzed discreetly next to her keyboard. Casting a quick, surreptitious glance at the screen, she recognized a message from Andy, with 'O'Jete' popping out as the subject. The ongoing saga was far from over. She maintained her focus on the interview setting aside her curiosity.

Sheila explained the advocacy and funding intricacies with clarity. "A portion of the funding has been sourced from the state's General Fund. However, the majority has been derived from what's popularly known as the Legacy Fund. This fund was established following a significant decision by Minnesotans in two thousand and eight. They voted in favor of a constitutional amendment that raised the state sales tax by three-eighths of one percent. This pivotal move led to the enactment of the Clean Water, Land and Legacy Amendment. Remarkably, Minnesota stands out as the only state that has secured twenty-five years of dedicated arts funding in its Constitution, a commitment that extends through to two thousand and thirty-four."

"That's something, isn't it? How was that possible?"

Sheila continued, "The amendment passed because we formed a statewide coalition. We trained and rallied hundreds of arts advocates from all over Minnesota to lobby the Legislature. It was a unique collaboration, you could say, as we worked alongside environmentalists, outdoor sports enthusiasts, and artists, all united for a common cause."

"So, was it like a coalition of many unrelated people coming together for a common cause? Can you explain the results a bit better for our audience?"

Sheila nodded. "Yes and sure! The passage of the amendment actually tripled arts funding, distributing it statewide and enhancing access to the arts in every community. Between two thousand and eight and two thousand and nineteen, we saw arts event attendance in Minnesota more than double."

"Impressive! Now, for those who aren't typically art supporters, could you explain why supporting the arts is important?"

"Communities with active arts and culture sectors are healthier than those without because the arts bring people together."

"How so?"

"Look, the arts can be a window into other people's lives and to build understanding across cultures. The arts can help heal veterans with PTSD and support kids with learning disabilities. The arts do have economic impact. When people get together, they're likely spending money in stores, bars, and restaurants and that, right there, is the way to impact the economy."

"This reminds me of JoAnn Balingit, the ex-Poet Laureate of Delaware. She's all about how poetry actually builds communities. Big thanks for that memory jog, Sheila! And hey, shout out to JoAnn, if you're listening to us right now!"

"I believe I met JoAnn when visiting Delaware a few years ago. She's right. You can't engage in this kind of grassroots organizing without realizing the need to bring people from mere awareness to active involvement," Sheila continued. "It's crucial to explain clearly and concisely why a particular initiative is necessary. You also have to educate people about how to effectively use the levers of power and help them understand the extent of their own influence."

"Influence, advocacy, and politics, perhaps a bit of all of that, right Sheila? In any case, it's time for a music break. I'm thinking about the collaboration between the Colombian Maluma and The Weeknd on a 'Hawái' remix. Here we go!"

The first portion of the program went smoothly. Alexa was feeling more and more confident running the interview. After telling Sheila that the music break was going to take three minutes, she glanced briefly in Ella's direction and then quickly texted Andy back, *What's up with O'Jete?*"

Andy responded: *Rumors, he's @principal's office now!* The texting stopped as Alexa realized that they only had thirty seconds for the song to finish. The program needed to be brought back.

Following Ella's example, Alexa shifted the focus to Sheila's personal life as she resumed the program. She reintroduced Sheila to the audience and continued, "Let's shift focus for a moment. Could you share something personal about yourself with our audience?"

Alexa noticed a thumbs-up icon pop up on Zoom from Ella, accompanied by a brief message in the chat box: *Doing great!* Feeling encouraged, Alexa quickly replied with a smiley emoji in the chat.

"You're asking about my personal life, Alexa?" Sheila inquired, with a hint of curiosity.

"Yes, exactly," Alexa confirmed, refocusing her attention on Sheila to capture the more intimate details of her life story.

"Well, besides arts advocacy. I'm a painter, mostly working with acrylic on board. I love kayaking, I dabble in woodcarving, and I'm actively involved with the Minnesota Council of Nonprofits. I also served on the board of the two thousand and twelve Minnesota United campaign, protecting the rights of all Minnesotans to marry. How's that for starters?"

Alexa, impressed, replied, "That's quite a diverse and inclusive set of interests!"

Sheila continued, "After college, I worked for a publishing company where the boss was cheating people by receiving manuscripts and then stealing them, rewriting them a little bit, and publishing them as his own work. So, I felt like I had participated in evil by working for this guy." Sheila paused, taking a sip of her coffee, as if briefly lost in memories of that time.

Regaining her composure, Sheila went on, "On the final day of my contract, I decided to make a change. I drove to the Capitol, thinking it was the place where I could counteract the negativity I had been a part of. I believed that meaningful work could be found there. So, I queued up for secretary interviews and, fortunately, got hired. My philosophy is that your goal in life is to be useful. I just followed my nose until I ended up where I needed to be."

Both Alexa and Sheila shared a light-hearted laugh over the comment. Alexa, with a smile, remarked, "Your family's spirit of activism definitely shines through in you. Should we all be following our noses as well?" Alexa explained, "*Latinisimo* is interviewing inspiring individuals like yourself, guiding people like me in choosing relatable career paths. In researching for this interview, it felt like everyone's eager to uncover the 'secret sauce' behind your successful advocacy. Could you shed some light on that for our audience?"

"Secret sauce? Really? Oh well… let me better quote Max De Pree, who's a businessman, a writer, and the son of Herman Miller from the office furniture company. A leader is a person who has followers. 'The first responsibility of a leader is to define reality. The last is to say thank you. In between the two, the leader must become a servant and a debtor.'"

Alexa was intrigued. "Could you please expand on that?"

"Sure. Let me put that in the context of nonprofits. Your primary job is to inspire and motivate people to align with your mission and participate with others in achieving it. You have to know what is happening outside of your own silo so you can marshal everyone to move in the same direction."

"How can you actually achieve that? I mean, how do you marshal people in the same direction?"

"So much is dependent on personal relationships, whether you are talking about constituents, founders, or community leaders. You have to be in the room with as many people as possible, so you have a deep knowledge of what is happening in the field."

Alexa was curious about the interplay between advocacy and politics in Sheila's career. "It seems like advocacy and politics are closely linked in your career. Would you say advocacy is easy?"

Sheila, displaying her pragmatic approach, responded, "No, it's not easy and it definitely takes time. Advocacy and politics connect but are different worlds. Advocates can convince elected officials about the importance of a cause if well informed about the issue at hand."

She then added a personal insight. "If I were to choose between being an elected official, or a city manager. The city manager is a way better job. Because you have lots of influence over how the public is served but you do not get all the problems that elected officials get. It is the people behind the scenes that really get things done. I think it's better to be the one making a difference quietly than the one always in the spotlight on TV shows."

Alexa, genuinely surprised by Sheila's perspective, said, "Really? I never thought about that angle."

Sheila nodded, her expression reflecting a mix of earnestness and frustration. "People think that politics is about screaming at each other, which is so unproductive. It's not about getting things done at all! People need to calm down and look at community problems and see what they can solve on a small scale. Stop thinking about the world as being America and think about the world as being your neighborhood."

Alexa absorbed Sheila's words and nodded thoughtfully. "So, you're suggesting a shift towards more localized solutions, right?"

Sheila reaffirmed, her voice laced with conviction. "Exactly. I believe that over time, people will grow tired of endless disputes and start craving real solutions. Those who are quietly resolving issues, rather than causing disruptions, are the ones who truly matter now."

"Collaboration seems a bit complicated these days, don't you think?"

With a chuckle, Sheila added some lighthearted wisdom to the conversation. "There are always crabby people in every crowd, but I've learned that the more time you spend with those who are collaborative and positive, the better things become. The crabby complainers become isolated. I tend to gravitate to people who are engaged. It is a lot harder to solve problems when you are alone than when you are in a group. Since there is always a scramble for resources, you can optimize resources by working together."

Alexa, curious about Sheila's future plans, inquired, "With your successful career coming to a close, what are you looking forward to doing next?"

As Sheila contemplated her response, Alexa noticed a visible change in her demeanor. Sheila's face relaxed, her eyes lighting up with anticipation for the future.

"After twenty-five years, it's time for a reset," Sheila began, her voice revealing excitement. "I'm planning to spend more time on my passions—painting, wood carving, and hopefully traveling when possible. I see a world of new opportunities waiting for me after a good, long rest. First, I am going to be in Arizona for a while. I am looking at a sabbatical year so I can travel, work on my artistic practice—and get used to being an artist once more."

Sheila's expression lit up with a playful grin. "I might just follow my nose again, which should be a lot of fun. I'll try something new, and if it clicks with me, I'll dive deeper into it." She mimed grabbing something from the air, her eyes twinkling with mischief. "But if it doesn't suit me," she continued, dramatically dropping her hand as if letting something go, "I'll just drop it and head off in a whole new direction." Alexa, watching Sheila's expressive movements, burst into laughter. In the chat, Ella joined in the fun, sending a *LOL* along with a string of laughing emojis.

Sensing the interview had reached its natural endpoint, Alexa warmly concluded, "Sheila, I can't thank you enough for joining us today. This has been a truly insightful conversation." With a grateful smile, she clicked off the recording, yet stayed connected on the call.

Ella reactivated her camera and microphone, beaming with pride. "Wow, Alexa, that was fantastic work!"

Sheila turned her attention to Ella on the screen, her expression one of approval. "Ella, you've got a star in the making here! Alexa has applied everything she's learned. We'll catch up soon!" With a final friendly nod, a distinct click signaled Sheila's departure from the session.

Ella's voice was filled with encouragement. "Alexa, you truly excelled today. You're wrapping up your internship with *Latinisimo* on an incredibly high note. Now, go ahead and enjoy your well-deserved weekend!" Alexa could feel the empowerment radiating from Ella's words.

"But, before you sign off," Ella said, smiling, "how about we grab lunch to celebrate? I'm eager to hear about your future plans."

For a brief moment, Alexa's mind flashed back to her first meeting with Ella a year ago. *What a change… this Ella… I like a lot!* Without hesitation, Alexa replied, "I was actually thinking the same. How about next week?"

Ella's face lit up. "Perfect, it's a date!" she exclaimed, and with that, she promptly disconnected.

Alexa turned off her camera and microphone, her mind shifting to Andy's text. But first, she reminded herself to secure the interview. She methodically saved the interview and transcript, ensuring everything was backed up before sending the mp4 file to Ella for WDEL's archive.

Then she finally replied to Andy, *Hi! Sorry. Just finished my first solo @Latinisimo! Nailed it! O'Jete talk tomorrow?*

Andy's quick response came through, *WOW!!! Congrats!! Talk tomorrow. Night!*

Alexa's text exchange was interrupted by her mom's call from the dining room. "Alexa, dinner's ready! We have green enchiladas, and we're just waiting for you."

"Coming, Mom! Just washing my hands," Alexa replied, her curiosity about O'Jete momentarily set aside for family time. Dinner with her family, especially her mom's green enchiladas, was not something she would miss. *The news about O'Jete will be the highlight of tomorrow.*

CHAPTER 13

ALEXA'S CHOICE

After dinner, Alexa reflected on her time with *Latinisimo* and her growing friendship with Ella. It had been an unexpectedly productive year, leaving her feeling different, empowered in a way she hadn't experienced before. *I feel like I can really do stuff now!*

Latinisimo and Ella had broadened her horizons, introducing her to people she never imagined she'd meet. The memory of her initial, not-so-smooth conversation with Ella came to mind, but it was quickly replaced by excitement for their upcoming lunch. Then Andy popped into her thoughts. She dialed his number.

"I know it's late, but I wanted to connect with you. What's up?"

"O'Jete is gone. It's official," he said.

"What? Gone... gone for real?"

"Yes. His office has a printed announcement. He wrote that he's leaving and that the college application process will continue with upcoming help."

"Are you sure? This is huge if true, Andy. I can't believe he's out. Sadly, it doesn't come as a total surprise. By the way, guess what! I just got news from the universities I applied to. You won't believe this, but I was accepted to my top three choices. My parents and the entire family are thrilled. I'm over the moon!"

"I knew it, Alexa! That's not surprising at all. I'm so proud of you!"

"And how about you?"

"I'm still waiting to hear back from my applications, but I'm feeling pretty hopeful about them. It's just taking a bit longer. I'll let you know as soon as I hear something. Let's talk tomorrow."

Alexa lay in bed, mulling over the news about O'Jete. I bet he'll still be there on Monday. I can't be that lucky, she thought. Turning off the light, she quickly fell asleep.

The next morning, Alexa woke up with thoughts of the O'Jete issue still swirling in her head, the conversation with Andy had only increased her curiosity. As she joined her family for breakfast, the familiar comfort of home and the lively chatter around the table temporarily pushed her concerns to the back of her mind. She savored the warm, homemade pumpkin pancakes and the rich aroma of freshly brewed coffee. Family time around meals is tradition amongst Latinos regardless of location.

Yet, as breakfast wound down and the conversation ebbed, her thoughts inevitably drifted back to the O'Jete situation. It occurred to her that Rudy might have some additional insights. Recalling their past conversations, she felt a twinge of curiosity and, perhaps, a hint of the old connection they shared. Finishing her orange juice, she decided to call Rudy, wondering what he might know about the unfolding drama.

"Hi Alexa! What's going on? Are you good? It's super early for a Saturday!" Rudy's voice came through, tinged with tiredness.

"Morning, Rudy! Yeah, I'm just really curious about this whole O'Jete thing. Got any more scoop on it?" Alexa asked, getting straight to the point.

Rudy's tone turned more serious. "Oh, right, the O'Jete drama. There's a solid chance he's gone. You should've seen the principal's reaction when I showed her that crazy video from the site I mentioned before. She even asked me to send her the link. No clue what's gone down since then, though."

"Definitely, we'll catch up with the O'Jete drama at school, I bet. So, what's new with you?" Alexa asked, eager to switch to a lighter topic.

Rudy's tone hinted at something more as he spoke, "Hey, you free to grab coffee and chat? Got some stuff to share. You down for hanging out today or maybe tomorrow?"

Alexa, curious and slightly hopeful about the sudden invitation, replied, "Yeah, today works for me. Just hit me up with the time and place."

Rudy's message about meeting for coffee at their usual spot later in the day stirred a mix of nervousness and hope in Alexa. She couldn't help but wonder if this meeting signaled a possible rekindling of their relationship. The thought of reconnecting with the new and improved Rudy filled her with a blend of excitement and curiosity.

Their favorite coffee shop, adorned with festive Christmas decorations, exuded a warm and welcoming ambiance. Twinkling lights hung from the ceiling, and a small, beautifully decorated tree stood in one corner. The scent of cinnamon and coffee filled the air, mingling with the soft melodies of holiday tunes playing in the background.

Alexa arrived first, ordering her usual green chai latte, and found a cozy spot near the window. She watched the light snow gently falling outside, her thoughts drifting to the possibilities this meeting might bring.

Rudy entered five minutes past the hour, his face lighting up upon seeing her. "It's so good to see you!" He greeted her warmly. "I'll just grab something to drink. Be right back."

Returning with his drink, Rudy sat down, a serious yet open look on his face. "Alexa, you've been such a positive influence in my life. In a way, I should thank you for our breakup."

Alexa's heart skipped a beat in hope and anticipation.

Rudy continued, his eyes reflecting deep introspection. "After we ended things, I went through a rough patch. It forced me to reassess who I was and what I wanted from life. Then, a friend introduced me to Voto Latino, and that changed everything." He paused, his passion for the cause evident in his expression.

"I was instantly drawn to their mission. Working with them, helping Latinos realize their voting power and its impact… it's been transformative. We're awakening a sleeping political giant, Alexa."

He took a sip of his soda, then shared the most exciting news. "And now, there's this incredible opportunity. I've been offered a position in Washington, D.C., along with a scholarship to study Political Science at Georgetown University!"

As Alexa sat across from Rudy, a storm of emotions played out inside her. Each word he shared about his future—the big move to Washington, D.C., the scholarship at Georgetown— filled her with pride for him. Yet, it also quietly echoed the end of something she hadn't even realized she'd been hoping for.

She watched Rudy, his eyes shining with dreams and ambition, and felt a swirl of happy-for-him and sad-for-her. This wasn't a chat about getting back together; it was about him stepping into a new chapter, one that didn't include her.

Taking a deep breath, Alexa forced a genuine smile. "That's awesome, Rudy. Seriously, you've totally earned this," she said, her voice a mix of cheer and a hint of sadness. Her heart was doing this weird thing—being super stoked for him but also feeling a pang for what might have been.

In the cozy coffee shop, amidst the holiday vibes and soft background music, Alexa was hit with the truth—they were heading in different directions now. It was like saying goodbye to a part of her life but also giving a quiet cheer for whatever came next, for both of them.

She took a deep breath, regained her composure the best she could, and started talking. "I am so happy for you, Rudy! You deserve only the best. I have seen how much you have grown up recently. The job and scholarship in D.C. are consequence of your hard work. Congratulations, from the bottom of my heart!"

Rudy could not contain himself any longer and embraced her long and tight. They both began crying.

"I want you to know that I am doing this for you and me. I love you, Alexa. You helped me find my voice. I am a better person because of you. I want to be the best version of me for our future together. We'll be in touch for sure. This isn't goodbye but a prolonged pause. If we're meant to be, we will!"

Alexa smiled and touched his face tenderly. "I love you too, Rudy. You're right. I once heard that if something is truly yours it will get back to you. Let's both set each other free and see if we come back. But if not, we will always be friends."

And just like that, in the midst of their heartfelt conversation, Alexa and Rudy transitioned from being exes to becoming the best of friends. There was an unspoken understanding between them, a shared hope that maybe, just maybe, the future might bring them back together. But for now, they were content to let time unfold their story

Throughout the week, Alexa was surprisingly at peace with how things turned out with Rudy. The more she thought about it, the more she felt at ease. Their relationship had shifted, sure, but it was still a meaningful part of her life. Just as she was getting ready to head out with her mom for some grocery shopping, her phone rang. It was Ella, bringing a new angle to her already eventful week.

"Hey, Alexa! Hope you're doing great. Got a minute to talk?" Ella's voice came through the phone, sounding cheerful.

"Hey, Ella! Yeah, I'm good. What's going on?" Alexa responded, curiosity piqued.

"So, I've got this cool idea for our dinner," Ella began, her excitement palpable. "There's this new spot in center city Philly, famous for its amazing Latin American dishes. I've been dying to check it out and immediately thought of you. What do you say we give it a try this Friday? I can swing by and pick you up."

Alexa's spirits lifted at the suggestion. "Oh, that sounds amazing, Ella! Count me in. I'm really excited to try it out with you!"

On the following Friday, Ella took the opportunity to visit Alexa's home, keen to meet the supportive parents of her outstanding

intern. She warmly greeted Alexa's parents, Leonardo and Cristina, with heartfelt thanks. "I really appreciate the incredible and promising young professional you've raised," Ella said sincerely. "She's been an immense asset to *Latinisimo*."

Leonardo and Cristina, delighted to finally meet the mentor who had significantly influenced Alexa's development, expressed their own gratitude. "Seeing Alexa thrive and grow under your mentorship has been a joy for us," Leonardo said with a grateful smile.

Cristina, with a touch of excitement, then offered, "Ella, we'd love to give you a small token of our appreciation. Alexa told us you enjoy strong coffee, so we've got something special for you." She presented Ella with a package of coffee from Veracruz, renowned for its quality. "We hope it's to your liking!" she added.

Alexa knew Ella would enjoy the gift from a region known for its exceptional coffee.

After a few minutes of pleasant conversation and shared laughter, Alexa and Ella bade farewell to her parents and set off for Philadelphia, ready for their anticipated dinner together.

Arriving in Center City Philadelphia, Alexa and Ella were greeted by the city's vibrant pulse. The streets were a lively blend of historic charm and modern buzz, with people moving about energetically under the evening lights. They soon reached their destination, nestled amidst the lively cityscape.

As Alexa stepped into the restaurant, she was immediately captivated by its warm and lively atmosphere. The walls were a canvas of vivid murals, depicting various Latin American landscapes and cultural scenes in bright, engaging colors. The lively beats of salsa and merengue music filled the air, perfectly complementing the vibrant decor and setting a festive mood for their dinner.

Near the entrance, a beautifully crafted nativity scene caught Alexa's eye. It was a thoughtful addition, reminding visitors of the Christmas season's deeper significance amidst the festive atmosphere. The entire setting was a delightful blend of cultural vibrancy and holiday cheer, creating the perfect backdrop for their dinner.

Finding their table, Alexa took a moment to appreciate the animated and bustling setting of the restaurant. The smells of spices and cooking meats from the kitchen were like an instant invite to a flavor party. Picking what to eat was a whole adventure in itself. Alexa flipped through the menu, each dish sounding so good that she had a hard time deciding. Everything just sounded absolutely mouth-watering.

They started with a round of tapas—small plates of empanadas, ceviche, and plantains that were a feast for both the eyes and palate.

Ella raised her glass of non-alcoholic sangria. "To a year of great achievements and new beginnings!"

Alexa clinked her glass against Ella's. "And to incredible mentors and friends!"

Their conversation flowed effortlessly. Ella reminisced about Alexa's early days at the studio. "Remember your first interview? You've come so far since then."

Alexa let out a laugh, remembering how she felt in those days. "Oh man, I was a total bundle of nerves at the start! And you, Ella, you weren't exactly the warmest cookie in the jar back then. But look at us now! You've turned out to be an awesome mentor and a cool friend. I've learned heaps from you, and let's not forget all those incredible guests we've had. It's been quite a ride, huh?"

"Oh yeah! Switching gears, how are things going with your college applications and essays? That can be quite the process, right?" Ella inquired, genuinely interested in Alexa's progress. "Lourdes mentioned she's been helping out here and there."

As they delved into the rich and aromatic Valencian paella, Alexa's face lit up with enthusiasm as she shared her discovery. "So, I recently came across rehabilitation engineering and it totally blew my mind! It's like all the stuff I love—tech, helping people, creativity—all mashed up into this one amazing field. It's exactly what I've been looking for without even knowing it! I was accepted to my top three choices." Alexa paused for a second. "I'm actually aiming for MIT."

Ella nodded, her face beaming with pride. "Congrats! That's the spirit! Finding what clicks for you is everything. It sounds like you're onto something really special. So happy for you!"

They ended their meal with the "bocadillo con queso," a delicious blend of salty cheese and sweet guava paste, a classic taste of Colombia. Sipping on Cuban coffee and enjoying the last of the sangria, they chatted about the future.

As Ella and Alexa left the vibrant heart of Center City Philadelphia, the city's festive lights faded into the background, giving way to the tranquil December night. They drove along the highway, the car's headlights cutting through the darkness, guiding them back to Delaware. Outside, the world was a serene landscape of winter beauty, with trees bare against the starry sky and the occasional house twinkling with Christmas decorations.

Inside the car, the soft melody of Diego Torres' 'Color Esperanza' played, setting a reflective mood. Alexa gazed out of the window, her mind alive with possibilities. "I've been thinking a lot about diving deeper into rehabilitation engineering after finishing at MIT," she mused aloud. "There's this program for a master's degree at the University College London that really caught my attention. It could be an incredible opportunity to study abroad and really specialize in this field."

Ella, sharing in Alexa's excitement, quickly called Lourdes Puig to relay the news of Alexa's potential venture overseas. Her voice was filled with pride and enthusiasm. "Lourdes, guess what! Alexa is studying rehabilitation engineering at MIT, no less, and then she plans to deepen her knowledge by pursuing a master's in the same field in London afterward. How do you like that!"

As they continued their journey, the peaceful night outside was a stark contrast to the flurry of thoughts and dreams swirling within Alexa. She felt a deep sense of gratitude for her experiences with *Latinisimo* and the guidance from Ella, which had opened her eyes to new paths and possibilities. The road stretched out before them like the expansive night sky above—vast and open, sprinkled with stars that seemed to mirror an avenue of possibilities. Alexa's heart soared with hope and excitement, energized by the endless potential that the future held.

On her bus ride home after a year away, Alexa felt a mix of exhaustion and excitement. She was busy responding to an email from a Latino student who had started following her journey on Instagram. Alexa noticed her following had been growing steadily, attracting more attention without her even trying.

Subject: My Journey to MIT as a Dreamer

Hi there,

Thanks for reaching out to me! It's always great to connect with fellow students who are navigating similar paths.

I noticed your question about how I, as a Dreamer, got into MIT. I'm more than happy to share my experience with you. MIT has an inclusive policy towards

DACA and undocumented students. They evaluate applications from undocumented and DACA students just like they do for all other students. This means your application is considered based on your academic achievements, personal qualities, and potential, regardless of your citizenship status.

One of the biggest concerns for us Dreamers is often the financial aspect. Fortunately, MIT is committed to providing financial support. They offer need-based financial aid that covers the entire demonstrated need, including tuition, housing, and other personal expenses. This support is crucial as it allows students like us to pursue our academic goals without the burden of financial stress.

Applying to MIT or any other university as a Dreamer can be daunting, but it's definitely achievable. It requires determination, hard work, and the right resources. Don't hesitate to reach out to the admissions office of the universities you're interested in to understand their policies for DACA and undocumented students.

Remember, your immigration status doesn't define your potential or limit your aspirations. With dedication and the right support, prestigious institutions like MIT are within your reach.

If you have any more questions or need guidance, feel free to reach out. I'm here to help!

Best,
Alexa

Before sending off the email, Alexa took a moment to add some useful links. She included information about MIT's financial aid options for DACA and Undocumented Students, as well as their admissions guidelines, knowing these resources could be invaluable for the student she was corresponding with.

After attaching the links, Alexa hit send on the email. As she did so, she found herself reflecting on the past year. It had been a period full of challenges that had pushed her both academically and personally, yet it was also a time of great achievement and notable academic success. She was eager to share all of these experiences and accomplishments with her parents, Cristina and Leonardo, who were just as enthusiastic and curious to hear about every aspect of her journey.

They planned to meet her at the downtown Wilmington bus station, a familiar and bustling hub situated just catty-corner to the train station. The station, with its constant flow of travelers and the rhythmic coming and going of buses, held a sense of anticipation and reunion. The area was a snapshot of the city's pulse—surrounded by the hum of urban life, streets lined with a mix of modern and historic buildings, and the ever-present backdrop of the train station's comings and goings.

Throughout the eight-hour bus ride to Wilmington, DE, Alexa and her parents had been in constant touch, exchanging countless texts. Each message built up the excitement for their imminent reunion, a moment they had all been eagerly awaiting. As the bus neared the station, Alexa's heart swelled with the thought of seeing her parents and sharing all the tales of her adventures and accomplishments.

"¡Hola mi'ja! ¿Como estás? We miss you so much!" Cristina's eyes were covered with tears. "¡Que flaca estás, Alexa! ¿Estás comiendo bien? We have pozole in your honor that Tía Maria prepared for you. We invited Ella and Lourdes. They were already there by the time we came to pick you up."

"¡Mi'jita! ¿Como estás?" Leonardo asked. "¡Te queremos mucho! ¡Te extrañamos tanto!" Leonardo couldn't contain his tears anymore. "We're so proud of you Alexa! ¡Eres un ejemplo para la familia mi'ja! Give me your luggage to put in in the trunk for you. La maleta mi'ja, gracias! Ahora, por favor ¡cuéntanos todo!"

Alexa knew that a single pozole dinner with her family wouldn't be sufficient to share everything with everyone. Fortunately, with the posadas just around the corner, she was looking forward to more opportunities to catch up. Each posada would offer ample time to exchange stories amidst food, ponche, and piñatas. She was also excited about the chance to reconnect with Ella and Lourdes. Adding to her excitement, Rudy and Andy had just texted her to confirm their attendance at the posada a week after her arrival, making the event even more eagerly awaited.

Alexa gave her parents a big hug. "¡Gracias… por todo!" She was profoundly grateful. Her heart was content. It felt good to be home. At the end of the day her success was also the success of a family rich in love.

Alexa, the dreamer, was making her dream a reality. She was sure challenges would come, but for now, it was time to celebrate with her loved ones.

REFERENCES

1. Baker, S. K. [TELEDUCTION], (2014, Jun 26). *Whispers of Angels* [Video] YouTube, WITN presents Content Delaware, https://youtu.be/vmE1202iBJM

2. Balingit, J. (2015, April 1). The language of home: Poets mine their childhood. *delaware online*. https://www.delawareonline.com/story/life/2015/04/01/language-home-poets-mine-childhood/70768244/

3. Barlette, K. G. (2018, August 27). 20 things you don't know about me: Havidán Rodríguez, UAlbany president. *Times Union*. https://www.timesunion.com/living/article/20-things-you-don-t-know-about-me-Havid-n-13184887.php#photo-16063966

4. Barrish, C. (2020, February 11). At Del. exhibit, art therapy provides expressive outlet, solace to people with disabilities. *WHYY*. https://whyy.org/articles/at-del-exhibit-art-therapy-provides-expressive-outlet-solace-to-people-with-disabilities/

5. Berdan, K. (2021, January 20). Sheila Smith talks about her legacy — and 25 years of change — with Minnesota

Citizens for the Arts. *Twin Cities Pioneer Press*. https://www. twincities.com/2021/01/10/sheila-smith-talks-about-her-legacy-and-25-years-of-change-with-minnesota-citizens-for-the-arts/

6. Considine, B. (2021, January 11). Interview: MCA Executive Director Sheila Smith & the road ahead. *Twin Cities Arts Reader*. https://twincitiesarts.com/2021/01/11/interview-mca-ed-sheila-smith-the-road-ahead/

7. Davis, Z. (2018, April 9). The magic of ArtsFest. *UDaily*. https://www.udel.edu/udaily/2018/april/artfest-center-disabilities-studies-art-therapy-express/

8. Delaware Division of the Arts. (2019). Governor's Awards for the Arts. https://arts.delaware.gov/governors-awards/

9. Delaware Division of the Arts (n.d.). JoAnn Balingit, writer & educator. https://delaware.gov/artistroster/artistProfile. php?aid=491

10. Eichmann, M. (2021, January 18). King's speech: Delaware students emulate MLK in spoken word contest. WHYY PBS NPR. https://whyy.org/articles/kings-speech-delaware-students-emulate-mlk-in-spoken-word-contest/

11. Espeland, P. (2021, February 26). After $563 million in funding for the arts, Sheila Smith steps down. *MinnPost*. https://www.minnpost.com/artscape/2021/02/after-563-million-in-funding-for-the-arts-sheila-smith-steps-down/

12. Guantanamera. (2021, July 12). In Wikipedia. https:// en.wikipedia.org/wiki/Guantanamera

13. Hillenbrand, K. (n.d.). JoAnn Balingit Interview, with Kaite Hillenbrand. *Connotation Pres an online artifact.* https://connotationpress.com/poetry/1178-joann-balingit-poetry

14. Huet, L. (2016, December 5). "It's the joy that I see in their eyes": Delaware children with disabilities create mural. *WDEL.COM.* https://www.wdel.com/news/its-the-joy-that-i-see-in-their-eyes-delaware-children-with-disabilities-create-mural/article_4a271052-bb38-11e6-8f52-0b035b8ed2a3.html

15. Jaime, K (n.d.). Forging a Path to Leadership: Dr. Havidán Rodríguez. Latino Leaders. https://www.latinoleadersmagazine.com/januaryfebruary-2018/2018/2/28/forging-a-path-to-leadership-dr-havidan-rodrguez

16. JoAnn Balingit (n.d.). *Bio.* http://joannbalingit.org/bio/

17. JoAnn Balingit (2013). *Words of House Story.* http://joannbalingit.org/2013/books/words-for-house-story/

18. Krogstad, J. M. (2016, July 18). 5 facts about Latinos and education. *Pew Research Center.* https://www.pewresearch.org/fact-tank/2016/07/28/5-facts-about-latinos-and-education/

19. La Red Health Center (2021). *Chief Operations Officer. Rosa Rivera.* http://www.laredhealthcenter.org/index.cfm?ref=40110&ref2=7

20. Little Patuxent Review. Book Review: JoAnn Balingit's Forage. https://littlepatuxentreview.org/2012/01/23/book-review-joann-balingits-forage/

21. Lourdes I. Puig, Ph.D. (n.d.). [LinkedIn page]. Retrieved January 15, 2022. *LinkedIn.* https://www.linkedin.com/in/lourdes-i-puig

22. Martinez, A. & Cheridan, C. (2021, January 26). Women making gains in STEM occupations but still underrepresented. *United States Census Bureau.* https://www.census.gov/library/stories/2021/01/women-making-gains-in-stem-occupations-but-still-underrepresented.html

23. MLKVoice4Youth (n.d.). https://mlkvoice4youth.org/about-us

24. National Endowment for the Arts. (n.d.) Poetry Out Loud. https://www.arts.gov/initiatives/poetry-out-loud

25. Náñez, D. M. (2020, Jan 7). Latinos make up only 1% of all local and federal elected officials, and that's a big problem. *USA Today Online.* https://www.usatoday.com/in-depth/news/nation/2020/01/06/aoc-julian-castro-underrepresented-hispanics-aim-change-politics/4253316002/

26. Klosterman, O. (n.d.). Havídan Rodríguez: A Leader in Disaster Research. *OΔK National Headquarters.* https://odk.org/havidan-rodriguez-a-leader-in-disaster-research/

27. Ostrowski, D. (2016, November 17). At TEDxWilmington talk, teen brought crowd to tears. *DelawareToday.* https://delawaretoday.com/life-style/at-tedxwilmington-talk-teen-brought-crowd-to-tears/

28. Plaza, R. (2016, August 16). Video production companies finding business niche. *Delaware Business Times.* https://delawarebusinesstimes.com/news/features/video-production-companies-finding-business-niche/

29. Poets & Writers Directory (n.d.). *JoAnn Balingit.* https://www.pw.org/directory/writers/joann_balingit

30. Purcell, G. (2019, October 24). Reading School Board hires homegrown assistant superintendent. *69News WFMZ-TV.* https://www.wfmz.com/news/area/berks/reading-school-board-hires-homegrown-assistant-superintendent/article_8e3775de-f60e-11e9-bf28-0fcdef4ae5a6.html

31. Raye Jones Avery (n.d.). Raye's Story. https://rayejonesavery.com/raye/

32. Reece, T. (2019, October 16). The Get Inspired! Project – Dr. Yamil Sánchez Rivera. *Berks County Living Magazine.* https://berkscountyliving.com/people/get-inspired-project/the-get-inspired-project-%E2%80%93-dr-yamil-sanchez-rivera/

33. Ross, J. (2020, December 29). A force behind Minnesota's Legacy Fund, arts advocate Sheila Smith retires after a quarter-century. *Star Tribune.* https://www.startribune.com/a-force-behind-minnesota-s-legacy-fund-arts-advocate-sheila-smith-retires-after-a-quarter-century/573497872/

34. Sayre, A. (2021, July 20). Explaining 'Patria y Vida,' The Song that's defined the uprising In Cuba. *NPR, WHYY.* https://www.npr.org/sections/altlatino/2021/07/19/1017887993/explaining-patria-y-vida-the-cuban-song-defying-an-evil-revolution

35. Steptoe, T. (2021, May 18). Marvin Gaye's 'What's Going On' is as relevant today as it was in 1971. *Smithsonian Magazine.* https://www.smithsonianmag.com/

history/marvin-gayes-whats-going-relevant-today-it-was-1971-180977750/

36. TELEDUCTION. About us. http://teleduction.com/about.html

37. TELEDUCTION. *Estamos Aquí: We are here.* https://www.teleduction.com/order/teleduction-estamos-aqui-are-here-ind.html

38. Thomas, B. (1999). Sharon Kelly Baker, Emmy Award-winning filmmaker. *UD Messenger.* http://www1.udel.edu/PR/Messenger/00/1/sharon.html

39. University at Albany, State University of New York. *Biography. Dr. Havidán Rodríguez is the 20th President of the University at Albany, State University of New York (SUNY).* https://www.albany.edu/president/about/biography

40. University of Delaware, Biden School of Public Policy & Administration (n.d.). Maria P. Aristigueta. Faculty. https://www.bidenschool.udel.edu/people/faculty/mariaa#BiosBodyContent5

41. UD Interdisciplinary Science Learning Labs. (2016, March 18). *Lisa Bartoli: Discover Delaware - Health, Humanities, and Human Rights* [Video]. YouTube. https://youtu.be/-f3IQFRs_1E

42. Vargas, J.A. (2018). *Dear America: Notes of an undocumented citizen.* New York, NY; HarperCollins Publishers.

43. Voto Latino. (2021). About. https://votolatino.org/about/

44. Weiner, Y. (2021, February 28). Sheila Smith of Minnesota Citizens for the Arts (MCA): Five things you need to

know to successfully lead a nonprofit organization. *Authority Magazine.* https://medium.com/authority-magazine/sheila-smith-of-minnesota-citizens-for-the-arts-mca-five-things-you-need-to-know-to-successfully-91249ebafd62

45. WITN Channel 22. (2018, November 29). Teleduction's powerful documentary: "A dream deferred". https://www.witn22.org/2018/11/29/teleductions-powerful-documentary-a-dream-deferred/

ACKNOWLEDGMENTS

The author profoundly thanks the interviewees for their time, editorial input, and accuracy corrections provided for each chapter featured in this novel. All interviewees are listed below in the order they appear in the novel, along with the time their interview took place.

- Lisa Bartoli on February 10, 2021
- Havidán Rodríguez on January 28, 2021
- Lourdes Puig on January 13, 2021
- Raye Jones Avery on January 26, 2021
- Yamil Sánchez on February 3, 2021
- Sharon Baker on January 27, 2021
- Maria Aristigueta on January 22, 2021
- JoAnn Balingit on January 15, 2021
- Jane Rubini on February 4, 2021
- Rosa Rivera on January 20, 2021
- Sheila Smith on January 15, 2021

ABOUT THE AUTHOR

Guillermina Gonzalez, a dynamic individual whose diverse professional background and personal experiences reflect a rich tapestry of cultural influences, career achievements, and community engagement, embodies the vibrant spirit of exploration and discovery. From her dynamic roles in multinational corporations to her passionate advocacy in the nonprofit sector and academia, Guillermina's journey reflects the power of versatility and the pursuit of meaningful work beyond conventional boundaries. Her commitment to understanding societal trends, coupled with a deep-rooted passion for community service and civic engagement, resonates with young readers seeking to make a difference in the world. Guillermina's multifaceted interests offer a relatable lens through which readers can explore their own passions and aspirations for personal and professional growth. Overall, Guillermina's debut novel offers a blend of inspiration, cultural insight, and practical wisdom that can resonate deeply with young adults and those navigating their own paths of self-discovery, academic pursuits, and aspirations for the future.

Are you interested in contacting Guillermina? If so please check her LinkedIn page https://www.linkedin.com/in/drguillerminagonzalez-11339329/ or email her at connect.guillermina@gmail.com